Pursuing his Viscountess

Courting *the* Unconventional

Laura Beers

1

ENGLAND, 1814

Mr. Evander Addington could read the boredom on his students' faces as clearly as if it had been scrawled across the lecture hall's stone walls. He had been speaking for well over an hour on the rise of the Ottoman Empire—an important topic, but admittedly one of the more uninspiring chapters in their syllabus. Even he, who found history endlessly fascinating, struggled to infuse the material with enough enthusiasm to keep the students engaged.

A palpable sense of relief swept through the room as the bell rang across the quad. Chairs scraped back, books snapped shut, and the hall emptied in a flurry of movement and murmured goodbyes. Evander watched them go without resentment. Some eras of history stirred the soul. Others simply had to be endured.

He gathered the worn volumes from the lectern and tucked them into his battered leather satchel. Slinging it over his shoulder, he took one last look at the now-empty hall. Despite the dull topic of the day, a quiet pride filled him. He had earned this post and the right to be called a Fellow of University College, Oxford. At only five and twenty, he had achieved what many only dared to dream.

Stepping outside, the crisp wind immediately threatened to send his cap flying. He caught it just in time and adjusted it firmly atop his head. The afternoon light was soft, casting long shadows over the cobbled quad.

As he approached the building that housed his office, the heavy oak door creaked open, and Professor Muir—broad, bearded, and slightly breathless—stepped out with a sheaf of notes in hand.

"Good afternoon, Fellow Addington," Muir said with a slight incline of his head.

Evander returned the gesture. "And to you, Professor. Are you off to enlighten young minds with the magic of physics?"

"Indeed, I am. Newton's Laws await." Muir gave a wry smile. "However, I do hope my students will be more engaged than they were during last week's lecture."

Evander chuckled. "I wish you luck. Mine looked as if they'd expire from boredom by the end of the lecture."

"Grim but necessary," Muir said with a theatrical sigh. "The fate of all professors—burdened with truth, cursed with students."

"And blessed with endless piles of essays," Evander added dryly. "If you happen to discover how to have a personal life in between lectures and reviewing students' work, do let me know."

"If I do, I shall write a monograph."

They shared a brief, companionable smile before parting ways.

Climbing the narrow staircase to the second level, Evander adjusted his satchel and headed down the dim corridor. The building was quiet, save for the occasional creak of the old timbers underfoot. As he turned the corner, he halted abruptly. His office door stood slightly ajar.

He distinctly remembered locking it.

A flicker of unease passed through him. Quietly, he approached and listened. There were noises—rustling papers, the subtle creak of wood. He pushed the door open and froze.

Seated at his desk, rummaging without a trace of shame, was the last person he expected to find.

"The devil take it—Father?" Evander blurted out, stunned.

The Earl of Everwyck looked up, entirely unbothered by the intrusion he was committing. His dark eyes calmly assessed his son.

"I've been waiting for over an hour," he said, as if that justified his trespass.

"And you filled the time by invading my privacy?" Evander asked sharply, stepping into the cramped room.

His father gave a dismissive nod. "Your office is smaller than I imagined. Dreary, too."

Evander clenched his jaw. He couldn't argue the point. The room was modest at best, barely large enough to accommodate the desk, two chairs, and a bookshelf that was filled to the brim. Still, it was his, and it had taken years of hard work and scholarly dedication to earn.

"I thought you were a Fellow now," his father said with his usual trace of condescension.

"I am. Offices don't magically expand the moment one is appointed," he replied, knowing perfectly well the subtle barbs were far from over.

His father rose and wandered over to the window, gazing out over the quad. "At least you've got a decent view."

Evander removed his academic gown and hung it beside his cap before finally lowering himself into the chair opposite his father. He studied the man—his rigid bearing, the lines etched into his face, the familiar coldness in his expression. They had never been close, and time had only widened the rift between them.

"Is Mother unwell?" he asked suddenly, the thought striking him with fear.

His father's gaze faltered. For the briefest moment, a shadow passed over his face. "Your mother is... surviving. The physician is uncertain how long she has."

Evander exhaled, shoulders sinking beneath the weight of the news. He had watched for years as illness chipped away at her strength. But hearing that the end might be near struck a blow deeper than he had anticipated.

"I've written to you," his father said, folding his arms. "You've ignored my letters."

"I've been occupied," Evander replied, not looking at him.

"Too occupied for family?"

"I never said that."

"You didn't have to," came the curt response. "I'm here because there's something that must be discussed."

Evander braced himself. He fully expected a rebuke about his career—about how his place was not in lecture halls but managing estates and maintaining appearances.

But as he looked at his father, he noticed something unfamiliar—weariness. The proud lines of his face sagged slightly, and for the first time, he appeared aged. Human.

His father pulled out the second chair and sank into it. "It's about Bryon."

Of course it was. Bryon, the golden child. The heir. The one who could do no wrong, while Evander's accomplishments were dismissed as willful defiance.

His father hesitated. "Bryon and Lord Harwood sailed to India to oversee the indigo plantation that we had recently purchased. I received word that illness struck the passengers and they both passed away."

Evander's breath caught. He stared at his father, trying to

reconcile the words with reality. Despite their differences, he had never wished harm to Bryon.

"Are you certain?" he asked, voice rough.

"Yes." Tears glistened in the earl's eyes, and his voice broke as he said, "I received confirmation three days ago."

Evander blinked, unsure what stunned him more—the news of his brother or the sight of his father crying.

"Does Mother know?" he asked.

"No," came the quiet reply. "I haven't told her. I fear what it might do to her."

Evander turned his head away, willing himself not to break. The urge to weep surged within him, but this wasn't the time or place. He would grieve in solitude. For his brother. For his mother. For the past that would never be reclaimed.

His father's tears were gone when he looked back, replaced by a mask of firm resolve.

"You will need to come home," he said flatly. "You are my heir now. You will need to take your rightful place."

Evander recoiled slightly, his mind rebelling. He had built a life here. Oxford was his sanctuary, his future. How could he make his father understand now when he had never succeeded before?

"I have obligations here," he began slowly.

"You have a greater one now," his father replied simply, as if that explained everything.

And with that, the room seemed to close in around him. Everything he had worked for—everything he was—stood on the edge of a precipice.

Evander shot to his feet and began pacing the length of the narrow office, his footsteps muffled by the worn carpet beneath his boots. The room, small to begin with, suddenly felt suffocating.

"I can't just leave," he declared. "I'm in the middle of the term. I have lectures to give, papers to grade, and students depending on me."

His father scoffed, rising from the chair with a dismissive wave of his hand. "This work"—he gestured vaguely at the shelves and papers surrounding them—"is hardly essential. You're teaching uninterested boys about long-dead kings and crumbling empires. You need to come home and help me run the estate. That's where your focus should be. That's what truly matters."

"My work does matter," Evander shot back, his voice taut with suppressed fury. "It matters to me, and to the students who actually want to learn."

His father's lip curled slightly, his tone patronizing. "You no longer need to labor for your keep. Bryon is gone," he said, his voice hitching slightly. "The responsibilities fall to you now. Frankly, this academic pursuit was always beneath your station."

"Working in academia is perfectly respectable for the younger son of an earl."

"Perhaps," his father conceded with a shrug. "But I had hoped you might choose a more dignified path. Become a barrister. At least then you'd be engaging in something useful. This history nonsense..." He shook his head. "It was always a diversion."

Evander turned away, eyes closed, trying to gather his composure before his temper got the better of him. They had danced this dance before, and each time it had ended with harsh words and wounded pride.

"I never wanted to be a barrister," he said.

"Pity," his father muttered under his breath. "I've already spoken to the Master—"

Hoping he misheard his father, he asked, "Pardon?"

"I spoke to Master Griffith earlier this morning," his father said, slow and deliberate, as if he had done him a favor. "I explained the circumstances, and he was quite understanding. He agreed that you would need to resign from your post immediately."

"You had no right to do that." Evander's voice rose, the edges fraying.

His father's eyes narrowed. "I had every right. You are my son. And with Bryon gone, you are the heir. This childish rebellion of yours has gone on long enough."

Evander took a step back, as though struck. The sheer arrogance, the presumption—it was unbearable. "You went behind my back. Interfered with my career, and my life, as though it were yours to control."

"I know this is sudden," his father said, his voice softening in a way that felt entirely false, "but you have a duty now. To your family. To your name. And whether you like it or not, that includes letting go of these... indulgences."

"I don't want it," Evander ground out. "Any of it. The title. The estate. The obligations. I built a life here, on my own terms."

"And now it's time to abandon that fantasy," his father snapped. "You're a grown man, Evander. Stop playing at being a schoolmaster and come home. Your mother needs you. The tenants need you. I need you."

But Evander had already turned towards the door. His hand gripped the knob with white-knuckled restraint. He opened it slowly and stood aside. "It's time for you to leave, Father."

His father's brows lifted. "Evander—"

"I said *leave*." His voice rang with finality, brooking no argument. "I need time to think. And I can't do that with you standing in my office, dismantling everything I've built."

For a moment, neither man moved. Then, with a sharp inhale and a bitter shake of the head, his father stepped past him and out into the corridor.

Evander shut the door firmly behind him.

And only then, with no one left to see, did he allow himself to lean against the wall, his eyes closing against the storm of emotion rising in his chest.

His whole life had just been upended.

And he had never felt so alone.

Lady Olivia Kendall strolled along one of the meandering paths of Hyde Park, the afternoon sun filtering through the leafy canopy above. Her Pomeranian puppy, Finnegan, zigzagged before her with unrelenting enthusiasm, tugging insistently at his leash.

"Finnegan," she chided with a laugh, tightening her grip, "must you weave about so? You are determined to see me sprawled in the dirt, aren't you?"

The puppy glanced up at her with wide, mischievous eyes and, if she didn't know better, she would have sworn he was grinning. Troublesome little beast. Why had she allowed herself to be persuaded into adopting him? He was unruly, obstinate, and wholly impractical.

And yet, she adored him.

Suddenly, Finnegan plopped down beneath the wide-spreading shade of an old oak, his sides heaving as he began to pant furiously.

"Come along, Finnegan," she coaxed, giving the leash a gentle tug.

He did not budge.

Olivia placed her hands on her hips and stared down at him with exaggerated disapproval. "You are a worthless dog."

In response, Finnegan promptly rolled onto his back and lay there with dramatic stillness, tongue lolling to the side.

Annie, her maid, who had been trailing behind at a

respectful distance, stepped forward, concern creasing her brow. "Would you like me to carry him for you, my lady?"

Olivia shook her head with a wry smile. "No need, Annie. I can manage."

Annie bobbed a curtsy and retreated once more as Olivia bent to scoop up the small, fluffy burden.

Finnegan nestled contentedly in her arms, utterly unrepentant.

"Well, who is walking whom, I wonder?" she murmured, pressing a kiss to the top of his head before continuing her stroll.

As she turned down a more secluded path that curved gently towards the Serpentine River, her gaze fell upon a solitary figure seated on a bench. Mr. Evander Addington sat motionless, his gaze fixed on the water, his expression distant and drawn. A black armband adorned his sleeve.

Olivia slowed, concern blooming in her chest. Something was most definitely wrong.

She veered from the path and approached him quietly. He didn't glance up as she neared, and even when she lowered herself onto the bench beside him, his eyes remained fixed on the rippling water.

Her voice was soft. "May I ask… who passed?"

He answered without hesitation. "Bryon."

The name struck her like a blow. Her breath caught. "No," she whispered. "How?"

"He passed away from illness while traveling to India. He was traveling with Lord Harwood," he revealed. "They both did not make it."

She sat back, arms tightening around the puppy now squirming in her lap. There had been a time, not so long ago, when she had fancied herself in love with Lord Harwood. But that future had been stolen when he had married another.

"I'm sorry for your loss," she said quietly, because it was all she could say.

Evander finally turned to look at her. His eyes were glassy, and it made her heart ache. "And I am sorry for yours. I know what Harwood once meant to you."

"He did mean something," she admitted. "But not anymore. Not in the way he once did."

He nodded faintly, emotion flickering across his face. "Society will know soon enough about my brother. Word always travels quickly when there's a title involved."

Olivia glanced at the armband. "Is that why you're in Town and not at Oxford?"

"My father summoned me home," he said, bitterness creeping into his tone. "Now that Bryon is gone, I'm the heir to the earldom."

"But… what of your fellowship?"

Evander let out a short, humorless laugh. "It no longer matters. I'll have to resign. My future has already been decided for me."

She reached out instinctively, resting her hand on his arm. "But you fought so hard for that position."

"And for what?" he asked, turning away. "It's over. Everything I built… all for nothing. Now I have a new path."

Silence stretched between them. Olivia gently lowered Finnegan to the ground, giving the wriggling puppy space to explore the grass.

"Do you want to resign?" she asked.

Evander's shoulders tensed. "Want?" He gave a bitter shake of his head. "What I want is irrelevant. My brother is dead, and duty waits."

She rose as he did, instinctively matching his movement. "Evander—"

He held up a hand. "Forgive me. I know I'm dreadful company."

"You've no reason to apologize. We've known each other since my hair was in braids and we climbed trees in our pantaloons."

That won a faint smile from him. "Those were simpler days."

"They were." She hesitated. "Is there anything I can do?"

His smile faded. "No one can help. It's only been eight hours since I received the news, and already I feel like I'm drowning."

"Have you told your mother?"

"Not yet. But I will soon. We'll go into mourning... as we ought."

He sighed heavily and looked as if he might leave, but then Finnegan jumped up onto the bench, barking twice before collapsing in a fluffy heap.

Evander blinked at the small dog. "When did you acquire a creature like this?"

"Shortly after I married," she replied. "My mother insisted I needed something to focus on."

He bent down to pet the puppy's head. "I read in the newssheets that your marriage was annulled."

"It was," she confirmed. "Given that I was deceived into marrying a woman, the courts found in my favor rather quickly."

"Was your dowry returned?"

"Yes. Lucinda has been... oddly obliging. Likely trying to curry favor with the judge before sentencing."

Evander straightened. "She must have been quite convincing for you not to suspect."

Olivia huffed. "I was a fool."

He looked at her seriously. "Don't be too harsh with yourself. You're not the first, nor will you be the last. The world is full of masks and misdirection. Entire novels have been penned on the subject."

She scooped Finnegan back into her arms. "Your literary references are not helping."

"I never claimed to be good at this," he said with a faint smile. "Grief has dulled my wit."

"Well, we're a fine pair, then," she replied.

Evander extended his arm. "Shall we walk a bit?"

"I suppose we ought," she agreed, looping her arm through his as they returned to the path. "My poor puppy is good for only the shortest of walks."

"He does have rather dainty feet," he said dryly.

She laughed. "When my sister-in-law, Dosia, first saw him scurry across the room, she shrieked and said she thought he was a rat."

Evander chuckled. "A very well-groomed rat, at least."

As they continued down the path, side by side, neither of them felt inclined to speak. The silence, though heavy with grief and regrets, was not uncomfortable—but rather the silence of old friends, grieving together.

By the time they reached the south exit of Hyde Park, the late afternoon light had begun to soften, casting long shadows across the path. Olivia slowed her steps and turned to face Evander.

"I wish you the very best, Evander," she said, sincerity woven through each syllable.

He tilted his head slightly, a somber echo of his usual charm. "And I, you."

There was a moment of hesitance as she searched for words that might bring him comfort. "If there's anything I can do during this time—truly, anything at all—"

"I know." He offered her a faint smile, one that didn't quite reach his eyes. "Thank you, Livy. You've always been a true friend to me."

Finnegan squirmed in her arms, restless and eager for attention. Olivia lifted the small dog with a playful lift of her brow. "Would you care for a dog? He is in desperate need of a more disciplined household."

Evander's eyes held amusement. "I must agree with Lady Wilton. That is not a dog. That is... something else entirely."

She pressed Finnegan protectively against her chest. "How dare you! He has feelings, you know."

"And my father," Evander added, "would likely mistake him for a rat and order his immediate execution."

"He is not a rat," she declared. "He is a noble creature of refined breeding and delicate constitution."

Evander chuckled, a sound that warmed the air between them for a brief instant. Then, he gave her a respectful bow. "Until we meet again."

"Good day, Evander."

She remained where she stood, watching him disappear down the street. His shoulders sagged slightly, and his stride lacked the determination she had always associated with him. He looked lost in thought—or perhaps simply lost. Her heart ached at the sight.

If only there were something she could do.

With a sigh, she turned and made her way home. She entered through the front gate and ascended the gravel drive. The front door opened just before she reached it, revealing Sterling, the ever-composed butler.

"My lady," he greeted with a slight bow. "I trust your outing was pleasant?"

Olivia handed Finnegan over with a resigned expression. "Will you see that he's fed? I believe he's positively famished after our long, exhausting promenade."

"Of course. I shall do so at once," Sterling said before departing from the entry hall to do her bidding.

Alone in the entry hall, Olivia paused. Her gaze drifted upward to the grand staircase, but she turned instead towards the back of the house, heading for her brother's study. As she passed by ancestral portraits, she noted how each solemn face seemed to stare down at her with equal parts judgment and curiosity.

The door to Richard's study stood open. She approached, but just as she stepped forward, a giggle floated out.

Olivia rolled her eyes and muttered under her breath, "Newlyweds."

Undeterred, she entered. Richard and Dosia were seated side by side behind his desk. Ledgers and papers were strewn in front of them, but they seemed to have eyes only for each other.

"Please tell me I'm interrupting something inappropriate," Olivia drawled.

Both turned at the sound of her voice. Only Dosia had the grace to look the slightest bit abashed.

"Sister," Richard said, smiling, "to what do we owe the pleasure?"

She sank into one of the chairs opposite the desk. "I saw Evander in Hyde Park just now."

At once, Richard's expression turned grave. "How is he?"

"Not well," Olivia replied honestly. "He's… unraveling."

Turning to Dosia, Richard explained, "His brother—Viscount Westmere—died at sea, along with his friend, Lord Harwood."

Dosia gasped softly, her eyes widening. "Lord Harwood… not the same one who—?"

"Yes, the very same," Olivia said before fixing a pointed look at Richard. "You knew about Bryon and didn't tell me."

He winced. "I didn't think it was my place to do so."

Olivia shook her head. "You should have told me."

"How are you holding up?" Dosia interjected.

With a small, dispassionate shrug, Olivia replied, "It hardly matters now."

Dosia's eyes narrowed with quiet sympathy. "You loved Lord Harwood once. It's all right to mourn him."

But Olivia didn't want sympathy. Not now. Not when her thoughts were so muddled and her emotions felt like distant echoes of what they once were. "Can we speak of something else?"

Richard seized the opportunity with evident relief. "As it happens, we were just considering taking a break from the accounts."

"We were?" Dosia asked in surprise.

"Yes," he replied, his lips twitching, "we have that... important meeting to attend. Urgently."

Dosia's laugh was light and indulgent. "How could I have forgotten?"

Olivia stood, shaking her head. "You two are incorrigible. You've only just returned from your honeymoon, and you act as though you're still on it."

A new voice chimed from the doorway.

"Leave them be, Olivia," her mother said with a smile. "They've only been married a few weeks."

"Thank you, Mother," Richard said graciously, helping Dosia to her feet. "We'll see you both at dinner."

Olivia glanced out the window. "I swear, if this keeps up, I shall enter a convent for the foreseeable future."

"There's no need for theatrics, dear," her mother responded. "We simply need to find you a new hobby—or perhaps a new scandal—to keep you occupied."

"No more scandals," Richard declared. "I daresay this family has weathered enough of them to last a generation."

Olivia walked towards the door. "Very well. I suppose I shall have to find some new way to occupy my time until I officially cross the threshold into spinsterhood."

"You are not a spinster," her mother remarked.

"Not yet," Olivia allowed, pausing with her hand on the doorframe. "But I am five and twenty and quite unattached. And now, with the added humiliation of having been deceived into marrying a woman…" She gave a mirthless laugh. "Well, let us simply say that I have provided Society with ample fodder."

"Olivia…" her mother began, the familiar note of gentle reprimand in her voice.

But Olivia didn't wish to hear it—not the sympathy, reassurances, or delicate encouragement to hold her chin high and endure the snubs with grace. There was no polite way to reframe what had happened. She had been tricked—utterly, spectacularly—and the scandal was well deserved.

Before her mother could continue, Olivia lifted her chin. "I think I shall lie down before dinner. The fresh air has quite exhausted me."

Without waiting for a reply, she stepped out of the study, grateful for the reprieve. She was pleased for Richard and Dosia—truly, she was. But the way they looked at each other and spoke with quiet affection and shared laughter… it stirred something raw within her. A longing she didn't quite know how to name anymore. She had thought she had found that kind of love with Lord Harwood. But he had chosen someone else, and the wound still throbbed faintly beneath her composed exterior.

Her brief, disastrous marriage to Lucinda had only further cemented the belief that she was not meant for love. At least not the kind that lasted.

Perhaps she should get a cat or two and embrace her spinsterhood.

2

Evander stood before the familiar façade of his ancestral townhouse, his gaze lingering upon the grand, three-storied structure of whitewashed stone gleaming beneath the gas lamps. A delicate iron railing encircled the property, its ornate design echoing generations of refinement and wealth. One day, this house—and everything it represented—would be his. That knowledge sat heavy upon his shoulders.

But there was no time to indulge in sentimentality. His duty awaited, however reluctant he might be to embrace it. No amount of longing for a different life would change what had already come to pass.

Drawing a steadying breath, he approached the front steps. Before he could knock, the door swung open. And there stood Gillingham, the family's tall, black-haired butler, clad in his immaculate livery. His mouth curved in what might have been intended as a smile but came off instead as a grimace of sympathy.

"Good evening, my lord," Gillingham intoned with a shallow bow.

My lord.

The words landed like a blow.

Evander froze upon the threshold, the truth settling over him with brutal finality. He was Lord Westmere now—not by triumph or merit, but because his elder brother was dead. The ache of that truth pressed hard against his ribs.

He had been raised to be the spare. The shadow. The son meant to step forward only if tragedy struck.

And now—here he was.

Gillingham closed the door behind him and stepped back, offering a respectful distance. No doubt he understood that Evander would need time to collect himself.

But there was little point in delaying the inevitable.

"Where is my father?" Evander asked, voice clipped.

"In his study, my lord."

With a nod of acknowledgment, Evander prepared to face the man who had summoned him home from a life he had carved for himself—one not dictated by duty or title.

As he turned to depart, Gillingham spoke again. "If I may, I have assigned Ramsey to serve as your valet."

"Very good," Evander replied. His tone was neutral, though a faint bitterness stirred within him. He had not required a valet in years, not since taking up residence in a modest flat near Oxford. There had been no room for such luxuries, nor any desire to rely upon his father's wealth. After completing his studies, he had refused even a single shilling of family money. He had wanted to prove that he could make his own way in the world.

And yet... here he was.

His future no longer his own.

He moved purposefully through the corridors of the townhouse, his footfalls muffled against the thick carpets. Reaching the rear of the house, he saw that the door to the study stood ajar.

His father was hunched over the desk, spectacles perched upon his nose as he reviewed a stack of estate accounts with a frown of concentration.

Evander straightened his shoulders and entered. "Father."

The earl looked up at once. "Good. You are here." His tone was brisk, formal, as though nothing monumental had changed between them. "Have you resigned from your post at Oxford yet?"

"I intend to do so tomorrow."

"Then simply write a letter of resignation. We will have a messenger deliver it to the Master."

Evander took another step into the room, jaw tightening. "I would prefer to speak to the Master in person."

His father leaned back in his chair, one brow arched. "That is a waste of time."

"It is my time to waste."

The earl gave a derisive snort. "I do not understand your reasoning, but very well. Now, there is something you must sign."

Crossing to the desk, Evander lowered himself into one of the leather chairs. "What is it?"

His father reached for a thick stack of papers. "Your marriage contract."

Evander stared, momentarily stunned. "I beg your pardon?"

Holding up the sheaf of documents, his father continued. "Bryon was to marry Lady Jemima Wakefield. The contract had not yet been finalized, but now that obligation passes to you."

"Bryon was to marry Lord Harwood's sister?" Evander asked, incredulous.

"Yes. And now you shall do so." His father extended the papers towards him. "All that remains is your signature."

Evander held up both hands. "I will not marry Lady Jemima. We would not suit. She is spoiled, cruel, and entirely too pretentious."

"What young lady of the *ton* is not?" came the dismissive reply.

An image flashed in Evander's mind—Livy. Ever since their youth, he had admired her. Not merely for her beauty, though she possessed that in abundance, but for her gentle spirit, her quick wit, and her kindness. She had the rare gift of making him laugh even in the darkest of times. If he were to marry anyone, it would be her. However… Livy had never seemed to see him as more than a friend.

Eyes narrowing, he gestured at the contract. "I will not sign those papers."

His father regarded him with exasperation. "You have a duty to this family."

"I am well aware of my duty," Evander replied evenly. "It is the very reason I am here. But that does not mean I will sacrifice my future to a woman who has never concealed her contempt for me."

"It is different now. You are the heir."

"Is that supposed to make it better?" Evander asked, voice sharpening. "Lady Jemima has always treated me as beneath her notice—as though I were an inconvenience."

His father sighed, clearly losing patience. "You are making this into more than it is. Lady Jemima's dowry is twenty thousand pounds. We need that money to repair the estate and secure our holdings."

"Surely there are other young women with comparable dowries," Evander countered. *Livy,* he thought. He knew for a fact that her dowry was generous.

"Do not be difficult. Sign the contract and marry the chit."

"No." His voice rang with finality.

His father's gaze hardened. "This defiance will lead to ruin. You are my heir, and you will do as I command."

"I will honor my duty—provided it does not require the destruction of my own happiness."

With a frustrated gesture, his father spread his hands. "Look around you! Everything I do—every decision I make—is to ensure your future."

"Then permit me to propose an alternative. If I marry another young woman with a twenty thousand pound dowry, surely that would suffice."

His father scoffed. "The only other such young woman is Lady Olivia. And she is wholly unsuitable as your wife."

"I disagree," Evander said, voice low and firm. "She is my friend and we would suit far better than I ever would with Lady Jemima."

His father's lip curled. "Lady Olivia may be a marquess's daughter, but she is scandal-ridden. Duped into marrying a woman disguised as a man. What sort of fool allows such a thing to happen? Hardly a proper match."

"Do not believe everything the newssheets print. There were other circumstances—ones you cannot begin to understand."

"Regardless," his father snapped, "I forbid it. You will marry Lady Jemima. That is final."

But if his father believed that a single command would sway him, he was sorely mistaken.

Evander rose from his seat, his back rigid. He would not surrender his future—his chance at happiness—for a loveless, contemptuous marriage.

Not for duty.

Not for twenty thousand pounds.

Not for anyone.

Standing over the edge of the desk, Evander planted his hands firmly upon its surface and demanded, "I will decide whom I will marry—*I*, and I alone."

His father's expression darkened, deep grooves etching across his brow. "And what of Lady Jemima?" he demanded. "She is expecting an offer of marriage from you."

Evander straightened, folding his arms across his chest. "Does she even wish to marry me?"

The earl gave a dismissive wave. "Of course she does! You are heir to an earldom. What more could she want?"

With a weary sigh, Evander stepped back from the desk, adjusting the edges of his waistcoat as though to shake off the suffocating conversation. "I want more from a marriage than social advantage or financial gain."

His father snorted in derision. "You want *love*?" he said, voice dripping with scorn. "What are you—a chatty young woman bewitched by those absurd romance novels? Next, you'll be telling me you dream of moonlit walks and sonnets!"

Evander lifted his gaze heavenward, a muscle twitching in his jaw. *Why,* he thought bitterly, *must every conversation with Father descend to this?* They could barely remain civil for five minutes before harsh words overtook them. It was this ceaseless tension that had driven him to leave the townhouse years ago.

Brushing past the desk, he turned towards the door. "I should see to Mother."

"She is resting," the earl replied tersely. "I had a sleeping draught prepared for her."

Evander halted mid-step, glancing back over his shoulder. "Have you told her about Bryon yet?"

At this, his father's composure faltered. A flicker of pain crossed his features, quickly masked by a grimace. "Not yet," he admitted. "I fear the news may be too great a blow. I am... truly concerned it could kill her."

Evander's heart twisted at the thought. His parents had entered into a marriage of convenience. Still, they had always shown one another a quiet respect, a kind of steadfast tolerance that had deepened into something akin to fondness over the years. He had long suspected his father's infidelities, whispered of in Society's drawing rooms, but had never broached the subject. His mother had borne it with grace, and for that, he respected her all the more.

"You must tell her," Evander said, voice firm.

The earl rose slowly from his chair. "I was hoping... that you might do it."

Evander turned fully now and asked, "Why me?"

"It might soften the blow, coming from you," his father replied, gaze averted.

Coward, he thought. His father, so commanding when ordering marriages and managing estates, sought now to hide behind his son rather than deal with a grieving wife.

But this was his mother. And despite the distance he often kept from this townhouse, despite all the grievances he harbored towards his father, he loved her deeply.

Drawing a long, resigned breath, Evander bowed his head slightly. "I will do it."

His father's shoulders sagged, the tension visibly draining from him. "Thank you, Son," he said, voice carrying a rare note of genuine relief.

"Now, if you will excuse me, I need to settle into my bedchamber."

As he turned towards the door, his father called after him. "Would you like Bryon's bedchamber? It is much larger than yours and it offers a fine view of the gardens."

Evander paused mid-step. His heart constricted at the suggestion.

No.

He might have inherited his brother's title and his responsibilities, but he would not take his brother's place in life so easily.

Turning his head just enough to glance back, Evander said, "No. My own room will suffice."

Without waiting for a reply, he strode from the study. The hollowness in his chest deepened with every step. The future awaited him, shaped by duty and loss, but at least, in this small matter, he would hold fast to what little choice remained to him.

Olivia sat alone at a corner table in the circulating library, her fingers lightly tracing the gilt-edged pages of one of her favorite French romance novels. The soft murmur of whispered conversation and the occasional rustle of turning pages surrounded her like a gentle cocoon.

Sunlight filtered through the tall windows, illuminating the dust motes that danced lazily in the air.

She had left the townhouse directly after breakfast, unable to endure the suffocating concern written so plainly on Dosia's face. Her sister-in-law meant well—truly, she did—but Olivia could not bear such attentiveness, not today. She needed space to think, to sort through the jumble of her heart. *I am perfectly fine,* she reminded herself, though her throat tightened at the thought of it. Lord Harwood belonged to her past now. He had made his choice, casting her aside without so much as a backward glance. She would not waste her tears on a man so unworthy of them.

Still, her eyes blurred as she tried to focus on the words before her. She was just about to surrender the effort when the chair opposite her scraped softly against the wooden floor.

Startled, Olivia looked up to see Lady Jane settling gracefully into the seat with an impish smile.

"Good morning," Jane greeted as she adjusted the straw hat that sat slightly askew on her head, covering her blonde curls.

"Good morning," she replied slowly. "I admit I did not expect company."

"I thought I might find you here," Jane said brightly. "At least, I hoped I would."

A faint smile tugged at Olivia's lips. "Does your father or brother know you are here?" she asked with a raised brow.

Jane's smile dimmed a fraction. "They know I am visiting the circulating library. They are not aware, however, that I intended to converse with you." She leaned forward conspiratorially, lowering her voice. "I recently discovered that my maid has been tattling on me to them. I left her sulking in the coach."

Olivia couldn't help but laugh softly. "Splendid move." She closed her book with a deliberate snap. "How are you faring?"

"I am well," Jane answered, a little too quickly.

Olivia fixed her with a pointed gaze. "The truth, if you please."

A sigh escaped Jane as her shoulders sagged. "My father is attempting to marry me off to the Duke of Brackenford."

Olivia wrinkled her nose in distaste. "But he is positively ancient."

"I know," Jane whispered with a shudder. "I hope he will soon find another suitable match for me."

"You do have a say in the matter," Olivia reminded her.

Jane's expression turned bleak. "That is easy for you to say. My father and brother govern every aspect of my life. I have no choices, no freedoms." She glanced around the room as if wary of being overheard. "It is no different for most women of our station."

"Have you ever defied them?" Olivia asked.

Jane looked horrified. "Heavens, no!" Her eyes widened. "I scarcely dare."

Olivia shook her head with quiet resolve. "You deserve more out of life, Jane."

Her friend managed a weak smile. "Perhaps. But I wouldn't even know where to begin." She reached across the table, her fingers brushing Olivia's hand. "But enough about me. I am more concerned about you."

Olivia arched a brow. "Whatever for?"

Jane gave her a pointed look. "I read in the newssheets that Lord Westmere and Lord Harwood perished."

"That they did," Olivia said calmly, though her fingers tightened slightly around the book.

"And I know you had feelings for Lord Harwood."

"*Had* being the operative word," Olivia replied. "He cast me aside and married another. I have made my peace with it."

Jane did not look convinced. "It is perfectly natural to grieve him."

"I refuse to give him another moment's thought," Olivia said firmly, though her voice wavered ever so slightly. "The way he treated me... I would not wish that cruelty upon my worst enemy."

"Livy—"

She raised a hand, forestalling her friend's sympathy. "You need not fret over me. I have a dog now. In fact, I am considering acquiring a cat or two."

"Cats? Whatever for?" Jane asked, bewildered.

Olivia's lips twitched into a grin. "I may as well embrace spinsterhood fully."

"You are only five and twenty," Jane protested. "Hardly destined to be a spinster."

"Ah, but who would want to marry a woman with an annulled marriage?"

Jane gave a little shrug. "The right man would. Are you not the one who always insisted that love conquers all?"

"Not anymore," she admitted. "Love is dead—or at least reserved for the lucky few who manage to find it. It is a little more than a game of chance."

Jane's gaze flicked to the book Olivia had been reading. "If that is truly how you feel, why are you reading romance novels?"

Olivia gave a weary smile. "Because it is pleasant to escape into another world, even for a few moments. Within the pages of a book, love still triumphs."

Jane reached for her hand again. "What happened with Mr. Smith was not your fault. He deceived you."

Olivia turned her gaze away, her throat tight. She knew her friend meant well, but such reminders only deepened her shame. Heartbroken by Lord Harwood's betrayal, she had allowed herself to be swept away by Mr. Smith's lies—all the way to Gretna Green. The consequences of that folly still haunted her.

"I know," she whispered. "But it does not make the memory any less bitter."

Jane straightened in her chair, brushing a stray curl from her shoulder with a determined flick of her wrist. "Then we shall speak of something else," she declared. "Politics, religion, or the weather?"

A laugh escaped Olivia's lips. "Not the weather. Never the weather."

Just then, a sudden commotion drew their attention to the side door leading to the salon. The door swung open, and a small gaggle of finely dressed ladies emerged in a flurry of muslin and lace. Their heads were bowed close together, and their fans fluttering to conceal mischievous smiles. Gentle laughter drifted through the air as they swept through the circulating library and out onto the street.

"I wonder what that was all about," Jane murmured, her gaze following the retreating group with undisguised curiosity.

Olivia tilted her head towards the now-quiet salon door. "That particular room offers a refuge," she explained. "It is where women gather to speak of matters they dare not utter in the drawing room. No chaperones are listening in, and no gentlemen are minding their sensibilities."

Before Jane could reply, a familiar voice sounded from just behind them. "Good morning, ladies."

Olivia turned in her chair to see Miss Winslow standing nearby, her fashionable bonnet tilted at a charming angle. Blonde curls framed her porcelain face, and her blue eyes sparkled with polite warmth.

"Good morning," Olivia returned the greeting with a courteous smile.

Jane followed suit, though her smile faltered slightly, not quite reaching her eyes. "Were you in the salon?"

"I was," Miss Winslow replied with an elegant nod. "Though I did little more than listen. One can learn the most interesting things by simply remaining silent." She leaned in slightly, as if sharing a confidence. "I confess, I never imagined I would hear women discussing politics so freely—and so passionately—among themselves."

Olivia gave a small sigh. "It is a shame our opinions must be hidden away in dark corners, spoken only in whispers, lest we offend the delicate pride of men."

Miss Winslow's smile deepened, and she gave a thoughtful nod, setting her curls in motion. "Perhaps one day that will change," she said. "Now, if you will excuse me, I must not be late for my appointment with the modiste."

Jane's gaze lingered on Miss Winslow's retreating figure. Her expression grew wary. "I would advise caution when dealing with Miss Winslow."

Olivia arched a brow. "Why is that? She seems harmless enough—pleasant, even."

Jane met her gaze. "That is precisely her intent. Her innocent act is well practiced. She is far more calculating than she appears."

"And how do you know this?" Olivia asked, curiosity piqued.

Jane hesitated, tension creeping into her posture. "I cannot say."

"You *cannot*—or you *will not?*" Olivia pressed gently, her eyes narrowing with interest.

Jane's fingers twisted the ribbons of her reticule. "Promise me you will be careful in what you say to her," she urged.

Olivia waved a dismissive hand. "You need not worry. I hardly imagine Miss Winslow has any real interest in me. Frankly, I am surprised she even spoke to me at all, considering she is rumored to be the Diamond of the First Water this Season."

Rising from her seat, Jane said, "I must leave before my maid takes it upon herself to storm the library in search of me."

Olivia stood as well. "Thank you for daring your family's disapproval to visit me."

Jane lowered her gaze, her voice wistful. "I wish I possessed the strength to truly defy them. But I do not—not yet."

Olivia reached out and gently squeezed her friend's hand. "You are stronger than you believe. One day, you will see it."

A soft smile played at the corners of Jane's mouth. "I hope you are right."

"I am right," Olivia said firmly, her tone softened with affection. She reached once more for her book. "And perhaps—one of these days—you will dare to read one of the scandalous French romance novels I so dearly love."

"I wouldn't dare," Jane protested.

With an amused smile, Olivia extended the book across the table. "You should," she urged. "Do one thing each day that reminds you that you are alive."

For a long moment, Jane stared at the book as if it were a forbidden treasure, and indecision warred on her features.

Slowly, tentatively, she reached out and took the book from Olivia's outstretched hands.

"I suppose I could manage a page or two each day," Jane murmured, as if speaking the idea aloud would somehow make it safer.

"That is a fine start," Olivia said, her voice encouraging. "And who knows? You may soon find yourself reading far more than that."

Jane hugged the book to her chest as though it were a secret she had to guard. Her shoulders lifted with a breath of resolve. "I will do it," she said, her gaze steady now. "I will."

A faint smile touched Olivia's lips as she watched her friend walk away. Jane was being brave—more so than she realized. To even consider defying the expectations of her father and brother required a quiet kind of courage. Olivia admired her for it, even envied her resolve in that moment.

She herself was fortunate; she knew it. Richard, for all his protective instincts, did not shackle her with endless restrictions. He granted her certain freedoms. He encouraged her love of learning, her curiosity, and even her occasional stubbornness. In many ways, she lived a life freer than most women of her station.

And yet...

As she reached for another book on the table, a hollow ache stirred in her chest—a sensation as subtle as it was persistent. *Why,* she wondered, *did she still feel as though some essential part of her was missing?*

She traced an idle line across the margin of the page with her fingertip.

Lord Harwood had been a mistake—a bitter one. The scandal with Mr. Smith had only deepened her sense of isolation. She told herself she was content, that she had moved beyond the heartbreak and disgrace. Yet beneath her composed smile, something within her remained... unmoored.

Drawing a slow breath, Olivia straightened her spine and turned the page deliberately. Books offered escape. Perhaps, today, they would also offer solace.

Still, the question remained, whispering at the edges of her mind: *What part of herself had she lost—and how would she ever reclaim it?*

3

Evander sat in the shadowed corner of White's, half-sunk into the worn leather of an armchair, a glass of brandy cradled loosely in one hand. The muted din of conversation and the clink of glasses barely touched the edges of his awareness. He had come here hoping that drink might dull the edge of grief and resentment that gnawed at him—but thus far, it had failed to oblige.

Another swallow burned down his throat, leaving behind a bitterness that had nothing to do with the liquor. He stared at the amber liquid with narrowed eyes. He knew well enough that he had no right to wallow. Any number of men would trade places with him in a heartbeat. Heir to an earldom. Wealth. Influence. A place secured among the *ton*. But none of it had been his choice. He had carved out a life of his own—one he had valued, one that had mattered to him.

Now it was gone.

He shifted in his seat, the movement drawing his attention to the black armband stark on his sleeve. A small, dark emblem of loss. Of change. Of a future he neither wanted nor was prepared to accept.

Bryon.

A familiar ache tugged at his chest. His brother's absence weighed heavily, but if he was honest with himself, that sorrow was complicated. Grief mingled with an odd, unwelcome sense of relief. Bryon had never been kind. He had scorned Evander's pursuits, belittled him at every opportunity. Reminded him at every turn that he was second-best, the spare.

But Evander had never wished him dead.

He drew in a slow breath, eyes half-closed, when a familiar voice intruded.

"You look like death."

Evander glanced up. Lord Bedford and Lord Westcott stood before him, concern softening their usual affable expressions.

"I have had better days," Evander murmured. He gestured wearily to the empty chairs near him. His friends took the invitation without hesitation, settling into the opposite wingbacks.

"How are you faring?" Bedford asked.

Evander let out a breath and lifted one shoulder in a half-hearted shrug. "As well as one can expect, I suppose."

"That didn't answer my question," Bedford pressed.

Evander glanced away, fingers tightening around the brandy glass. "I didn't want this life."

Bedford's gaze softened with understanding. "Neither did I, but here we are. We do our duty and carry on." He offered a faint smile. "Besides, there are certain advantages to being a lord. Our word carries weight. People trip over themselves to win our approval."

Westcott gave a low chuckle. "I hate to say it, but I agree with Bedford. Being a lord isn't so terrible."

"I preferred my life in academia. It was simpler... predictable," Evander said.

Bedford nodded solemnly. "You worked hard for your place as a Fellow. That doesn't have to vanish overnight. Could you not finish the term before stepping away?"

Evander exhaled heavily. "That's no longer an option. My father expects me to begin working on the estate accounts immediately." His voice was flat with resignation.

Before anyone could respond, Lord Wilton and Lord Alcott approached the table, both looking faintly winded as if they had come straight from another engagement.

"I came as soon as I got your message," Wilton said, taking a seat beside Bedford.

Evander met Wilton's gaze. "How is Olivia faring with Lord Harwood's death?"

Wilton's expression darkened. "She says she is well enough, but she hides her feelings too easily."

"That she does," Evander agreed softly, a flicker of sympathy stirring within him.

Wilton tilted his head. "Tell me, why did Harwood accompany your brother to India?"

Evander huffed, a dry sound devoid of humor. "It seems Harwood had acquired a few indigo plantations. He intended to assist Bryon with ours."

Alcott let out a low whistle. "Indigo. A swift path to fortune, but it leaves the land barren in its wake."

Evander gave a weary nod. "I know little about the trade. But my father insists I must learn."

"Will you travel to India?" Wilton asked.

"No." The word came out sharp, bitter. "My father will not risk losing his only heir."

Wilton placed a steadying hand on Evander's shoulder. "I know your path seems bleak just now. But it will not always be so."

"Since when did you become a blasted optimist?" Evander muttered.

Wilton's smile warmed. "Since I married Dosia. She's taught me to see the world rather differently."

"I daresay it was a fortunate thing you abducted her, then," Bedford quipped with a grin.

Wilton chuckled. "It was undoubtedly the smartest thing I've ever done. Though she was less than pleased when she learned the truth."

"I can imagine no woman would welcome such circumstances," Alcott remarked.

"True enough," Wilton agreed. "But Dosia is forgiving and I may have purchased more than a few pieces of jewelry to ease her ire."

At that moment, a short server approached the group. "Would any of you gentlemen care for refreshment?"

Drink orders were placed, and as the server departed, Alcott turned his attention back to Evander and said, "The good news is, you haven't a sister to manage."

"Hear, hear," Wilton agreed.

Alcott sighed theatrically. "They are maddening creatures, robbing us of peace and reason with every passing day."

Evander felt his shoulders loosen slightly, the edges of his mouth twitching upward. "What has Charlotte done now?"

"She is far too independent for a girl of eighteen," Alcott grumbled. "Always scribbling away in that blasted notebook of hers."

"She is young," Bedford offered.

"Yes, and she's up to something," Alcott asserted. "I'm certain of it, but I simply cannot discern what."

"Perhaps you're imagining things," Westcott suggested.

"That's precisely what she wants me to think," Alcott declared. "I ought to marry, find a wife who might keep Charlotte in line."

Wilton nodded sagely. "A wise course, indeed, but choose carefully. The wrong match brings nothing but a lifetime of misery."

Alcott leaned back in his chair, considering Wilton with a

mischievous gleam in his eyes. "I suppose I could always abduct a wife, just as you did."

Wilton looked heavenward. "I didn't abduct Dosia at random. There were extenuating circumstances, as you well know."

Bedford grinned. "Yes, yes, you were somehow deceived by a woman wearing men's clothing. A tale for the ages."

Wilton huffed. "Lucinda was rather convincing, I'll have you know. I had no reason to suspect otherwise. And besides"—he glanced pointedly at Evander—"I thought we were here to cheer up Addington—er, Westmere, now."

Evander stiffened at the sound of his new title. "I have not yet grown accustomed to being called Westmere."

Wilton offered a sympathetic smile. "Well, you had best grow accustomed to it, for it is yours now, whether you like it or not."

With a resigned sigh, Evander reached for his glass and tossed back the remaining contents. The brandy seared down his throat, leaving behind only a deeper sense of hollowness. He set the empty glass down with a dull thud.

"I should go," he said. "My father has tasked me with delivering the news of Bryon to my mother."

"Why you?" Bedford asked.

Evander's mouth twisted into a humorless smile. "He believes she will bear the news better if it comes from me."

"Coward," Alcott muttered beneath his breath.

"Well said," Evander agreed. "My father is many things, but when it comes to my mother, he is strangely... tender. He fears the shock of this might kill her."

Wilton's expression softened into something close to pity. "If there is anything you need—anything at all—you need only ask."

"Thank you," Evander said, rising to his feet. His shoulders sagged beneath the weight of duty and loss. "The sad thing is that I do not yet know what to ask for."

Bedford stood as well. "I'll walk you out."

Together they made their way through the club's opulent halls and out into the cool night air.

As they approached the main doors, Evander spoke. "Tell me—how did you do it? Walk away from academic life so easily?"

Bedford exhaled slowly, as if recalling a distant ache. "It wasn't easy. I always knew the title would be mine one day, but... not so soon. My uncle and father passed within months of each other. I had no choice."

Outside, the lamplight flickered against the damp pavement. Evander paused by his waiting coach, the horses stamping impatiently.

"I may have complained about my post at the university," he said softly, "but I loved it. Every lecture, every debate, every late night spent over dusty volumes. It gave me purpose. It challenged me."

Bedford clasped Evander's shoulder firmly. "I know. But in time, you will find a new purpose. Think of the good you might do in the House of Lords, when the opportunity comes."

Evander turned to him then, frustration breaking through the façade of calm. "You know my father. He can be tyrannical. How am I to survive this without losing myself?"

Bedford's expression tightened with understanding. "Your father is stubborn, true—but so are you. Do not let him forget who you are, nor let yourself forget it."

Evander's voice grew strained. "Easy for you to say. Your father was generous with his affection. Mine... has always found me lacking." His gaze dropped. "At least I still have my mother... for now."

With quiet conviction, Bedford dropped his hand. "Life

tests us in ways we never expect, but you are stronger than you know."

"I don't feel strong," he said, the words slipping out before he could stop them.

Bedford studied him for a long moment, his expression grave. "Sometimes," he said, "we have no choice but to be strong. Whether we feel it or not."

"I had everything planned," Evander admitted, his voice rough with the weight of shattered dreams. "I built my life, my future, with care—every step deliberate. And now... now I stand on a path I cannot see the end of. That uncertainty terrifies me."

"Then don't look too far ahead. My advice is to take one day at a time. Some days, that is all you can do."

For a moment, Evander said nothing, his thoughts tangled and heavy. Then he tipped his head in a quiet gesture of gratitude. "Thank you, Bedford."

His friend responded in kind, understanding passing between them without need for further words.

Evander stepped towards his waiting coach, and the door shut with a soft thud. The vehicle lurched forward, merging into the flow of traffic along the gaslit street.

He leaned back against the worn velvet of the bench. His eyes drifted closed for a moment as exhaustion pressed down upon him. A wild, fleeting impulse seized him. He could tell the driver to keep going—past Mayfair, past the boundaries of Town, into the countryside beyond. To drive and drive until the weight of duty and grief could no longer find him.

But he knew better. Running would not solve what awaited him. It would only worsen it.

No.

He drew in a slow, deliberate breath. *I must face this. Face my father. Face my mother. Face this new life I did not choose.*

And above all, he hoped he might do so without losing the man he had spent years becoming.

Olivia exited her bedchamber and descended the staircase. She had been rudely awakened that morning by a particularly insistent bird that had taken up residence on the windowsill just outside her chamber. After tossing about in bed with the pillow pressed over her head to no avail, she had at last surrendered to the morning and decided to join her family for breakfast, though it was hardly a choice she embraced with enthusiasm.

As she entered the dining room, a shaft of sunlight illuminated the long table set with gleaming silver and steaming dishes. Seated together at one end were her brother and Dosia as they read the newssheets.

"Good morning," Olivia greeted.

Richard looked up with a boyish grin. "Olivia, I am astonished to see you awake at such an indecent hour," he teased, folding his newssheets.

"I thought I might grace you both with my presence at this godforsaken time," Olivia replied airily, moving to sit across from them.

Dosia glanced up with a warm smile. "It is nearly noon."

"My point exactly," Olivia quipped, settling into her chair and placing a starched linen napkin upon her lap with a sigh of exaggerated weariness. "You two wake far too early. I daresay you make a habit of it."

"I happen to enjoy seizing the day," Richard said cheerfully. Too cheerfully. "Dosia and I have already been for a ride this morning."

"How very joyful for you," Olivia murmured, reaching for a

cup of thick, fragrant chocolate. She took a long sip, savoring the warmth.

"You are remarkably pleasant today," Richard teased.

"I nearly committed murder this morning," Olivia replied. "A small bird has taken it upon itself to perch outside my window and chirp incessantly. Day and night."

Richard set the newssheets aside, eyes twinkling. "You could always shut your window."

"And be denied fresh air? Absolutely not. I refuse to let the bird win," she replied with a shake of her head. "However, I have given considerable thought to the possibility of serving bird for dinner."

"You most certainly will not," Richard said, a grin tugging at his mouth.

Olivia sighed dramatically. "You are right. If I were to dispatch one bird, I would surely provoke the wrath of its kin. A veritable avian uprising would follow, and I should never sleep again."

Richard chuckled. "You have clearly spent too much time pondering this."

"Oh, I have," Olivia admitted with a nod. "As I lay in bed this morning, I devised no fewer than five methods of silencing the wretched creature."

"Five?" Richard repeated.

"Indeed," she said. "Though I must confess, none were entirely humane." She took another sip of chocolate. "I do like birds in general. But there are limits to my patience."

Richard glanced at Dosia, an exaggerated look of concern in his eyes. "Do you think Olivia is bottle-weary this morning?"

His wife laughed. "Not at all. She makes perfect sense to me."

"Traitor," Richard said lightly.

Reaching for his hand, Dosia smiled. "Never, my love.

Besides, I have long suspected that birds are not as innocent as they appear. They know precisely what they are about."

Richard lifted her hand to his lips, eyes gleaming with fondness. "How is it I did not know this about you before we wed?"

"You never thought to ask my opinions on birds," Theodosia replied, her tone playful.

"No, I did not," Richard murmured. "But I shall endeavor to ensure no feathered fiend disturbs your slumber, my lady."

Olivia rolled her eyes. "I preferred it when you two were perpetually at odds. It made for far better entertainment."

Richard released Dosia's hand and leaned back in his chair. "And how do you intend to occupy your day, dear sister?"

"I thought to call upon Lady Everwyck," Olivia replied. "Evander mentioned her health is declining."

A voice from the doorway interrupted them. "I shall accompany you."

Olivia turned to find her mother entering the room. "Very well," she said. "But may I ask why? I usually call alone."

Her mother moved to the end of the table, smoothing her dark blue skirts before taking a seat. "Circumstances are different now."

"In what way?" Olivia asked, brows knitting together.

Her mother's tone was patient but firm. "Evander is now the heir. It would be highly inappropriate for you to call unchaperoned."

Olivia frowned. "I am visiting Lady Everwyck—not Evander. And our families have been friends since I was a child."

Richard cleared his throat. "Mother is correct. Your reputation is already... fragile. We must take care not to worsen matters."

Olivia sighed. "Perhaps I should simply remain here and resign myself to an utterly uneventful existence."

"Be serious, Olivia," her mother admonished. "You must

accept that these are the consequences of your choices. You eloped to Gretna Green with Mr. Smith."

A flush crept up Olivia's cheeks. "Thank you for the reminder," she said coolly.

Her mother's expression softened. "I know this is difficult. But we must weather this scandal—together."

Richard bobbed his head. "The *ton* is a fickle beast. In time, another scandal will capture their attention."

"Wonderful," Olivia said dryly, picking up her fork.

As Olivia pushed the food about her plate, her appetite all but vanished, and the familiar wave of guilt rose in her throat, bitter and unrelenting. It was her fault—*entirely her fault.* Her foolish decisions had not only ruined her own prospects but cast an unwelcome shadow over her family as well. Richard was determined to repair the damage she had wrought, to shoulder the burden she had placed upon them, but it was not his responsibility. It was hers. And she alone must find a way to set things right.

But *how*?

The question haunted her waking thoughts, as relentless as the bird that had driven her from sleep. She could think of only one clear solution—marriage. A well-made match could begin to restore her tarnished reputation. But who among Society would risk even the appearance of courting her now? No one would dare. Her name had become the subject of drawing room whispers and smirking glances. The thought of enduring more of that empty pretense made her stomach twist. Better, then, to simply step aside from Society altogether. To embrace spinsterhood, fade into the background, and allow her family's life to resume untroubled by her presence.

No one would miss me if I did.

Dosia's voice pulled her from her dark reverie. "Do not give up hope, Olivia."

Olivia looked up. "It is far easier to forgo hope than to believe there is any bright future left for me."

"You do have a future," Richard interjected. "I will find a way to fix this."

She forced a faint smile to her lips. He meant well—he always had. That was what she loved most about him. "Thank you," she replied softly, knowing there was no use arguing with him. They were both far too stubborn to sway one another.

Their mother glanced at the long clock in the corner of the dining room. "Shall we be off?" she asked, rising gracefully to her feet.

Olivia took a final sip of her chocolate and stood. "Yes, I think a visit to Lady Everwyck would do me some good."

"I am certain it will do her good as well," her mother said. "She often complains of the tedium of her bedchamber."

Richard rose with them and caught Olivia's gaze. "You will be just fine."

She lowered her eyes to the floor, her heart too heavy to meet his optimism. "I wish I could believe that," she murmured, before following her mother from the dining room.

In the entry hall, as they waited for the coach to be brought round, her mother spoke again. "How is Evander faring?"

"He is as well as can be expected," Olivia answered. "But I know him. He is struggling beneath it all."

Her mother's lips pressed into a thin line. "I know you wish to help him, my dear, but it might be best to distance yourself."

"And why is that?"

Turning to face her daughter fully, her mother's expression softened with compassion. "You carry a scandal about you. And Evander has only just inherited his title. Do you truly wish to see the gossips sharpen their tongues against him as well?"

The words stung because they rang with truth. "No. I do not," she responded.

"I say this not to wound you," her mother continued. "But

because I know how much you care for him. Protecting him may mean stepping back—for now."

Olivia swallowed hard. Her mother was right, as painful as it was to admit. She would not be the cause of more hardship for Evander. She loved him too dearly to see his name dragged through the mud alongside hers.

At that moment, Sterling appeared and opened the door. "The coach is ready, my ladies."

Together, they stepped outside and entered the coach. As the door shut and the vehicle moved forward, Olivia turned her gaze to the passing streets beyond the window. How had her life come to this? All because of one terrible mistake. One reckless, foolish moment when she had believed Lord Harwood's promises.

The journey passed swiftly, and soon they arrived before the grand stone façade of the Everwyck townhouse. The coach drew to a halt, and they disembarked. Ascending the wide steps, her mother knocked firmly upon the door.

It opened almost at once. The butler greeted them with a courteous bow. "Lady Wilton. Lady Olivia. You are most welcome."

"Is Lady Everwyck receiving callers?" her mother inquired.

"Her ladyship gave strict instructions that you were always welcome," the butler replied. "Please follow me. I shall show you to the parlor."

"She is not in her bedchamber?" Olivia asked.

The butler led them down the corridor, replying over his shoulder, "Lady Everwyck requested a change of scenery this morning."

"I suppose she is entitled," Olivia remarked with a faint smile.

They had just reached the parlor door when a familiar figure approached from the far end of the corridor. Evander. His expression flickered with surprise when he saw them.

"Olivia. Lady Wilton," he greeted, drawing nearer. "What brings you here today?"

"We've come to visit your mother," Olivia replied.

"That is most kind of you," he said sincerely. "Do you call upon her often?"

"As much as time permits," Olivia answered.

Evander stopped before them, his gaze resting on hers. "I have no doubt that she cherishes your visits."

"She has always been kind to me. It is the least I can do. And her wit is as sharp as ever, even if her body betrays her."

"Here—allow me." Evander opened the parlor door.

As Olivia moved to follow her mother inside, she felt a light touch on her arm. She turned to find Evander beside her, his voice hushed. "I need your help."

"Always," she replied without hesitation.

His jaw tightened. "I have not yet told my mother about Bryon. Would you remain with me when I do?"

She met his gaze steadily. "I would be honored."

"'Honored' is not the word I would use," he muttered, releasing her arm but lingering close.

"Then let us do it now. Together."

His lips curved faintly. "Thank you. I can always count on you."

"Yes, you can."

Before they could speak further, her mother's voice rang out from within the parlor. "Are you two quite finished? We are here to visit Lady Everwyck, not to gossip in the hall."

Evander straightened. "I assure you, Lady Wilton, we are not gossiping."

"Come along, then," her mother said, gesturing them to enter with a wave of her hand.

4

Evander followed Olivia into the parlor, his steps slowing as he took in the familiar room. Sunlight filtered through the tall windows, casting a soft glow over the worn but elegant furnishings. His mother sat near the hearth, a shawl draped about her shoulders, her frame far too slight beneath its folds. The moment she saw them, her face brightened with a weary smile.

"Olivia, dear," she called, extending both hands. "What an unexpected surprise."

Evander stood back for a moment and watched as Olivia crossed the room and clasped his mother's hands warmly. The affection between the two women was evident. Yet as he observed the scene, his heart tightened. His mother's fingers were thin and fragile in Olivia's grasp. Her once vibrant black hair now carried streaks of silver that seemed more pronounced than ever. Her every movement, even her smile, seemed to cost her effort.

He swallowed hard. How many moments had he wasted, thinking there would always be time? And now, he was no longer certain how many such moments remained.

Olivia and Lady Wilton settled on the settee across from his mother. Evander remained by the door, uncertain if he could compose himself enough to join them.

His mother's gaze shifted towards him. "Do you intend to join us, or loiter by the doorway?" she asked, her tone laced with gentle amusement.

A rueful smile tugged at his lips. "I will join you," he said, and crossed the room to sink into an armchair near the settee.

"Wonderful," his mother replied. "Now, let us have a little *tête-à-tête*. I find I am most curious about Olivia. How are you faring, my dear?"

Olivia straightened, folding her hands primly in her lap. "I am well," she replied—though her voice lacked its usual brightness, a note of strain beneath the polite words.

As she conversed with his mother, Evander studied her closely. No matter how often he saw her, she unsettled him. She was by far the most beautiful woman he had ever known—not simply for her countenance, but for her spirit. She haunted his thoughts, whether he wished it or not. And he loved her. Madly. Hopelessly.

But she did not feel the same.

And so he kept his silence, content to remain in her presence and hope, in some unguarded moment, that her heart might one day soften towards him.

His mother's voice interrupted his reverie. "Evander?"

He started and realized too late that he had been staring at Olivia. A sheepish smile curved his lips. "I do beg your pardon. My mind wandered."

His mother tilted her head, eyes twinkling. "Do tell us—what is so fascinating about Olivia?"

The smile on his face deepened into a playful grin. "I was wondering if perhaps she is a witch."

Olivia arched a brow. "And why would you think that?"

Placing a hand dramatically over his heart, he said,

"Because she has bewitched me, and it is the only reasonable explanation."

As he had hoped, Olivia rolled her eyes. "That was dreadful," she said lightly. "I do hope you have not used that line on other women."

"I have not," he said. "You are my first attempt."

"Well, pray do not repeat it. One cannot go about accusing young ladies of witchcraft—not even in jest."

Evander leaned back in his chair, his grin lingering. "You used to be far more mischievous."

"I am still mischievous," she bantered.

"Are you?" he teased. "I recall a time when you and I concocted the most dreadful mixtures out of mud and berries in the gardens."

"We were children," Olivia remarked.

"Perhaps, but you did once believe that drinking the potion would grant you the power to fly."

A wry smile touched Olivia's lips. "I remember. I also remember breaking my arm attempting to prove my point."

Lady Wilton interjected with a fond sigh. "Poor Olivia was confined to her bed for weeks while her arm mended."

"And yet," his mother added with a chuckle, "she was back to climbing trees the moment she was able. We should have tied bells around the two of you. At least then we might have known where you were at any given moment."

Lady Wilton nodded. "Indeed, we could scarcely keep them apart whenever we were at our country estates."

His mother's eyes softened as she looked at him. "When Evander left for Eton, I feared he might attempt to smuggle Olivia away in one of his trunks."

Olivia perked up. "I would have gladly gone! It would have been far preferable to being left in the care of my governess, Miss Laverton."

"She was highly recommended," Lady Wilton attempted.

"Highly dull, more like it," Olivia replied. "I would often sit by the window, counting how many steps it would take to reach freedom."

Lady Wilton shook her head. "You exaggerate, as always. Miss Laverton was an excellent governess."

"Was she?" Olivia asked. "I distinctly remember seeing her skip away after our final lesson—as if she had been released from captivity."

Lady Wilton huffed. "Perhaps she was driven to it by your questions. I seem to recall you asked her to explain... certain matters concerning animal mating."

Olivia looked wholly unrepentant. "She claimed to have been raised on a farm. I wished to test the breadth of her knowledge."

Lady Wilton frowned. "Genteel young ladies do not speak of such things."

"Whyever not?" Olivia countered. "It is a part of life. An essential one."

"Let us choose another topic before we scandalize Diana," Lady Wilton said firmly.

His mother laughed, a warm sound that seemed to lighten the room. "You forget that I have known Olivia since the day she was born. There is nothing she might say that could shock me."

"You are most kind, my lady," Olivia replied, casting a triumphant glance at her mother.

Evander chuckled softly. "That does not mean you should test the limits."

Abruptly, Olivia rose and met his gaze. "Shall we take a turn about the room?"

He rose at once. "I would be honored."

They began a slow circuit of the parlor, their voices lowered.

"When do you intend to tell your mother about Bryon?" Olivia asked.

His chest tightened. "I suppose now is as good a time as any."

"I am sorry," she said gently. "How can I help?"

He glanced at her, gratitude flickering in his eyes. "Just stay with me. That will be enough."

She gave him a small, steady nod. "Your mother seems weaker than when I last saw her."

He swallowed slowly. "Every day she fades a little more. I hate to burden her with this... with the truth about Bryon."

"It was in the newssheets," Olivia said. "How have you kept it from her?"

He winced. "The household staff is shielding her. Her eyesight has deteriorated to the point that she can no longer read the newssheets herself. I suspect her maid conveniently skipped over that article."

Olivia's expression was one of concern. "You carry so much on your shoulders, Evander. But you are not alone."

Their gazes met for a moment longer than necessary. And in that fleeting exchange, Evander allowed himself a single, silent hope—that one day, her words might mean more than comfort alone.

His mother's voice pierced the quiet space between them. "What are you two conspiring about in hushed tones?"

Evander halted mid-step and turned slowly to face her. Olivia did the same, her expression smoothing into polite composure, though her hand lingered lightly at his elbow in silent support.

"I have something to tell you, Mother," Evander said. "And I fear it will not be easy for you to hear."

His mother's brow creased slightly. "Are you and Olivia engaged at last?" she asked, a hopeful gleam momentarily brightening her eyes. "Because if so, I must say—"

"No. No, no... absolutely not," Evander said quickly, hands rising in an almost panicked gesture.

Olivia turned her head sharply, her eyes wide with mock offense as she bumped his shoulder. "Truly, Evander. A simple *no* would have sufficed."

He gave a sheepish chuckle, running a hand through his hair. "My apologies. I meant no slight, I assure you."

"I know," Olivia replied, the corners of her mouth lifting slightly. "Still. A little less horror in your tone next time, perhaps."

Evander gave her a grateful glance, then turned back to his mother. His humor faded as the gravity of the moment returned. "Mother... it's about Bryon."

At once, the lines on her face deepened. Her lips pressed into a thin line. "What about Bryon?"

Evander drew a slow, steadying breath, though it did little to ease the heaviness in his chest. "Illness swept through his ship on his journey to India, and he did not survive."

His mother stared at him, unmoving. The silence stretched for several long seconds.

"Are you certain?" she asked at last, her voice a mere whisper.

"I am."

For a moment, she remained very still. Then her gaze dropped to her lap, and Evander saw the telltale glimmer of moisture in her eyes just before the tears began to fall in earnest.

He crossed the room in an instant and dropped to his knees beside her, reaching for her trembling hand.

"I'm here, Mother," he murmured, his voice thick with emotion. "You are not alone."

Olivia appeared at his side. She drew a dainty handkerchief from her reticule and held it out. His mother accepted it and dabbed at her cheeks, though the tears kept coming.

The parlor fell into a hush, broken only by the sound of her unsteady breathing and the tick of the long clock by the wall.

After a long silence, his mother turned to the maid sitting quietly in the corner. Her voice was raw but composed. "I wish to retire to my bedchamber."

The maid stood at once and crossed the room.

Evander squeezed his mother's hand. "Allow me to escort you."

She withdrew her hand slowly. "No. I wish to be alone."

"But—"

"You have guests," she said with effort. "Please, Evander. See them out properly."

"There is no need for ceremony. We can see ourselves out," Lady Wilton interjected.

His mother's chin lifted faintly. "There is no excuse for bad manners, even in grief."

Lady Wilton gave a respectful nod. "Very well."

As the maid helped his mother to her feet and quietly led her from the parlor, Evander remained frozen where he knelt. His throat burned. He blinked rapidly, but the tears gathered, nonetheless.

Olivia knelt beside him, gently pressing another handkerchief into his hand.

He looked down at it, then at her, his lips twitching. "How many of these do you keep in your reticule?"

She gave a half-smile, her tone light but her eyes tender. "I'm a lady, Evander. I must be prepared for anything."

"Thank you," he murmured.

Olivia leaned in ever so slightly. "You did well."

He lifted his gaze to hers, searching her eyes as though they alone could confirm what he could not yet believe. "Did I?" The question was whispered, raw with uncertainty.

"Yes," she replied. "Your mother needs time to absorb the weight of what you've told her about Bryon."

He exhaled slowly, the tightness in his chest loosening a fraction. Then, as if remembering himself, he straightened and extended his hand. “Come, let me see you to the door.”

Her fingers slipped into his, and he helped her stand. “I must say,” she said, “I thought it rather rude that you had not done so already.”

Evander knew precisely what she was doing. She was trying to lighten the mood, and he appreciated her more for it. And therein lay the danger—for friendship such as theirs was something he could not bear to lose.

Later that day, Evander stood outside his mother’s bedchamber, his fist poised to knock but hovering uncertainly in the air. Through the thick door, he could hear the faint sound of weeping—soft, muffled sobs that wrenched at his heart. He closed his eyes for a moment, as if doing so could somehow ease her grief or give him the strength to face it. How desperately he wished he could take her pain upon himself, to spare her this agony. But no such power existed.

Drawing in a breath and summoning his courage, he knocked gently. The sobs quieted, leaving an eerie stillness in their wake. A long moment passed before he heard her voice, fragile but composed. “Enter.”

He opened the door and stepped into the dimly lit chamber. The heavy drapes had been drawn tightly shut, allowing only the thinnest slivers of late afternoon light to seep through. A small fire burned low in the hearth, casting flickering shadows across the walls. The scent of lavender, faint and faded, mingled with the smoke of the fire.

His mother sat upon the settee before the hearth, her figure small and forlorn. She wore a black gown and tear tracks glistened on her pale cheeks, though her eyes were now dry and distant, fixed upon the flames.

"Why is it so dark in here?" Evander asked softly, his voice breaking the hush of the room.

She blinked and glanced about as if noticing her surroundings for the first time. "Is it?" she replied absently, as though the question scarcely mattered.

Evander crossed to the window and drew the drapes apart. Sunlight streamed in and he turned back. "Much better," he murmured.

Yet his mother remained where she was, unmoved, her gaze returning to the hearth. New tears welled in her eyes and slid silently down her face.

Evander's heart constricted. He strode to the settee and lowered himself beside her, reaching out to take her trembling hand in his.

"How can I make this better?" he asked earnestly, his voice rough with emotion.

She wiped at her tears with a handkerchief, though it did little good. "You cannot, my dear child," she whispered. "No one can. Losing a child... it breaks the heart in ways no words can mend. I simply need time to carry this sorrow."

He swallowed hard. "Has Father come to see you?"

A faint, wistful smile touched her lips. "No. But I would not expect him to. Your father has never been able to bear the sight of my tears. He may wear a stern exterior, but his heart is tenderer than he lets on."

"Father?" Evander echoed, skeptical.

She managed a faint chuckle. "Yes, your father. I know you two are often at odds, but do not mistake his severity for coldness. He is a good man."

Evander doubted that, but he did not want to argue with her. Not now. So instead, he squeezed her hand. "Can I fetch you anything? Tea, perhaps, or a blanket?"

She shook her head. “No. Having you here is enough. I was merely thinking of all that has been lost with Bryon’s passing. I shall never see him marry, never hold his children in my arms.” Her voice broke on the words. “And... I may not even live to see you wed and find happiness.”

He grasped her hand more firmly. “You are going to live a long time yet, Mother,” he said, willing it to be true.

She gave him a wan smile. “Pish-posh. We both know my health is failing. The doctor has not tried to soften his words. I do not have much longer.”

Silence fell between them and Evander felt his throat tighten. “I... could marry,” he offered, the words spilling out unbidden.

She looked at him with new interest. “Are you courting anyone?”

“No. But Father has been pressing me to marry Lady Jemima. I could—if it would bring you peace...”

She raised a hand to halt him. “Absolutely not! That girl is terrible. You would be miserable, and I would not see you sacrificed for convenience. I never understood what Bryon saw in her.”

“I think it was her dowry that caught his attention,” Evander offered.

His mother gave a weary sigh. “That would explain it. If I were to choose, I have always thought you and Olivia would suit one another.”

The mention of Olivia made his heart skip, though he schooled his features into neutrality. “Olivia and I are merely friends.”

“Perhaps,” she said knowingly. “But friendship is a fine foundation for marriage. It is more than your father and I began with.”

He hesitated. “Father has forbidden me from marrying her.”

"Because of the scandal?" she asked bluntly.

"Yes."

His mother's expression darkened with a hint of defiance. "And do you intend to obey him?"

Evander released her hand and leaned back with a sigh. "No, but—"

"Then why not ask her?" she interrupted, her gaze bright with sudden resolve. "The *ton* would be far more forgiving if she married the heir to an earldom. It would shield her from further harm, and it would bring me comfort to know you were with someone who could truly make you happy."

"Mother..." Evander began, taken aback. "Surely you cannot mean for me to wed her out of duty alone."

"I would be more at peace if I knew you were wed, yes. But more than that—I have seen how you look at her, Evander. Do not deny it."

He looked away. "We are friends," he murmured.

"The best of friends."

"We were, when we were younger. Now... we each lead separate lives. I scarcely see her."

Her gaze met his, filled with quiet understanding. "I know I ask much of you, my son. But think on it—for my sake."

Before he could respond, a soft knock sounded at the door. A moment later it opened, and his father stood in the threshold, his bearing uncharacteristically tentative.

"How are you, Diana?" he asked, his voice gentler than usual.

A thin smile touched her lips. "I am well enough."

"Would you... would you care for me to read to you before dinner?" he offered awkwardly.

"I would like that," she replied.

The earl looked visibly relieved and stepped farther into the room.

Evander rose. "I should go."

"Must you?" his mother asked.

He bent to kiss her cheek. "I will return tomorrow. Do try to get a good night's sleep."

She nodded. "Think on what I said, Son."

"I will," he promised. With a respectful nod to his father, he slipped from the room, his mind and heart both heavier than when he had entered.

As Evander strode quickly down the corridor, he found that, to his own surprise, he was not at all opposed to the idea of marrying Olivia. Why should he be? He loved her. He always had, though he had spent years convincing himself otherwise. The thought of binding his life to hers did not fill him with dread, but with longing. And yet... how would she respond if he were to offer for her now?

Knowing Olivia, she would resist. She would balk at the notion, convinced he acted from pity or duty, rather than affection. And worse—the question that gnawed at him most remained. What if her heart still belonged to that scoundrel, Lord Harwood? Olivia might wear a mask of indifference in public, but he had seen the shadow behind her smile. He knew she had suffered far more than she ever allowed others to see. Could he truly bear to marry her, knowing she might never return his love?

But then, unbidden, an image of his mother rose in his mind—pale and fragile, her voice trembling with sorrow and resignation. He knew time was slipping away from her, faster than any of them wished to admit. If marrying Olivia would bring his mother even a modicum of peace, then he would do it. He would do whatever it took. And if it meant spending the rest of his life gently persuading Olivia to accept his suit—and perhaps, in time, to love him—so be it.

With a renewed sense of determination, he exited through the main door. His steps quickened as he made his way down the pavement. Olivia's townhouse was not far, and he had no patience for waiting upon the coach to be brought round. The brisk air cleared his thoughts even as it heightened his nerves. As he walked, he rehearsed speech after speech in his mind—words that might persuade her, soothe her doubts, and assure her of his sincerity. None of them seemed quite right.

His breathing was slightly labored by the time he reached her townhouse. He ascended the steps and raised his hand to knock.

The door opened almost at once, and the butler greeted him with practiced civility. "Lord Westmere, do come in," the man said, opening the door wide.

Evander stepped into the familiar entry hall just as Wilton was descending the staircase, an eyebrow arched in surprise. "Westmere. What brings you by at this hour?"

"I need to speak to Olivia," Evander replied, his tone clipped with purpose.

Wilton gave him a considering look. "She is dressing for dinner," he informed him. Then, with a more welcoming air, he added, "Would you care to dine with us this evening?"

"I would not wish to be an imposition."

"Nonsense," Wilton responded, turning to the butler. "Inform the cook that Lord Westmere will be joining us for dinner."

The butler inclined his head. "Yes, my lord." With that, he departed to carry out the order.

Now alone with Wilton in the entry hall, Evander found his friend's gaze fixed upon him, sharp and appraising. "Dare I ask what this is all about?"

"I would prefer to speak privately."

Wilton gestured towards the drawing room. "After you," he said with a nod of encouragement.

Once they had entered the drawing room, Evander closed the door behind them and turned to face his friend squarely. "I am going to offer for Olivia," he announced.

If Wilton was startled by this sudden admission, he gave no outward sign. Instead, he merely said, "It is about time."

"Pardon?"

Wilton's mouth twitched into a knowing smile as he crossed his arms over his chest. "You two were inseparable as children. I have long suspected there was more between you than either of you cared to admit. I believe you would suit very well."

Evander dragged a hand through his hair. "As you know, my mother is dying. She wishes to see me wed before she passes—she says it will ease her mind." His voice grew softer. "And if I marry Olivia, I might help restore her reputation. She deserves that much."

"Yes, you could," Wilton agreed. "It would be a most advantageous match for her."

"Do you think she will agree?"

Wilton gave a small shrug. "Olivia can be... unpredictable. I rarely presume to guess what she will do. But it is not as though there are scores of gentlemen beating down our doors to court her, especially not after what happened. Still, know this: if you truly mean to offer for her, do not speak as though you are doing her a favor. Olivia would never accept such terms."

Evander's jaw tightened. "I would never insult her so. I would be a good husband to her. I only hope she can come to believe that."

Wilton studied him for a moment, then gave a short nod. "Then I wish you luck, my friend. You will need it."

"How did you convince your wife to marry you?"

Wilton chuckled. "There was some groveling involved," he confessed with a grin. "But more than that—I loved her so deeply that I set aside my pride and spoke to her from the heart. That, I think, is what won her over."

Before Evander could ask more, the door opened, and both men turned.

Olivia entered the room with graceful ease. She wore a pale

blue gown with a delicate white net overlay that complemented her fair complexion to perfection. Her blonde hair was swept up in an elegant style and two soft curls framed her face.

"Evander," Olivia greeted him. "What a pleasant surprise."

He stepped forward until he stood directly before her, the words he had rehearsed on the walk over suddenly fleeing his mind. "I was hoping to speak with you," he managed.

Olivia tilted her head slightly, her gaze sparkling with curiosity. "It sounds rather serious."

"It is," he admitted, clearing his throat in an attempt to steady his nerves.

"Then perhaps I ought to fetch my serious hat," she teased, her eyes dancing with mischief.

A chuckle escaped him despite his tension. "You are a minx."

Placing a light hand upon his sleeve, she said, "I was merely trying to make you laugh. I know the burdens upon your shoulders of late have not been easy to bear."

"No, they haven't," he confessed, his voice roughened by fatigue and grief.

She held his gaze steadily. "But you will get through this. You are the strongest man I know."

Wilton interjected with mock indignation. "What about me, Sister?"

Olivia dropped her hand from Evander's sleeve and turned towards her brother. "I stand by my statement."

Wilton placed a dramatic hand over his heart. "That wounds me."

Before more could be said, Lady Wilton appeared at the threshold and announced, "Sterling informs me that dinner is ready. Shall we adjourn to the dining room?"

"That is an excellent idea," Wilton replied, offering his arm to his wife. "Westmere will be joining us for dinner."

Lady Wilton's smile warmed further as she met Evander's gaze. "My lord," she murmured politely.

"Please," Evander replied with a small bow, "you must call me Evander. All my friends do."

"Then you must call me Dosia," she responded.

Evander returned her smile. "It would be my pleasure."

As they began to make their way towards the dining room, Evander fell into step beside Olivia. His heart thudded in his chest as he leaned slightly towards her and said in a quiet voice, "We shall speak after dinner."

Olivia glanced up at him, her smile light and teasing. "Then I have something to look forward to."

As they entered the dining room, Evander could scarcely take his eyes off her. He had always been fascinated by Olivia, completely and breathtakingly fascinated by her. She was his future. He was certain of it now, more than ever.

But would she feel the same?

5

Olivia sat at the long, rectangular dining table, the low murmur of conversation swirling around her like distant music. Yet her thoughts remained fixed on her mother's voice, those sharp, sensible words still ringing in her mind: *You mustn't spend so much time with Evander. It will only encourage gossip.*

A fresh wave of guilt washed over her. She had loved Evander as a friend for as long as she could remember. He had been her companion in childhood, her confidant in youth, and her solace through recent trials. But now... the world demanded more caution. For his sake—for his future—she would have to do the unthinkable and step away from their friendship.

The decision pressed on her heart like a stone. *Tonight will be the last,* she resolved. *I shall cherish this evening, one final memory before I sever the tie.*

With that melancholy thought, she forced herself to look at him. Evander sat next to her, the candlelight emphasizing his handsome face. His strong jaw, straight nose, and that unruly, dark hair of his—still curling at the nape of his neck as it always had. She remembered all too well how, as a girl, she had once laughed and tangled her fingers in those curls. She quickly averted her gaze, heart tightening.

Dosia's voice broke through her reverie. "Olivia? Are you well? You have been staring at your venison for quite some time."

Startled, Olivia blinked. Her tongue, quicker than her judgment, betrayed her. "I was merely thinking of Evander's hair," she replied without a thought. "It is... curly."

Laughter rippled down the table as Evander looked up, amused. "Indeed," he said. "I inherited the curls from my mother."

"I like it," Olivia said, and immediately regretted the words.

"Good." His blue eyes gleamed with teasing warmth. "Should I return the compliment? Your hair is... rather blonde."

A reluctant smile tugged at her lips. "It is, but it is far from curly."

"And yet, I am exceedingly fond of it."

"You only say that because I complimented your hair," she countered.

He leaned towards her, his voice lowering conspiratorially. "This is a delightful game. What else do you like about me?"

Olivia shook her head. "You are being insufferably cocky tonight."

He waggled his brows playfully. "You started it, Livy. I am merely seeing it through."

"Now I regret saying anything," she stated. "I hereby retract my compliment."

"You cannot. You've said it. It is mine to keep."

"Then I *un*say it."

Evander leaned back in triumph. "Too late. My admiration for your hair stands unshaken."

At the head of the table, Richard cleared his throat. "As

diverting as this conversation is, I was inquiring about Westmere's opinion on the bill I am drafting."

Evander immediately grew serious. "Yes, of course. I am in full support of your efforts. I intend to encourage my father to vote in favor."

"I hope so," Richard said, lifting his glass. "It will take every ounce of influence to see it through Parliament."

Dosia placed a gentle hand on her husband's arm. "I think it is admirable that you are seeking to raise the working ages in the workhouses."

"The Tories do not agree," Richard replied with a grim smile. "They argue that the foundling homes are already overburdened."

"You will persuade them," Dosia said with quiet conviction.

Their gazes locked. "I love you."

"And I you," she replied softly.

Olivia rolled her eyes. "Can the two of you manage three seconds without professing your love?"

Richard arched a brow. "Why does it trouble you so, Sister?"

"I care for Evander," she said with forced nonchalance. "But I do not see the need to parade it about the table."

Evander tilted his head. "I would not object if you declared your affection—once or twice."

Olivia sighed. "Very well. I care for you."

"That sounded dreadfully insincere. Do try again," Evander responded.

With exaggerated patience, she repeated, "I care for you."

Evander laughed outright. "No. I detect sarcasm. You must woo me with greater sincerity."

Olivia seized her wine glass. "I require a drink." She took a generous sip.

Dosia interjected with a laugh. "Come now, let us spare Olivia further torment. I fear she will finish the entire bottle."

"Thank you, Dosia," Olivia said with a grateful smile, setting her glass down. "Perhaps we might choose a new topic?"

Dosia glanced down the table. "I do hope your mother feels better by morning."

Olivia waved a hand in front of her. "She has taken laudanum for her headache. She will sleep well enough."

Richard leaned forward. "What shall we do tomorrow? A ride through Hyde Park? Or an evening at Vauxhall Gardens?"

Dosia's eyes lit up. "I vote for Vauxhall."

"Very well," Richard said. "After we attend to the accounts."

"Two things to anticipate," Dosia said with a pleased smile.

Richard turned to Evander and explained, "Dosia often assists me with the ledgers."

"I think it is brilliant," Evander declared. "Why should gentlemen hoard all the enjoyment of balancing sums?"

Olivia furrowed her brows. "You do not object to a woman working on estate accounts?"

"Not in the least," Evander said. "If memory serves, Dosia managed her family's estate admirably before her marriage."

"She did," Richard confirmed with pride. "And continues to do so."

"Eventually," Dosia added, "I hope to entrust my sister with our family's estate after she is released from prison."

Evander's expression softened. "How long will that be?"

"Four months," Dosia replied. "She was convicted of vagrancy, though Richard intervened and persuaded the judge towards leniency."

"That was generous of you," Evander said.

Dosia bobbed her head in agreement. "Only with Olivia's blessing."

Evander turned to Olivia. "That was most gracious."

Olivia shrugged. "Lucinda returned my dowry and sent an apology. It seemed sincere enough. I am not one to nurse grudges. Besides, I do believe four months among rats is punishment enough."

"The rats outnumber the prisoners three to one," Richard said grimly.

Olivia shuddered. "But I was adamant that Lucinda could not live with us upon her release."

"Entirely fair," Dosia agreed.

Just then, the footmen stepped forward, whisking away their plates and setting bowls of pudding before each person.

Olivia reached for her spoon and, after a moment's thought, glanced at Evander. "You mentioned you wished to speak with me?"

Evander hesitated, then said, "I would prefer to do so in private."

Olivia took a generous bite of pudding, swallowed, and met his gaze. "I am ready."

"Very well," Evander said, dabbing the corners of his mouth with a napkin. "Shall we take a turn about your gardens?"

Olivia pushed back her chair. "We may, but I should warn you that the birds may not prove welcoming."

"Oh?"

"I threw a pillow at one of them this morning," she shared. "The wretched creature insisted upon serenading me from my windowsill at an unholy hour."

"I think I can withstand a few disgruntled birds."

"You should not be so cavalier," Olivia replied. "If they were ever to rise up in revolt, we would surely be outnumbered."

Rising to stand, Evander extended his hand towards her. "Then I shall take my chances... though I can say I wouldn't mind defending you from a flock of murderous sparrows."

Her lips curved as she allowed him to assist her to her feet. "My knight in shining—"

"But no armor," he said. "I have a nickel allergy. I get a terrible rash, and it is rather unsightly."

She laughed. "No armor, then."

As they started to leave the dining room, Richard's voice called after them. "Dosia and I will be watching you from the drawing room window."

"Why?" Olivia asked.

"To ensure you are properly chaperoned," came his reply.

"Very wise," Olivia said with a wry smile, slipping her hand into the crook of Evander's arm. "That way I shall not be tempted to run off to Gretna Green." She flashed a grin over her shoulder. "Oh, wait—I already did that."

Richard gave her a disapproving look. "We are joking about that now?"

"*I* am," Olivia responded. "You are still recovering." Then, with a conspiratorial glance at Evander, she added, "Come along. Let's do something scandalous."

"Olivia..." Richard growled a warning.

Once they passed beyond the threshold of the dining room, Olivia leaned towards him. "It is such fun to provoke my brother," she confessed with a mischievous smile. "But do not worry, your virtue is perfectly safe with me."

Yet Evander did not return her playfulness. She felt the subtle tension in his frame beneath her fingers as they strolled towards the gardens' doors.

Sensing the shift in mood, Olivia glanced up at him. "You are unusually stiff at the moment," she remarked. "Is something troubling you?"

"Nothing is wrong," he said, too quickly.

"You just seem... rather tense."

"I am not tense."

She decided to try another approach. "How is your mother faring?"

At that, his expression faltered, revealing the weary strain beneath. "As well as can be expected, given the circumstances."

"And how are you?"

A footman, discreet and silent, opened the back door leading to the veranda and followed at a respectful distance as they stepped into the cool night air. The faint scent of jasmine drifted on the breeze. They moved down a gravel path edged with clipped box hedges and summer blooms.

They walked in silence until Evander spoke. "I am afraid of letting everyone down."

Olivia's heart clenched. She halted, gently tugging his arm until he stopped and faced her. His features were shadowed in the moonlight, but the vulnerability in his gaze was plain.

"That isn't possible," she said, but he shook his head.

"I am being serious, Olivia." His voice roughened with self-reproach. "I know nothing about estate management. I can draft a lecture, debate policy, and command a classroom easily, but to take on my father's legacy? To manage the land, the tenants, the staff, the accounts..." He exhaled a ragged breath. "I am wholly unprepared to be my father's heir."

She met his gaze steadily. "You will learn."

"It is not that simple."

Taking a step forward, she asked, "Do you not remember how worried you were when you left for Eton? And again, when you went to Oxford. You were so nervous, so convinced you would not measure up to the other students." Her voice softened. "And look at you now. You became a Fellow at five and twenty, an accomplishment most scholars twice your age would envy."

For a moment, silence stretched between them. Then Olivia reached up and lightly touched his arm. "You have faced daunting things before, Evander. You will face this, too. And you will not face it alone."

He studied her face for a long moment, his expression guarded. Then, he asked, "Will you marry me?"

Evander was an idiot.

The realization struck him with a force that left him momentarily speechless. Why had he just blurted out a marriage proposal to Olivia? He had planned the perfect, well-crafted speech. So why had his words come tumbling from his mouth like an avalanche he could not stop?

He watched helplessly as Olivia reared back, her brows knitting in bewilderment. Her parted lips formed no words, only silent astonishment.

Closing his eyes briefly, he exhaled in frustration. "I boggled that quite nicely, didn't I?" he muttered.

Her voice, low and uncertain, broke the silence between them. "Did you truly just mean to offer for me?"

Opening his eyes again, he forced himself to meet her gaze. He could see the questions there—so many of them—and perhaps a flicker of hope, though he dared not trust it.

"I did," he said. "But before you say no—please—allow me to explain why I think we should marry."

She crossed her arms slowly over her chest, adopting a guarded stance. "Very well," she replied.

Drawing in a deep breath to steady himself, he began. "As you know, my mother is gravely ill. Her one wish is to see me married before she passes. And I—I cannot bear to disappoint her." His throat tightened, but he pressed on. "I thought that you... that we... would suit nicely." He ran a hand through his hair, tousling it further. "And... if you marry me, the *ton* will be less inclined to punish you for past events. My name will protect you."

Her brow arched. "Are you quite finished?"

"I am," he said, though the words stuck in his throat. He held his breath as he awaited her reply.

For a long moment, Olivia said nothing. Then she opened her mouth, closed it again, visibly struggling to form her thoughts. At last, she said, "You do not truly want to marry me."

"I do."

"No, you don't," she countered. "You need a wife whose reputation is beyond reproach. Someone the *ton* will embrace as your viscountess."

He stepped towards her, his voice firm. "I do not care what the *ton* says. I want to marry you."

She placed a hand lightly against his chest, her touch sending a ripple through him. But the smile she gave him did not reach her eyes. "I know what you are trying to do."

"And what is that?"

"You are trying to save me," she whispered. "But you must think of your own reputation now. Of your family's standing."

He caught her hand in his. "I am thinking of that. This was not solely my idea. My mother suggested it. She wants me to marry you."

"What of your father?"

He winced. "He may object for now. But he would come around... eventually. Especially once your dowry bolsters our coffers."

Olivia's gaze grew pained. "And what of the whispers? The stares that follow me everywhere I go? They are relentless."

"That matters little to me."

She slipped her hand free and stepped back. "You are the best of friends, Evander. But I cannot let you throw your life away for me."

"I would be throwing nothing away."

Her eyes shimmered with unshed tears. "And what of love?" she asked. "What of that? What if you grew to resent me because of it?"

He faltered. The words hovered on the edge of his tongue—*I love you. I always have.* But he swallowed them back, knowing she was not ready to hear them. "I could never resent you," he said instead.

A tear slid down her cheek. She brushed it away quickly, her composure faltering. "I think... it is best if we avoid one another for a time."

He stared at her, stricken. "I beg your pardon?"

"I care about you too deeply to risk jeopardizing your new position," she replied.

Reaching for her hand again, he said urgently, "No. I will not accept that. We are friends, Livy. I do not care who knows it."

"You say that now..."

"I will say it always. And it will remain no less true," he declared. "If you try to push me away, I will only come right back."

She smiled through her tears. "What did I ever do to deserve a friend like you?"

He grinned, leaning in. "I suspect you bewitched me the day you poured that mud over my head."

She laughed—a real laugh this time—and wiped her cheek. "You cannot go about accusing people of witchcraft. Though... I daresay it would be entertaining. I could fly about on a broomstick and concoct potions."

"I believe the broomstick part is a myth."

"That is the only part you take issue with?" she teased.

He chuckled. "Very well. I promise never to accuse you of being a witch again."

But her humor faded swiftly. "I cannot marry you, Evander."

"Why not? We would have such fun together. You are the only one who makes me laugh as you do."

"It would be selfish of me to say yes," she said, voice thick with emotion.

"Does that mean you are tempted?" he pressed.

She nodded slowly, her shoulders slumping. "Of course, I am tempted. I am five and twenty, and my reputation is in tatters. You may well be the only offer I shall ever receive."

"Then say yes. We will post the banns at once." His eagerness rang clear—and perhaps too forcefully. He could sense her wavering.

"I need you to be certain."

"I am certain."

She let out a breathless laugh, but it was without joy. "You are a viscount now. Every choice you make carries weight. Do you truly wish to tie yourself to a woman with an annulled marriage?"

"That means nothing to me. You were tricked, and everyone knows it."

"Not everyone is so kind or forgiving."

He leaned closer, his tone fierce with sincerity. "But I am not 'everyone.' You knew me when I was but the second son of an earl. The spare. And you never treated me differently."

"Why would I?"

"Exactly," he said with a small smile. "You are the wife I need."

She looked upward, as though the stars themselves might grant her wisdom. "You are good."

"That is because I am charming, handsome, and keeper of your secrets," he quipped. "Think of the disservice you will do to Society if we do not marry. Our children would be beautiful and brilliant."

"You make a fair point."

His expression sobered. "I do not wish to force you. Think on it. I will return tomorrow."

"What if you change your mind?"

"I will not. That I promise."

She bit her lower lip—a telltale sign of her inner struggle, one he had come to know well. He watched her with aching tenderness.

"You need not answer now," he added gently. "But do not dismiss the possibility outright."

She gave a small nod, tears glistening once more. "You are impossible," she whispered.

"And yet, here I stand," he replied, his gaze unwavering.

Turning her gaze towards the townhouse, Olivia asked, "Does Richard know that you were going to offer for me?"

"Yes," Evander replied. "And he was rather excited by the prospect."

Her lips pressed into a thin, resigned line. "I am sure he is more than anxious to be rid of me."

"You are wrong," Evander said. "Your brother loves you."

"Yes, but I have caused him no small amount of grief these past months."

He placed a reassuring hand upon her sleeve. "It is cold out here, and you do not even have a shawl. Come—we should go back inside."

As they headed towards the townhouse, Olivia remarked, "Your father would be furious if we did wed."

"All the more reason to say yes, then."

"He has never liked me."

Evander merely smiled. "That may have had something to do with the fact that you never listened to him," he replied. "And that you constantly ran off into the woodlands."

Looking entirely unrepentant, Olivia tilted her chin. "How else was I supposed to look for truffles?"

"We hired people to do that, you know," he reminded her.

"Yes," she said, "but if I wanted to keep them for myself, I had to find them and eat them before anyone discovered my stash."

Evander gave her a long, knowing look. "You used to hide them under your pillow and eat them at night."

"It was a delicious treat."

They stepped inside and made their way to the drawing room, where Wilton and his wife were already waiting.

As they entered, Wilton held out his hands. "Are congratulations in order?"

"Not yet," Evander responded. "But Olivia is considering it."

Wilton's brows shot up. "What is there to consider?" he asked, his voice rising in earnest. "This is the solution to all of our problems."

Olivia turned to face him fully, her back growing rigid. "It is *my* choice, Brother."

"It is," Wilton allowed, though his mouth pressed into a grim line. "However, I feel—"

Dosia, standing beside him, nudged him with her elbow. "Leave her be. It is Olivia's decision."

"Yes, but there is a very clear right and wrong answer here," Wilton muttered under his breath.

Sensing the growing tension, Evander inclined his head. "I feel this is a good time to take my leave." He gave a courteous bow. "I will return tomorrow."

Olivia turned towards him. "Allow me to walk you to the door."

"I would like that."

Together they left the drawing room, walking side by side until they arrived at the main door.

"Until tomorrow, Olivia," Evander said, holding her gaze.

"Goodnight, Evander."

He opened the door and stepped out into the cool night air. As the door closed behind him, he exhaled slowly. He felt confident that he had pleaded his case as best he could. But with Olivia, he never truly knew what she would do.

And that, perhaps, was why he loved her all the more.

6

Dressed in a pale yellow gown that complemented her fair complexion but did little to brighten her weary spirits, Olivia stepped from her bedchamber and into the quiet corridor. The faint scent of lavender from her bath lingered in the air, though it had done little to soothe her restless mind. She had scarcely slept since her thoughts were consumed by the proposal Evander had offered the night before.

It would be selfish to accept. She knew that. Yet the temptation gnawed at her resolve.

Marrying Evander would solve everything. His name would shield her from Society's censure. The whispers would cease, and the weight of guilt pressing upon her heart might finally lift. And she *did* love him, though not in the way a wife ought to love her husband. He was her dearest friend, which only made the prospect of a marriage of convenience all the more troubling. Could she sentence him to a lifetime of polite affection, knowing he deserved far more?

But oh, how easy it would be to say yes. A single word could erase the shame she had brought upon her family.

Descending the staircase with a hand lightly brushing the iron banister, Olivia came to an abrupt halt at the sight below. The entry hall was transformed—a riot of color and fragrance greeted her. Dozens of flower arrangements in crystal vases crowded the space, spilling onto tables and pedestals.

Sterling stood at the sideboard, deftly arranging yet another bouquet.

"Where did all these flowers come from?" Olivia asked, her voice edged with disbelief.

Sterling looked up, a faint smile tugging at his lips. "They are all for you, my lady. They have been arriving steadily since this morning."

Her brows rose. "All for me?"

He retrieved a card from among the blooms and handed it to her with a slight bow. "They are from Lord Westmere."

Curious, Olivia took the card and read the familiar, teasing script: *Say yes, and I will vanquish the bird that has been bothering you.*

A soft laugh escaped her before she could stop it. It didn't surprise her that Evander would remember the impudent bird that had plagued her windowsill.

Yes.

It would be so easy to say yes.

Before she could ponder further, Sterling reached down and produced a small brown box tied with a crimson string. "This package arrived with the flowers."

Accepting it, Olivia slipped the string free and opened the lid. Nestled inside, rich and earthy in scent, were black truffles. Her breath caught. He remembered everything, even her fondness for these little treasures.

Her mother's voice interrupted her reverie. "What is in the package?"

Olivia turned, revealing the box. "Truffles."

A blank stare met her words. "Did you say *truffles*?"

"I did." She offered a small smile. "Evander sent them. He... offered for me last night. This is his attempt to woo me."

Her mother's eyes widened with unguarded delight. "Evander offered for you?" she repeated breathlessly. "That is wonderful news!"

Olivia raised her hand. "I haven't accepted yet."

"Perhaps not, but you will," her mother replied with certainty. "This is your chance to reclaim your place in Society."

"I am aware. But can I truly trap him in a marriage of convenience?"

Her mother dismissed the concern with a wave of her hand. "Love can grow, my dear. And in time, it will. Now, we should begin planning a luncheon to celebrate."

Olivia pressed her lips into a thin line. "Mother, you are getting ahead of yourself."

"I am merely excited," her mother said brightly. "Imagine it—you, the wife of Lord Westmere. An heir to an earldom. Society will have no choice but to welcome you back with open arms."

With a small shake of her head, Olivia turned and headed for the dining room. She had heard enough. The decision had to be her own, free of her family's hopes and expectations.

Inside, she found Dosia and Richard already at the table, engaged in a quiet conversation. Richard rose when he noticed her, but Olivia waved him back down.

Taking her seat, she placed the box of truffles beside her.

Richard arched a brow. "What have you there?"

"A gift from Evander," she replied simply. "Truffles."

A smirk tugged at her brother's mouth. "Nothing says affection like a fungus."

Dosia laughed. "Leave her be, Richard."

"I do love truffles," Olivia admitted, a wistful smile touching her lips. "I used to scour the woodlands near our country estate for them. When I found any, I would sneak them to my room and savor them in secret."

"That is odd, Sister," Richard said with amusement, though his tone was gentle.

Before she could respond, her mother swept into the room and claimed her place at the head of the table. "I think we should have a family meeting."

Olivia groaned. "May I be excused from it?"

"Are you not family?" her mother countered.

"I am. But I already know where you all stand regarding my possible marriage to Evander."

Her mother gave her an innocent smile. "I am only trying to help."

A footman set a cup of chocolate before Olivia. She lifted it, the warmth seeping into her fingers. "Perhaps we could discuss something else."

Dosia perked up. "Would you care to join us at Vauxhall Gardens this evening?"

"I would like that," Olivia replied, welcoming the change of topic.

Richard interjected, "Perhaps we should invite Westmere, as well."

Surprisingly, Olivia found herself unopposed to the idea. Evander had an uncanny ability to lift her mood and he could always make her laugh, even when she least expected it.

"I will ask him," she said at last.

Satisfied, Richard returned to his newssheets.

Olivia, however, sipped her chocolate in thoughtful silence. The choice before her remained, as tempting as it was terrifying. And though her family clearly hoped for her to accept, the decision would be hers alone to make.

Dosia met Olivia's gaze. "I trust you slept well?"

Olivia gave a weary smile. "Not particularly. I had a fitful night." Her shoulders lifted in a slight shrug. "I suppose that is to be expected when one is wrestling with an impossible decision."

"That is hardly surprising," Dosia agreed. "You are carrying a great deal on your shoulders. No one could expect a restful night under such circumstances."

Richard lowered the newssheets he had been perusing. "It seems a simple decision to me."

Dosia gave her husband a pointed look. "It may be simple in *your* mind, but it is not *your* decision to make." Her voice was firm but kind. "Whatever choice Olivia makes, we will stand by her."

Olivia's throat tightened with gratitude, and she offered Dosia a faint smile. "Thank you. That means more to me than I can say."

"Of course." Dosia reached for her fork again. "Now, shall we plan something pleasant to occupy the morning? Would you care to visit the circulating library after breakfast? I find myself in desperate need of a new book or two."

A welcome distraction. Just the thought of escaping into the world of stories brought a small measure of relief. "I would like that," Olivia replied. "Very much."

A companionable silence settled over the room as they resumed eating. The clatter of cutlery and the quiet rustle of paper were the only sounds.

Then, after a long moment, Richard let out a loud groan. "It would appear, dear sister, that you have made the newssheets... again."

Olivia's heart sank. "What is it this time?"

Richard folded the newssheets and handed it across the table. "Read it for yourself. It's an article by Mr. Fairchild."

Dread coiled in her stomach as she took the newssheets and scanned the article. The words blurred slightly as her eyes flew across the damning lines. Finally, she sighed heavily and set the newssheets down. "How in the blazes did Mr. Fairchild learn of Evander's offer? It only happened last night."

"Language, dear," her mother admonished from her seat. "A genteel woman does not resort to such vulgar expressions."

Olivia chose to ignore the rebuke, her gaze fixed on the offending article. "Now I have little choice in the matter. If I refuse Evander, my name—and our family's—will be further dragged through the mud."

"There are far worse fates than becoming a viscountess," Richard remarked dryly.

Turning to Dosia, Olivia asked, "How did you know you wanted to marry my vexing brother?"

At once, Dosia's expression softened. "I loved him," she said. "The decision was easy. I would not have given up my independence for anyone else."

"But would you have considered a marriage of convenience if you had not loved him as you ought?"

Dosia considered the question carefully. "No. I would not have," she replied. "But everyone's path is different. You must choose what is best for you, not what anyone else expects of you."

A knot of dread twisted in Olivia's chest. She leaned back in her chair, her posture sagging beneath the weight of her thoughts. "I fear there will be no future for me if I do not marry Evander."

"There are worse things than becoming a spinster, you know," Dosia remarked.

Richard reached across the table and gave his wife's hand an affectionate squeeze. "Stop trying to dissuade her from marrying Westmere," he teased.

"I merely want Olivia to follow her heart," Dosia replied.

The grandfather clock in the corner chimed the passing hour, the deep tones filling the room.

Dosia glanced towards Olivia. "Shall we be off to the circulating library?"

Grateful for the escape, Olivia pushed back her chair. "Yes, please. I believe I am in desperate need of a distraction." She rose and reached for the box of truffles. "Let me put these in my bedchamber first."

Richard eyed the box with amusement. "Why not give them to the cook? Then we could all enjoy them."

Olivia grinned. "And deprive myself of the perfect midnight snack? I think not."

Richard shook his head in mock resignation. "Very well. Keep your fungus."

A faint laugh escaped her, and for the first time that morning, the heaviness in her heart lightened—if only by a fraction.

"*You offered for her*?"

Evander lifted his teacup with deliberate calm and took a sip, the faint clink of porcelain was the only sound in the tense dining room. Setting the cup back on its saucer, he met his father's thunderous gaze across the gleaming table. "If you are referring to Olivia, yes. I did offer for her."

His father's chair scraped back an inch as he jerked upright. "Are you mad?"

"No."

The elder man tossed the folded newssheets onto the table with a snap of his wrist. "Do you have any notion of what you have done?"

Evander reached for his fork and took his time cutting a bite of egg. "I do. I intend to marry Olivia or no one at all."

"You cannot be serious." His father's nostrils flared, the

veins at his temple pulsing. "Olivia is not a suitable choice for you."

"I disagree." Evander met his father's stare unflinchingly. "And I believe I made it clear that the decision of whom I marry is mine alone. Not yours."

A muscle twitched in the older man's jaw. "You would tarnish our family's reputation for this foolishness? Because that is precisely what will happen if you go through with this madness."

"You exaggerate, Father." Evander took a bite and chewed with studied patience.

"I do not," his father snapped.

Evander set down his fork. "Olivia is the daughter of a marquess and possesses a dowry of twenty thousand pounds. Hardly a scandalous match by any rational measure."

His father surged to his feet, his chair scraping harshly across the floor. "Yet she also eloped to Gretna Green with a woman masquerading as a man! The entire *ton* whispers about her."

"She was duped," Evander said. "That is not a crime."

His father threw up his hands. "No, but it is evidence of intolerable naïvety. She would make a terrible countess."

Evander sighed inwardly. His father's anger was no surprise. It was his standard weapon when his will was thwarted. "Father—"

"Enough." His father held up a commanding hand. "You will break this engagement at once. You will marry Lady Jemima. She is expecting your offer."

"Then she will be disappointed." Evander's voice remained level. "Furthermore, Olivia has not yet agreed to marry me."

"But she will."

Evander gave a faint shrug. "I hope so. But with Olivia, nothing is guaranteed."

His father stalked around the table, stopping close enough

that Evander caught the faint scent of tobacco and brandy clinging to his coat. "I know you have always been fascinated by that girl. Take her as a mistress if you must, but not your wife."

Evander's entire frame went taut. "I would never dishonor Olivia in such a way. She deserves far better than that." His gaze sharpened. "As does Mother."

A flicker of something—guilt, perhaps—flashed in his father's eyes. "You know not what you speak of."

"I think I do." Evander kept his voice low, but firm. "The entire house knows. Mother knows."

His father took an unsteady step back, color draining from his face. "Did you tell her?"

"No," Evander replied. "But it's no great secret, is it? You've hardly been discreet."

His father turned abruptly and walked to the window, clasping his hands behind his back. "I love your mother. But she has been… unwell for some time."

"Please." Evander's voice hardened. "Do not insult us both by attempting to justify yourself."

His father pivoted to face him. "I want you to understand."

"I do not." Evander tossed his napkin beside his plate. "You speak of protecting our reputation, yet you do not live as an honorable man yourself."

"It is not uncommon for men of my station—"

Evander cut him off, voice sharp. "Your wife is dying, and you would rather slip off to your mistress's bed. That is your justification?"

His father's mouth tightened. "Bryon understood."

"Well, I am not Bryon." Evander straightened to his full height. "And I never will be." He pushed back his chair with a scrape. "If you'll excuse me, I have a call to make."

"You are a fool, Son."

"With that insult, I bid you good day," he said as he strode towards the doorway.

"Have you begun reviewing the estate accounts?" his father called after him.

Pausing, Evander glanced back. "I have."

"Good," his father replied. "You will focus on the indigo plantation this quarter. The estate depends on its profit."

Evander arched a brow. "Are you certain that's wise? I know very little about indigo plantations."

"You had best learn—and quickly. The plantation's success is vital."

Evander tipped his head in acknowledgment and continued out.

In the entry hall, the butler handed him his hat and opened the door. Stepping outside into the morning air, Evander noticed a stout man in a brown coat loitering nearby. Their eyes met.

The man approached with determined strides. "Are you Lord Westmere?"

"I am," Evander replied warily.

Without preamble, the man reached into his coat and drew a knife, holding it low but menacing. "Mind your business and stay out of India."

Rearing back, Evander asked, "Pardon?"

The man stepped closer. "Sell your *Neel Kothi*—or else."

"I'm afraid I do not know what that is."

The man sneered. "Then learn quickly. You've no place meddling there. Do the right thing or it'll be the last thing you do." With that final warning, he retreated swiftly down the street.

Evander considered pursuing him, but thought better of it. The man was armed with a knife and that was not to be underestimated.

As he made his way towards Olivia's townhouse, his mind churned with questions. *What is a Neel Kothi?* And why did this man threaten him so brazenly on the street?

He arrived sooner than he expected, climbing the stone steps and knocking. The butler admitted him promptly, and he couldn't help but notice the profusion of fresh flowers he had sent filling the entry hall.

As if summoned by the thought, Olivia appeared from a side corridor. "Evander," she greeted.

He bowed. "Livy. You are looking lovely as always."

A playful smile touched her lips. "Flattery? And at such an early hour."

"It is the truth." He stepped closer. "I have always found you to be remarkably beautiful."

"That is kind of you to say..."

Speaking over her, he said, "Surely you must know how beautiful you are."

She pressed her lips together. "I am no beauty."

"You are wrong." He smiled. "You outshine every other young lady in any room."

A blush rose on her cheeks, and she looked down. "Is that why I am five and twenty and unwed?"

He moved until he stood before her and gently tipped her chin up. "Only because you were waiting for me to offer."

"About your offer..." She hesitated. "If you truly mean it, I will marry you."

A smile lit his face. "Nothing would make me happier."

She searched his eyes. "You must be certain. It is an advantageous match for me, but for you—what do you gain?"

He traced a light touch along her cheek. "I gain *you*."

"Be serious, Evander."

"I am," he replied. "I will post the banns at once. And in three weeks' time, you shall be my wife."

Her eyes shimmered. "Does your mother have that much time left?"

He swallowed hard. "I hope so."

"Then perhaps we should marry by special license."

His grin turned roguish. "What you are proposing is scandalous, but I like it. My father will despise the idea, which is an added benefit."

She laughed softly. "You are awful."

He reached for her hand. "Awfully in love with you."

Olivia visibly stiffened, her eyes widening ever so slightly. "You… love me?"

Realizing what he had just let slip, Evander's breath caught. *Fool,* he silently cursed himself. He shook his head quickly. "I do… as a friend." The words tumbled out too quickly. "It was merely an expression. Surely you have heard it before," he added, forcing a light tone in a desperate attempt to deflect.

"I haven't," she replied, her voice soft, almost wary.

"Then you need to get out more," he said with a faint, crooked smile.

To his relief, she didn't press him further. Her gaze dropped to her hands for a moment before she looked up again. "Should we tell my family?"

He opened his mouth to respond, but before he could utter a word, Wilton's voice cut through the air from the corridor. "There is no need. We overheard everything."

Evander dropped his hand from Olivia's and took a step back, scanning the corridor. *How had I not heard them approaching?* His instincts must have been dulled by the sheer weight of this moment.

Dosia and the Dowager Lady Wilton approached swiftly, their faces alight with joy. Dosia reached Olivia first, embracing her tightly. "We are so happy for you," she said warmly, her eyes shining.

Evander's gaze flicked to Olivia. Her smile was polite, her posture composed—but her eyes… they told another story. There was no spark of true happiness there, only a quiet resignation and a flicker of uncertainty. *She is marrying me out of duty, not love,* he thought grimly. But that would not deter him.

If it took days, weeks, or a lifetime, he would win her heart. *I will not let this be a practical arrangement. I will woo her until she sees we belong together.*

Wilton moved to his side. "Thank you," he said quietly.

Evander glanced at him, brow furrowed. "For what?"

"I know why you are doing this," Wilton replied, his tone layered with meaning.

Evander's pulse quickened. "You do?" he asked carefully, wondering if his friend had truly glimpsed the feelings he so carefully guarded.

Wilton nodded once, his next words carrying the weight of a warning. "Be true to her."

Meeting his gaze steadily, Evander replied, "I have every intention of doing so."

At that moment, a sudden scurry of movement drew their attention downward. Finnegan darted across the floor with uncontainable energy, paws skittering on the polished surface.

With a soft laugh, Olivia bent to scoop up the small dog and cradled him in her arms. "Isn't this exciting, Finnegan?"

Evander couldn't help himself. He reached out to stroke the little creature's head, but Finnegan beat him to it, lifting his chin and enthusiastically licking Evander's hand.

A soft chuckle escaped Olivia. "I see that Finnegan already adores you," she said, her voice lighter now.

"My father is going to hate Finnegan," Evander remarked, his words edged with almost gleeful anticipation.

"Should I not bring him with me to your townhouse, then?" Olivia asked.

Evander smirked. "On the contrary, you must bring him. And anything else your heart desires. After all, it will be your townhouse now, as well."

At his words, her smile faltered—just a fraction—but Evander noticed. He always noticed.

Her gaze wandered from him to the space around her, and

there was a wistfulness in her expression, a flicker of doubt clouding her features. *This is my home,* her eyes seemed to say.

Evander knew this would not be easy for her, leaving behind this townhouse and stepping into the unknown with him. But he would not rush her. In time, he vowed, she would not think of it as leaving home... but as finding a new one. With him.

7

The moon hung low in the sky as Olivia rested her head against the cool windowpane in her bedchamber. Tomorrow was to be her wedding day.

She ought to be filled with anticipation, perhaps even joy. Instead, a strange weight pressed against her chest. It wasn't fear—no, she trusted Evander implicitly. He would be a good husband, kind and honorable. That much she had never doubted. What gnawed at her was something far more complicated.

What if he came to regret it?

She knew Evander well—too well, perhaps. He was loyal to a fault and would sooner trap himself in a life of discontent than risk wounding another's pride. What if this marriage was more duty than desire? He claimed to want it, said it with such conviction, but would time erode that certainty? Would he one day look at her and see not a partner, but an obligation?

They had been thick as thieves growing up. He'd pulled her out of more trouble than she could count, and now he was doing it again. Saving her. Marrying her.

She blinked back the sting of tears and exhaled. Just then,

something sharp and small struck her cheek. "Ouch," she muttered. She glanced down and saw a pebble tumble to the floor. Perplexed, she peered out the window and spotted a familiar figure in the moonlit gardens.

Evander.

He stood in the shadows, one arm drawn back as if preparing to launch another stone.

She stuck her head out of the window. "Have you taken leave of your senses?" she whispered fiercely. "What are you doing?"

He grinned up at her, boyish and utterly unrepentant. "I came to talk to you."

"At this hour?"

"I had a feeling you'd be awake, second-guessing everything. I thought I might spare you the misery of overthinking."

Her annoyance dissolved into a sigh. Of course he knew. He always knew. "You were right," she admitted. "I could use someone to talk to."

"Then come down before I rouse the entire household with my abysmal aim."

She glanced down at her dressing gown, then turned back into the room. "Give me a moment."

Evander gave a mockingly courtly bow. "I await you with great impatience."

Suppressing a smile, Olivia crossed to her wardrobe and pulled out a soft muslin gown—plain, but easy enough to fasten without a maid. She slipped it on, then paused before the mirror. Her hair was slightly mussed from restlessness, pinned in a loose chignon with a few stubborn strands framing her face. It would do.

After tugging on her boots, she tiptoed into the corridor and padded silently towards the back stairs. The house was dark and hushed, the creak of the floorboards loud in her ears as she reached the door and slipped outside.

Evander was waiting on the veranda. He smiled as she approached—the smile that always made her feel seen, steady, understood.

"Well?" he asked softly. "How are you faring?"

She folded her arms. "I'm... anxious."

"That's perfectly reasonable," he said, his tone gentle. "Everyone gets nervous before they're shackled for life."

She arched an eyebrow. "You hit me with a rock."

He had the grace to look sheepish. "Yes, well. I needed to get your attention."

"With terrible aim?"

"But effective," he said with a rakish smile. "You're here, aren't you?"

"You're incorrigible."

He gestured towards a nearby bench. "Shall we sit? You can tell me all your doubts, and I shall heroically dispel them."

She let out a soft laugh and moved to sit down. "Are you absolutely certain this is what you want?"

"Yes," he replied as he sat next to her.

"You're doing this for your mother," she said. "What if you wake one day and resent the obligation?"

"I could never resent you," he said, his voice firm. "You're the one giving up everything. You're the one being whispered about. If anyone should be grateful, it's me."

"I'm not sacrificing anything," she remarked. "This marriage will restore my family's reputation. For that, I'll be forever grateful."

He studied her. "I know how you feel about love..."

She reached for his sleeve, her fingers brushing the fabric. "That was the old me. I don't feel the same."

"What changed?"

She looked away. "I thought I loved Lord Harwood. He made me believe it. He even proposed... in secret. No one knew but you."

Evander's jaw tightened. "Harwood is a scoundrel."

"And yet, you were friends."

"Not willingly. He was more Bryon's companion than mine. And I ceased speaking to him after what he did to you."

She met his gaze, moved by the conviction in his voice. "You've always been a good friend."

"I hope to be something more," he murmured. "Perhaps we'll fall madly in love, and have a boatload of children."

"A boatload?" she echoed with a mock gasp. "That's hardly reasonable."

"Perhaps not," he admitted. "But the trying will be... enjoyable."

Her cheeks turned pink. "Evander..."

"What? You're blushing?"

"You're being improper."

"I'm being honest." His voice softened. "But your virtue is safe. I won't rush you. We'll take things slowly—at your pace."

Looking down, she said, "We haven't even kissed."

"We could rectify that now."

She hesitated as she brought her gaze back up. "What if it feels... strange? Like kissing my brother?"

"Do you often kiss your brother?"

"Of course not. It's just an expression."

"Then allow me to offer you a new one. What if you kiss me, and everything changes? I do tend to have that effect."

She bit her lip before admitting, "I kissed Lord Harwood once. It was... underwhelming."

"Excellent," Evander replied. "That sets the standard very low. I've only to clear a small hurdle."

"You're not bothered by it?"

He shook his head. "Why should I be? Unless..." His expression sobered. "Do you still love him?"

Her spine straightened. "No. I see now that it was never love. He used me and discarded me."

Evander reached up, brushing a stray curl behind her ear. "You deserve better than that."

"I know," she said softly. "But then I ran off and eloped to Gretna Green—"

He cut her off. "That's in the past. Let it stay there. Stop punishing yourself for mistakes already paid for."

She looked at him, her heart aching in a strange, tender way. "You truly believe we could be happy?"

"I know we can," he said, his voice barely above a whisper.

Olivia tilted her head, her brow furrowing softly. "How can you be so certain?"

Evander shifted on the bench, turning to face her more fully. The gravel crunched lightly beneath his boot as he angled himself closer, their knees now just inches apart. The moonlight cast a gentle glow across his features, emphasizing the quiet determination in his expression.

"What is the foundation of any good marriage?" he asked.

She considered the question. "Friendship?"

A small smile curved his lips. "Precisely. And we have that. In abundance."

She couldn't argue. They had shared secrets, scraped knees, laughter and heartache, books and biscuits since childhood. If any match could be founded on companionship, surely it was theirs.

He leaned in slightly. "And it certainly doesn't hurt," he added, "that we are both ridiculously attractive."

A laugh caught in her throat, though it never quite escaped. Her heart fluttered in a way it never had before, not even during her most dramatic moments with Lord Harwood. She had never been this close to Evander, not like this. Not with the weight of a kiss hanging between them. There was an intensity in his gaze that made her pulse race.

She swallowed, her voice caught somewhere between breathlessness and disbelief.

Evander's eyes flicked to her lips, then back to her eyes. The warmth of his breath brushed her cheek. "May I kiss you?"

"You may," she whispered.

For a long, suspended moment, they simply stared at one another, the gardens around them utterly still. Then, slowly, Evander closed the gap.

And then, at last, their lips met.

It was soft at first, tentative. A question rather than a declaration.

But in that moment, something shifted within Olivia. Something warm, unfamiliar, and astonishingly real. It was unlike her kiss with Lord Harwood, which had been remarkably dull. This—this was different. There was no rush, no desperation. Just the warmth of Evander's mouth against hers, and the feeling of being entirely, irrevocably seen.

When he pulled back, his breath still mingling with hers, he looked at her carefully. "Well?" he asked, his voice rough with emotion.

She gave a small, almost shy smile. "It was definitely not like kissing my brother."

He let out a breath that sounded suspiciously like a laugh, though his gaze remained on her face. "Thank heavens," he murmured. "I've been waiting my entire life to kiss you."

"Truly?"

"There was always something about you. I suppose I've always known… but I was too much of a coward to admit it."

"Did it disappoint?" she asked softly, searching his face for any flicker of doubt.

His eyes dropped to her lips again, lingering. "No," he said, his voice hoarse. "It was better than I ever imagined."

Olivia felt something inside her tremble. Not in fear, but in anticipation. Her hands twitched in her lap, and she had to resist the sudden urge to throw her arms around his neck and kiss him again. Instead, she sat straighter, drawing a slow breath to steady herself.

"Good," she replied, managing to keep her tone calm, though her heart was far from it.

A comfortable silence stretched between them. They were engaged. It was a fact. In the eyes of Society, they belonged to one another already. Standing before the vicar was merely a formality. So she could just lean forward and kiss him. It would be so easy to do, but was she brave enough to do so?

"We don't have to rush anything," Evander said. "We'll take it one day at a time. But I meant what I said. I want this marriage. I want you."

Her breath caught again, but this time it wasn't anxiety that filled her—it was hope. Trembling and uncertain, perhaps, but alive.

And for the first time in days, she allowed herself to believe that happiness might not be a foolish dream, after all.

Evander rose and offered his hand. "You should get some rest. We have a big day tomorrow."

She slipped her hand in his and allowed him to assist her in rising. "Thank you for coming here tonight."

"It is what I do."

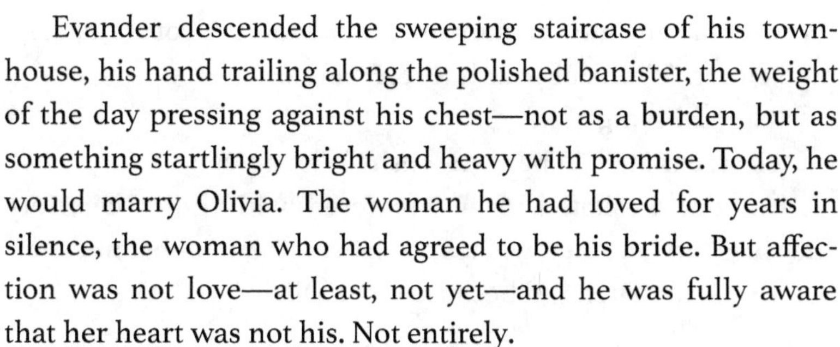

Evander descended the sweeping staircase of his townhouse, his hand trailing along the polished banister, the weight of the day pressing against his chest—not as a burden, but as something startlingly bright and heavy with promise. Today, he would marry Olivia. The woman he had loved for years in silence, the woman who had agreed to be his bride. But affection was not love—at least, not yet—and he was fully aware that her heart was not his. Not entirely.

But he would win it. In time.

As he stepped into the entry hall, the butler was already waiting, composed and solemn as ever.

"The coach has been brought around, my lord," the man announced with a slight bow.

"Thank you, Gillingham," Evander replied with a brisk nod.

He had told no one of his true intentions. There had been no formal announcement, no family gathering, no letters sent. It was safer this way—for now. If his father were to discover he was marrying Olivia this very day, there would be fury, not celebration. It was better to tell him after the fact and deal with the consequences then.

He stepped through the open door onto the front steps, only to find a familiar figure pacing beside the coach, arms crossed and expression tight with disapproval.

Evander halted mid-step. "Alcott? What are you doing here?"

Lord Alcott turned to face him, his mouth already set in a grim line. "I came to talk you out of this madness."

"And what madness might that be?"

"You can't marry Lady Olivia," Alcott declared.

Evander stared at him. "How do you even know about the wedding?"

"Wilton told me. We were boxing this morning," Alcott replied. "He was positively gleeful."

"And you are... not."

"I cannot stand idly by while another friend willingly throws himself into the parson's mousetrap," Alcott said, stepping closer. "Think of your future, Evander."

"I am thinking of it."

Alcott exhaled. "Then why rush? Why now?"

Evander hesitated, then answered with quiet certainty. "Because my mother wishes to see me settled before she... before it is too late. And because I love Olivia."

Alcott raised both brows. "You love her?"

Saying it aloud surprised even him with its clarity. "I do."

His friend studied him for a long moment, then nodded. "Then I'll come with you. I'll stand beside you at the altar."

Nothing surprised him more. "You will?"

Alcott glanced at the townhouse behind them. "I take it your family is unaware?"

"You would be correct," he said. "I would have told my mother, but her lady's maid said she had a difficult night and was not to be disturbed."

Alcott gestured to the open coach door. "Best we leave now, before I regain my senses."

With a quiet chuckle, Evander stepped into the coach, settling on one side as Alcott joined him across the way.

"I still don't like this," Alcott muttered. "I thought we would stand together and refuse to be shackled to wives."

Evander smiled. "I've changed my mind. If I must be shackled, I'd rather it be to Olivia."

Alcott gave him a long look. "I knew you had a soft spot for her. I didn't realize she returned your affections."

He winced. "She agreed to marry me for her reputation's sake, not out of love."

"She doesn't love you?" Alcott asked, brows drawn.

"Not yet," Evander admitted, "but I have a plan."

Alcott folded his arms. "Does this plan involve bribery or hypnotism?"

Evander smirked. "Neither. Just persistence. I'll show her, day by day, that I am the man for her. Eventually, she'll see it, too."

Alcott gave a low whistle. "That is risky."

"Perhaps. But necessary."

After a pause, Alcott added, "Whatever happens, I'm here. You have my support."

Evander looked at him, surprised by the sincerity. "That means more than I can say."

They fell into a companionable silence until Alcott asked, "Are you taking her on a wedding tour?"

"In time," Evander said. "But for now, I want to remain close. I'm not certain how much longer my mother has."

The humor faded from Alcott's expression. "I'm sorry, truly."

Before Evander could reply, the coach slowed, then came to a full stop before the chapel. Without waiting for the footman, he pushed open the door and leapt down, taking the steps two at a time, propelled by a mix of nerves and anticipation.

But when he entered the chapel, he found it empty.

His heart stilled.

Where was she?

He pulled out his pocket watch. He wasn't early, nor late. No, he was perfectly on time. Panic surged in his chest. Had she changed her mind?

A voice broke through his spiraling thoughts.

"She'll come," Alcott said calmly, appearing at his side.

Evander swallowed. "And if she doesn't?"

"Then you recover and move on."

He turned towards his friend. "You make it sound simple. I practically begged the Archbishop of Canterbury for a special license."

Alcott was about to respond when the door opened with a gentle creak.

And there she was.

Olivia stood in the doorway, bathed in soft light, wearing a simple pink gown embroidered with delicate white flowers. Her golden hair was swept into an elegant coiffure, two soft curls framing her face. But it was her expression that undid him—serene, composed, and utterly radiant.

And in that moment, he knew, without a doubt, that Olivia was the best thing that had ever happened to him.

Alcott bumped his shoulder. “You're staring.”

He didn't care.

Crossing the nave in long strides, Evander stopped before her. “You came.”

She smiled up at him. “I told you I would.”

“I know,” he said, his voice thick. “But Alcott had his doubts.”

“Not true,” came the retort from behind him. “I merely encouraged him to run while he still had the chance.”

Olivia tilted her head. “Why would you run?”

“Alcott has a well-documented aversion to matrimony,” Evander said dryly.

“Ah,” she said. “That explains everything.”

The chapel door opened once more, and in walked Wilton, Dosia, and the Dowager Lady Wilton. Wilton spread his arms dramatically.

“Shall we make this wedding official?”

Olivia rolled her eyes. “Please ignore my brother. He's far too excited.”

“We all are,” the dowager interjected.

As they stood near the chapel's entrance, Olivia cast a glance over her shoulder. “Is no one from your family here?”

Evander inhaled through his nose, not quite able to suppress the flicker of tension in his brow. “My father is... not enthusiastic about our union, to put it mildly. But my mother —” He gave a faint, wistful smile. “My mother will be overjoyed once she hears.”

Understanding flashed in Olivia's gaze. “Shall we get married, then?”

He offered his arm. “I am ready, if you are.”

Before she could respond, a tall, slightly stooped man in worn clerical robes approached them, spectacles perched on the edge of his nose. “Good morning,” he said, his voice crisp but warm. “I am Reverend Appleton, vicar of this parish. I understand there is to be a wedding?”

Evander nodded and reached into his jacket pocket, retrieving the neatly folded paper. “We have obtained a special license,” he said, extending it.

The vicar adjusted his spectacles and read it over with a slight nod. “Very well. Everything appears to be in order. If you’ll come stand with me at the front.”

As they moved up the aisle together, Olivia’s gloved hand rested lightly on his arm, but Evander could feel the tension radiating from her posture. Her back was stiff and her steps measured. He glanced sideways at her, heart clenching.

Was he asking too much? Was he being selfish?

Abruptly, he slowed to a stop, drawing her to a halt with him. Turning to face her, he whispered, “You don’t have to marry me, Olivia. Not if your heart isn’t in it.”

Her eyes met his with surprise, a flicker of uncertainty passing through them. “I told you I would.”

“You did,” he said. “But I want you to be happy. That is all I’ve ever wanted.”

She bit her bottom lip. “Marrying you is the sensible thing to do.”

His brow lifted slightly. “Since when have you been sensible?”

That drew a soft laugh from her, easing some of the strain from her features. “Fair point. I suppose it’s nerves. You’re the best man I know.”

From behind them, Wilton gave a theatrical cough. “Then you clearly haven’t met very many men.”

Olivia didn’t even look back. “My mother insisted that Richard attend,” she said lightly, ignoring her brother’s teasing tone.

Before Evander could reply, the vicar asked, "Is there a problem?"

Olivia turned back to him, eyes shining. "No. No problem at all." She looked at Evander and smiled, the kind of smile that steadied him. "I think today is a fine day to be married, don't you?"

He leaned forward and pressed a kiss to her cheek, his voice thick with emotion. "I do."

They walked the final distance to the front of the chapel together.

"Will the witnesses step forward?" Reverend Appleton called.

Wilton and Alcott moved forward, taking their places beside Evander. Wilton looked proud, while Alcott offered a resigned, good-natured shrug, though his expression was far softer than usual.

Evander barely registered the vicar's words. His mind and heart were consumed by the vision beside him—Olivia.

She was really going to be his wife.

They would face Society together. They would weather the awkwardness, the whispers, the doubts, and build something new. Something theirs.

"Evander?" Olivia's voice broke through his thoughts.

He blinked. "Yes?"

"The vicar asked you a question."

"Oh." He looked towards Reverend Appleton, flustered. "I beg your pardon. Would you repeat it?"

The vicar did not seem particularly amused. "Evander Addington, Viscount Westmere, wilt thou have this Woman to thy wedded Wife, to live together after God's ordinance in the holy estate of Matrimony? Wilt thou love her, comfort her, honor, and keep her in sickness and in health; and, forsaking all other, keep thee only unto her, so long as ye both shall live?"

"I will," Evander said quickly, his voice certain and full of conviction.

The vicar turned to Olivia. "Lady Olivia Kendall, wilt thou have this Man to thy wedded Husband, to live together after God's ordinance in the holy estate of Matrimony? Wilt thou obey him, and serve him, love, honor, and keep him in sickness and in health; and, forsaking all other, keep thee only unto him, so long as ye both shall live?"

"I will," she responded.

A wide smile broke across Evander's face, and it stayed there as the vicar pronounced the final words of the ceremony. It wasn't until the last line had been spoken that he leaned forward slightly and asked, "May I kiss the bride now?"

Reverend Appleton gave a tolerant nod. "It is not officially part of the ceremony, but... yes, you may."

Without delay, Evander cupped Olivia's cheek and pressed his lips to hers. It was not a passionate kiss, but one full of promise—warm and reverent, like a seal upon a vow spoken from the heart.

As he pulled back from the kiss, he whispered, "Thank you... for marrying me."

"Well, I had nothing else to do today," she replied with a mischievous look in her eyes.

He chuckled, the sound echoing faintly in the quiet chapel. There was something so Olivia in her irreverent reply, and he loved her all the more for it. In that moment, joy surged through him, deeper than anything he had ever known.

He had no idea what the coming days would bring—the whispers from Society, the strain of adjusting to married life, or the weight of trying to win her heart fully—but none of it seemed daunting. Not with her by his side.

8

Olivia sat across from Evander in the softly rocking coach, her gloved hands tightly clasped in her lap. Though she tried to keep her expression serene, a quiet storm of nerves churned within her. There was no reason to feel this unsettled, since Evander was her dearest friend, a man she trusted above all others. He had rescued her from disgrace and offered her protection under his name. She ought to feel nothing but gratitude.

And yet, beneath the surface of that gratitude lay an uncomfortable truth: she had ensnared him in a marriage born not of love, but necessity. Would he come to regret it? Would he, in time, come to resent her?

Evander's voice broke the quiet. "You are unusually quiet," he observed.

"I am," she admitted, without lifting her gaze from her lap.

Rather than press her, he shifted from his seat across from her and settled beside her on the padded bench. His nearness offered unexpected comfort.

"You need not fear for the future," he said. "I am here. And I always will be."

The words, simple as they were, provided her with immense comfort. She turned her head to meet his gaze, her lips lifting into a faint smile. "And your father? How do you think he'll respond to the news of our marriage?"

Evander winced. "With thunder, no doubt. But I will not allow him to be cruel to you."

She arched a brow. "You forget I know your father well. He blusters, yes, but his bark is far worse than his bite. I can handle him."

"Perhaps," he said, his jaw tightening. "But now you are my wife, and no one—least of all him—shall speak to you with anything less than respect."

She drew in a breath, startled anew by the sound of the word. *Wife.* "I am your wife," she echoed, more to herself than to him.

"That you are," he said with a crooked grin. "Don't tell me you've already forgotten?"

She laughed. "No. I remember the ceremony well enough. But it feels... strange. As if I have stepped into someone else's life."

"Not just anyone," he teased. "You are now the wife of the handsomest man in London."

She nudged him playfully with her shoulder. "You are certainly the cockiest."

He gave a theatrical sigh. "But can you blame me? Handsomeness of this caliber is a burden few can bear."

His banter worked its magic, as it always had. The tension in her shoulders eased, and for the first time since leaving the chapel, Olivia felt herself begin to breathe again.

"I will need to acquire some mourning clothes to grieve Bryon's passing properly," she remarked.

Evander shook his head. "We are newlyweds. That is cause for celebration, not a time for mourning. I would prefer if you wouldn't wear black."

"Are you quite sure?"

"I am."

The coach slowed, wheels crunching on gravel. Outside the window loomed a grand stone townhouse, its columns proud and stately in the pale afternoon light. Evander opened the door and stepped out, turning to offer his hand.

Once her boots touched the ground, he tucked her hand into the crook of his arm with familiar ease, guiding her towards the front steps. But with each step closer to the door, Olivia's breath quickened. The weight of what lay ahead settled on her chest. This was no longer a visit—it was her home now. Her future.

Evander must have sensed her hesitation because he gave her hand a gentle pat. "Just breathe," he murmured.

She obeyed, drawing in a deep breath. *This was her choice. Her decision. Her marriage.*

The door opened and Gillingham bowed politely. "My lord. Lady Olivia."

Evander led her into the entry hall as he revealed, "Lady Olivia and I are now married. She is to be addressed as Lady Westmere."

If Gillingham was surprised, he masked it with professional grace. "Yes, my lord." He turned to Olivia with a respectful nod. "My lady, welcome home."

Home.

The word clanged strangely in her mind. This was her home. Now, and forever.

But before she could reply, a voice boomed from the corridor beyond. "*You married her!?*"

Lord Everwyck, red-faced and formidable, stormed into view. Olivia dipped into a graceful curtsy. "Good afternoon, my lord."

He ignored her entirely, rounding on his son. "What in the blazes were you thinking?"

Evander held his ground. "This should not come as a surprise. You knew I intended to offer for her."

"Yes, but I thought I had time to dissuade you!" his father roared. "To make you see sense!"

Evander's expression hardened. "Which is why I secured a special license. I wanted to be married before Mother…" He faltered slightly. "Before she passes."

The mention of Lady Everwyck softened the elder man's face for a fleeting moment, but it was gone as swiftly as it appeared.

"It was a mistake," the earl said tightly.

"I disagree," Evander replied. "Now, shall we not properly welcome your new daughter-in-law?"

Lord Everwyck's eyes snapped to Olivia. "I am well acquainted with her."

"Excellent," Evander said with a thin smile. "That will spare us formalities. I'll take my wife to her chambers now."

But his father wasn't finished. His eyes narrowed on Olivia. "I trust you won't ruin our family's reputation as easily as you did your own."

The insult struck like a slap, but Olivia refused to let it show. Her spine straightened, her chin lifting.

Evander interjected, "That is enough, Father. You will speak to my wife with respect."

Lord Everwyck gave a derisive snort. "You're both fools. You'll regret this hasty marriage. Mark my words."

With that, he turned on his heel and stormed out of the entryway, his footsteps echoing down the corridor.

Evander turned to her, his expression laced with apology. "I'm sorry."

Olivia shook her head. "Don't be. Frankly, it went far better than I anticipated."

He gave a dry chuckle. "I suppose it bodes well for me that your expectations are so blessedly low."

Together, they ascended the sweeping staircase, Olivia's eyes lingering on the polished balustrade, the gilded sconces, and the thick carpet beneath their feet. At the end of the corridor, Evander paused before a carved wooden door and pushed it open.

She stepped inside and drew a breath. The room was warm and elegant. A four-poster bed draped in ivory silks, a velvet settee before the hearth, and lavender curtains framing tall windows. It was lovely. Far lovelier than anything she'd ever expected.

Evander leaned against the doorframe. "Does it meet with your approval?"

She turned to him, a smile touching her lips. "It is more than I expected."

He hesitated. "Would you like to rest before seeing my mother? I recall how fond you are of naps."

"I do love naps. But I can speak with her now, if you prefer."

"There's time," he said. "Take a moment for yourself. You've earned it."

Crossing to the bed, Olivia trailed her fingers over the silk coverlet. "Then I believe I shall close my eyes for a bit."

"As you wish," Evander said. "You're my wife now. You may have anything you like."

Wife.

There it was again—that word. She would have to grow used to hearing it. Saying it. *Living* it.

A yawn escaped her lips, and she lifted a gloved hand to stifle it. "I suppose I am a bit more tired than I thought," she murmured, offering Evander an apologetic smile.

His gaze was warm with understanding. "Then rest, Olivia," he encouraged. "We've had quite the day." With a soft click, he closed the door behind him, leaving her alone in the stillness of her new bedchamber.

She stood motionless for a moment, staring at the door. The

silence pressed in around her, a reminder that this was her new life now. *You did the right thing*, she told herself. If she repeated it often enough, perhaps she would begin to believe it.

She sank onto the edge of the mattress, the silk coverlet cool beneath her palms. She reached to remove her gloves, but a soft knock halted her movements.

"Enter," she ordered, sitting up straighter.

The door opened and in stepped Annie, her petite lady's maid, balancing two hat boxes in her arms. Wisps of blonde hair framed her round, familiar face.

"Good afternoon, my lady," Annie said cheerfully as she nudged the door closed with her foot.

A genuine smile broke across Olivia's face. "Annie! I'm glad to see a friendly face."

"I thought I'd bring these up first," Annie said, setting the boxes down with care. "Shall I start unpacking the rest of your things?"

"Not yet," Olivia replied. "I was planning to take a nap first."

Annie tilted her head. "And how are you faring, truly?"

Olivia offered a slight shrug. "I am... Evander's wife."

"I'm aware," Annie replied. "But that was what you wanted, was it not?"

"It was," Olivia admitted, smoothing the folds of her gown. "Still is."

Annie crossed the room and perched beside her on the edge of the bed, her expression probing. "Then what's troubling you?"

With a weary sigh, Olivia leaned back and let herself fall against the mattress, eyes drifting to the carved canopy overhead. "It's just... I don't know the first thing about being a wife."

Annie gave a soft laugh. "I don't think anyone does at first. I suspect it's something you figure out along the way."

"But ours is a marriage of convenience," Olivia said. "What if Evander regrets it? What if, one day, he resents me?"

The light humor drained from Annie's expression. "And what if you two end up deliriously happy?"

Olivia turned her head to look at her maid. "I'm being serious."

"So am I," Annie replied. "You've endured so much. Surely happiness isn't out of reach."

"But none of it would have happened if I'd been wiser. The scandal, the humiliation… it was all my doing."

"You were tricked—"

"I should have known better," Olivia interrupted, the words sharper than intended. "I let myself believe I could escape the consequences. I was a fool."

Annie appeared unbothered by the outburst. "You were heartbroken, my lady. After what Lord Harwood did… anyone would've lost their footing."

"That doesn't excuse it."

"No," Annie agreed. "But it means you're human. And perhaps you ought to offer yourself a shred of grace for that."

Olivia closed her eyes, as if willing the world—and her thoughts—to go still. But even behind the darkness of her eyelids, her mind offered no peace. The ache in her chest did not abate. Forgiveness was a balm she could freely offer to others, yet when it came to herself, she found it withheld. Why was that? Why did she so easily excuse the missteps of those she loved, yet punish herself relentlessly for every mistake?

She had survived heartbreak, public ridicule, and shame. And still, she could not let go of the familiar guilt. It wasn't just the scandal. It was the sense that she had disappointed those who mattered most. Her brother. Her friends. Evander.

Most of all… herself.

Annie rose from the bed. "Rest now, my lady," she said, her voice full of concern. "The unpacking can wait. Everything else can wait. We'll talk again later."

Olivia opened her eyes. "Thank you."

Annie gave a nod and slipped out, closing the door gently behind her.

Left alone, Olivia moved her head to lie on the pillow. Perhaps rest would help. And perhaps, when she woke, she could take the first step towards forgiving the one person she had always been hardest on: herself.

Evander's footsteps echoed down the long corridor, each stride tight with tension. He was about to have the most trying conversation of his life—and certainly the most volatile. His father was angry with him for marrying Olivia, but he didn't care. It was done. Now he needed to ensure that his father treated her with even the barest shred of decency.

Reaching the study, he paused only a moment before entering. The room smelled of ink, leather bindings, and tobacco. The earl sat hunched over a spread of ledgers at his imposing desk, quill scratching across parchment with determined strokes. He didn't look up.

"You are a fool, Son," came the biting greeting.

Evander crossed the threshold with a calm born of years of forced composure. "And why is that, Father?"

"Because you weren't thinking with your head when you married that girl. Olivia is not a suitable match."

"I disagree," Evander replied, moving to the high-backed chair across from his father and settling in. "She's the daughter of a marquess and brings a substantial dowry. Twenty thousand pounds, if you recall."

The earl finally raised his head, his expression thunderous. "And a reputation that's been dragged through the mud in every drawing room from Mayfair to Bath. Her presence will taint our name, and our family will become the subject of every dinner party whisper."

Evander leaned forward. "The scandal will pass. The gossips will find someone new to feed on by next week."

"You should have posted the banns. Followed proper convention. Given time, I might've talked some sense into you."

Evander scoffed. "That was precisely why we did not. I've no interest in delaying my future for your attempts at manipulation."

The earl's eyes narrowed. "Why do you insist on being so stubborn? You have a duty to this family—"

"I am well aware of my duty," Evander cut in, his tone sharpening. "And I've fulfilled it. I married."

The earl's voice rose. "To the wrong woman! I made promises to Lady Jemima's family—"

"Promises you made. Not I," Evander said firmly. "I owe Lady Jemima nothing."

For a moment, his father didn't say anything, his mouth tightening with unspoken fury. Then he gave a derisive snort. "Well, what's done is done. You'll live with the consequences."

"I expect nothing less."

The earl leaned back and waved his hand towards the ledgers. "Have you had a chance to review the figures for the indigo plantations?"

Evander stiffened. "As a matter of fact, yes. I was approached outside our townhouse yesterday. A man threatened me at knifepoint. He told me to stay out of India. Said I should sell our *Neel Kothi*."

His father blinked in irritation, as if swatting away an inconvenient fly. "I wouldn't put much stock in idle threats."

Evander's brow arched. "That is easy for you to say since a knife wasn't pointed at you," he said. "What is a *Neel Kothi*?"

The earl let out an exasperated sigh. "A *Neel Kothi* is a term for a factory that processes the indigo dye. You would know that if you'd spent any time learning about our affairs overseas."

Evander stared at him. "What exactly have you gotten us involved in?"

"A profitable venture," the earl replied tersely. "One that will bring us a fortune if properly governed. Stop asking foolish questions and start acting like the heir you now are."

The moment hung thick with unspoken accusations. Then the earl dipped his head and resumed his calculations, as though the conversation were already finished.

Evander rose slowly. "You will treat Olivia with respect, Father. She is your daughter-in-law now."

"Respect is to be earned, not given freely," the earl muttered, not bothering to look up.

Evander stepped forward, placing both palms on the desk and leaning in. His voice was stern. "I will tolerate many things from you. Insults. Condescension. Even your schemes. But I will not allow you to treat my wife with anything less than courtesy."

The earl finally looked up, his eyes blazing. "You dare make demands in my house?"

Evander's lips curved into a cold smile. "Yes, I would, especially when it pertains to Olivia."

A long silence passed before the earl's expression turned calculating. "You'd do well to remember your place. You are my heir."

"And you'd do well to remember," Evander said, standing tall, "that the spare has become the heir—and I have nothing left to lose."

Without waiting for a reply, he turned on his heel and strode from the study, leaving his father fuming behind him.

As he ascended the stairs, he spotted Olivia at the landing. She stood with one hand on the banister, worry etched in every delicate feature.

"There you are," she said, relief washing over her face.

"Here I am," he replied, reaching her side.

Olivia leaned in close, her voice touched with playfulness. "I think it would be wise if you wore a bell around your neck so I could always find you."

He chuckled. "Or you could ask Gillingham. He always knows my whereabouts."

She tilted her head as though considering it. "That could work as well."

"How was your nap?"

"It was... restful," she said, though her eyes studied him carefully.

He smirked. "That is the general purpose of a nap."

Her brow furrowed. "Something troubles you. You're tense."

"Observant, as always." He sighed, knowing it would be best to tell her the truth and be done with it. "I just spoke with my father."

"I take it the conversation did not go well."

He shook his head. "No. But then, they never do. He's furious that we married."

"I'm sorry."

He met her gaze. "Don't be. I forced your hand in marrying me."

Her fingers brushed his sleeve in a comforting gesture. "And in the midst of everything else, you're still mourning your brother."

The truth of her words struck deep. He looked away, throat tight. "Bryon was always the favored one. The golden son. I spent most of my life in his shadow, resenting him, if I'm honest. My father barely acknowledged me. When he did, it was only to criticize."

He took a breath and continued. "I thought that was just how fathers were... until I met yours. Lord Wilton treated me kindly, like I mattered, even though I was only the second son of an earl. It made me realize the kind of man I wanted to become."

She stepped closer. "My father thought highly of you."

Tears pricked his eyes, and he blinked them away. "You were lucky to have him."

"I was," she said, her voice tender. "He was the best of men."

"I grieved his passing more than I ever expected to," Evander admitted.

They stood close now, her hand still resting on his arm. It grounded him. Anchored him.

"I shouldn't complain," he murmured.

"You're not," Olivia responded. "And even if you were, you may always complain to me."

He smiled faintly. "You've always been there for me—even when my family was not."

"You're an easy person to be kind to," she said with a small smile. "Do you remember what we used to call your brother?"

A genuine laugh escaped him. "Viscount *Weirdmere*."

"He absolutely loathed it."

"He did. Which made it all the more enjoyable."

Her smile faded slightly. "Have you made arrangements for the funeral?"

"It's to be held tomorrow," Evander said. "But I don't expect you to attend. It isn't customary."

"I'd like to be there. For you."

His lips twitched. "My father will despise that. He believes women are too emotional for funerals."

"I don't have to come—"

"No, you misunderstood me," he said quickly, cutting her off. "I want you to come."

She nodded. "Then I will."

His heart warmed. "Have I told you how happy I am that I married you?"

"Well," she replied lightly, "give it time. You might come to regret it."

Something in her tone gave him pause. There was strain beneath the jest.

Leaning closer, he asked, "Why would I ever regret marrying you?"

She dropped her gaze, but not before he caught the flicker of pain in her eyes. "You saved me, Evander. But what did you get in return?"

"I got you," he said firmly. "You forget that it was my idea to marry. For my mother's sake, yes, but also for my own."

She tried to protest, but he pressed on.

"This marriage benefited us both. And I will never regret it. Because I married my best friend."

Her eyes shimmered with emotion. "I hope you're certain of that. Because you're stuck with me."

He grinned and offered his arm. "Good. Shall we go give my mother the happy news? I imagine she will be overjoyed."

Taking his arm, they walked the short distance to his mother's chamber. He lifted his hand to knock, then stopped.

"What's wrong?" Olivia asked.

Evander lowered his fist. "I never quite know what to expect when I visit my mother," he murmured. His voice dropped, thick with emotion. "And I don't want her to die."

The weight of that confession hung in the air.

Olivia turned towards him, her expression softening with understanding. "I know," she said. "But you should cherish the time you still have."

His eyes remained fixed on the door. "She's always been there," he said. "The only constant in my life. She never judged me... not once. She just loved me for who I was, not who I was supposed to be."

Without hesitation, Olivia reached for his sleeve and turned him to face her. "That kind of love doesn't disappear," she told him. "Even if she's no longer here, she'll still live on in you. You are her son, Evander."

His gaze met hers, and for the first time in years, he didn't try to hide the tears that welled in his eyes. They spilled over, carving silent paths down his cheeks. He didn't look away.

Then Olivia stepped forward and wrapped her arms around him. She held him as though she could anchor him through the storm. And he clung to her in return, burying his face in the curve of her neck, allowing himself a moment of vulnerability. In her arms, he felt steadied… protected. Loved.

In that moment, he knew that he would survive this. Because she would help him bear it.

A quiet creak interrupted them as the door to his mother's chamber opened. A maid appeared and said, "Oh, my apologies, my lord… my lady. I didn't mean to intrude."

Olivia gently stepped back, her arms falling to her sides. Evander immediately missed the warmth of her touch, but he gave no outward sign of it. Instead, he turned to the maid and composed himself.

"How is my mother?" he asked, voice slightly hoarse.

"She is sleeping—"

"No, I am not," came a familiar voice from within the bedchamber, laced with amusement. "I am simply resting my eyes. Now stop lurking and come in."

The maid stepped back and pulled the door open wide. "You heard her, my lord."

Evander gave a small smile and gestured for Olivia to enter first. He followed close behind.

Inside, the chamber was bathed in the soft golden light of the late afternoon sun. His mother lay propped up on a nest of pillows, her skin pale but her eyes bright. As soon as she caught sight of Olivia, her entire face lit up.

"My dear! What a delightful surprise," she declared.

Olivia approached the bed and leaned down to kiss the older woman's cheeks. "How are you faring, my lady?"

"I am still drawing breath, which is more than many can say," his mother replied with a weary smile, her voice dry but affectionate.

Olivia gave a soft chuckle and took a step back as Evander joined her beside the bed.

"We come bearing news," he said.

His mother looked between them with sudden interest. "Oh? What sort of news?"

Evander reached for Olivia's hand and intertwined their fingers. He lifted their joined hands slightly. "We are married."

For a moment, there was silence—then joy spread across his mother's face, bright and unrestrained. "What *wonderful* news! Oh, you must tell me everything—where, how, when—every detail!"

"There isn't much to tell," Evander replied with a sheepish smile. "We were married this morning at the chapel."

"Who was in attendance?" his mother asked.

"It was rather a small affair but Olivia's family came, as did Lord Alcott," he replied.

Turning to Olivia, his mother remarked, "I do hope this means your family approved of the union."

"That they do," Olivia confirmed.

"And what of your father?" she asked, addressing him.

Evander shrugged. "He was predictably appalled."

Her expression didn't falter. "He'll come around."

"I'm not holding my breath," he muttered.

"Well, then let me be happy for the both of us," his mother declared. She turned to Olivia and reached for her hand. "I always thought you two would suit each other."

Olivia's lips curved into a playful smirk as she glanced at Evander. "He is tolerable, I suppose."

His mother laughed—a genuine, delighted sound that filled

the room with unexpected lightness. Evander had almost forgotten what that laugh sounded like. "Now I can die in peace," she said with a contented sigh. "Knowing that you'll take care of one another."

"You are not going to die anytime soon," Evander said quickly, his tone firm.

A soft knock came at the door before it creaked open once more. A man stepped in carrying a worn leather doctor's bag.

Doctor Wentworth gave a courteous bow. "How is my most troublesome patient today?"

His mother pushed herself up higher on the pillows. "Still alive. Much to everyone's surprise."

The doctor looked amused. "That's more than satisfactory."

Evander reached out and placed a hand gently on his mother's frail shoulder. "We'll let you get on with your examination. We'll come back a little later."

His mother gave his hand a squeeze. "Thank you, my darling."

As he led Olivia out of his mother's bedchamber, he was pleased by his mother's reaction to his marriage, confirming what he had already known. He had done the right thing by marrying Olivia.

9

Olivia stood before the looking glass in her bedchamber, her gaze fixed on her own reflection as though trying to reconcile the woman she saw with the one she had always known. The gown she wore—a delicate shade of blue that complemented her fair complexion—fit her perfectly, but it was not the gown that made her appear different. It was the simple gold band now on her finger. It was the knowledge that she would be descending the stairs as a viscountess.

She didn't feel any different. And yet… everything had changed.

The memory of the kiss she had shared with Evander earlier drifted into her thoughts—unexpected, tender, and more stirring than she cared to admit. It had awakened something deep within her, something new and uncertain. But this was not the time to dwell on it, not when the responsibilities of her new role loomed large and unfamiliar.

"Will there be anything else, my lady?" Annie's voice broke gently into her reverie.

Olivia gave a small shake of her head and smoothed down the folds of her gown. "No, Annie. That will be all. Thank you."

Before Annie could retreat, a knock sounded at the door. She turned to answer it, revealing Evander standing just beyond the threshold.

He did not step inside, but his gaze traveled over Olivia with unhurried appreciation. "You look beautiful," he said, a smile spreading across his face.

Olivia couldn't help but return it. "And you look rather handsome yourself."

He struck a playful pose. "I'm delighted you noticed. I fear that my presence can be rather distracting. I feel it is only fair to issue a warning."

Olivia approached him, a teasing lilt in her voice. "Your cockiness truly knows no bounds."

"Careful, Wife," he teased, "one more smile from me, and you shall be entirely undone."

She stopped just before him, lifting her brows in feigned concern. "One more smile, and I shall require smelling salts—not from swooning, but from the exertion of keeping from laughing."

Clutching his chest in mock agony, he replied, "You wound me."

"Nonsense," she said, arching a brow. "Your ego is so well-padded, it likely didn't feel a thing."

He chuckled, the sound low and warm. "You have an unerring talent for humbling a man."

"And that," she said with a soft laugh, "is the duty of every devoted wife."

He extended his arm with a flourish. "In that case, shall I have the honor of escorting you to dinner?"

She slipped her hand into the crook of his elbow. "I would be delighted."

As they strolled arm-in-arm down the corridor, he asked, "How are you adjusting to married life?"

She gave a small shrug. "Considering I've only been married since this morning, I daresay I'm managing quite well."

"Have you had a chance to speak with our housekeeper, Mrs. Whitehall?"

"Not yet," she admitted. "I intend to do so tomorrow."

Evander glanced at her with quiet approval. "You are mistress of the house now, with my mother confined to her rooms."

"I know," Olivia said softly. "But I don't wish to overstep or make her feel displaced."

"I rather think she'll be relieved," he replied. "She needs rest, and I trust she'll find comfort in knowing the household is in capable hands."

Olivia nodded, touched by his confidence in her. "I shall do my best."

As they reached the stairwell, Evander added, "I may have taken the liberty of writing to your mother to inquire after your favorite dishes."

"You did?"

He puffed out his chest with exaggerated pride. "Indeed. It is the duty of every thoughtful husband to impress his new bride at dinner. I'm hoping such efforts might earn me another kiss."

Heat crept up her neck, but she kept her voice even. "You will have to try harder than that."

"Then what if I invited your family to join us this evening?"

Olivia stopped at the base of the stairs and turned to face him, eyes wide with hope. "Did you truly?"

"I did," he said simply.

A bright smile broke across her face. "Thank you. I didn't get the chance to properly say goodbye earlier."

"I suspected as much," he replied.

"You are very thoughtful."

Before he could respond, a familiar voice called from the drawing room. "Olivia!"

She turned to see Dosia standing in the doorway, her expression bright.

"Dosia!" Olivia greeted with delight as they crossed the room and embraced.

Richard followed, lounging with his usual self-assurance. "It's only been a few hours since we last saw her," he drawled.

Dosia shot him a look over her shoulder. "Yes, but now she's moved out, and I miss her dreadfully."

Richard stepped to Dosia's side. "I am more than willing to keep you company, my dear," he said, waggling his eyebrows.

Olivia rolled her eyes with a smile. "I do not miss that."

Richard grinned. "How are you faring in your new role?"

"I'm adjusting," Olivia admitted.

Their mother stepped forward, her posture proud but warm. "You'll do splendidly, Olivia. I've no doubt."

"Thank you, Mother." Olivia stepped forward to embrace her. "How are you bearing up, surrounded by these two lovers?"

Her mother's lips twitched with amusement. "It's not all bad." Then she turned to Evander. "Thank you for inviting us this evening. It was a thoughtful gesture."

"We had no wedding breakfast," Evander said, "so I thought this might serve as a small celebration."

"Will your father be joining us?" Olivia asked.

Evander shook his head. "He's dining at his club."

Olivia gave a slow nod. "Well, I won't pretend I'll miss his presence, but I suppose I ought to find some way to win him over."

"I wish you all the luck in the world," Evander said dryly.

Just then, the butler stepped forward and announced, "Dinner is served."

Evander offered his arm once more. "Shall we, Lady Westmere?"

They made their way into the grand dining room in silence. Candlelight flickered from the gleaming silver sconces along the paneled walls, casting a warm glow across the long, polished mahogany table.

Evander paused at Olivia's chair, the one set at the far end of the table, and pulled it out with a courtly gesture. She murmured her thanks and lowered herself gracefully into the seat. Once she was settled, he crossed to the opposite end and took his place.

Dosia broke the silence as a footman poured wine into her glass. "So, when do the newlyweds plan to embark on a wedding tour?"

Olivia reached for her own glass but hesitated as she lifted it. "I suppose that won't be until after…" Her voice faltered, her eyes shifting to Evander.

"Until my mother dies," he replied.

A hush fell over the room. Dosia's expression crumpled. "Oh, I'm terribly sorry. I hadn't meant to reopen a wound."

Olivia offered a quick smile, trying to soothe her sister-in-law's guilt. "It's quite all right. We understand you meant no harm. We simply wish to spend as much time as we can with Lady Everwyck while we still have the opportunity."

The footmen moved with silent efficiency, placing bowls of soup before each guest.

After a few moments of comfortable silence, Richard dabbed his mouth with his napkin and turned to Evander. "Have you resigned from your fellowship yet?"

Evander gave a small nod. "I did."

Though his voice was composed, Olivia could hear the strain beneath it, and her heart ached for him. She knew how much it had cost him—the years of study, the prestige, the sense of purpose. All surrendered in the name of duty.

"It's for the best," he continued, though the tightness in his tone betrayed him. "I am heir now, and it's time I turn my attention to the family's holdings and responsibilities."

"Sounds like you could do with hitting something," Richard said lightly. "You're welcome to join me at my boxing club."

"I just might take you up on that." Evander set down his spoon, then added almost absently, "What do you know of indigo plantations?"

Richard paused, his brow furrowing. He reached for his wine glass, took a sip, and then replied, "Quite a bit, actually. They're immensely profitable—but brutal. Those who own them can grow rich in just a few seasons, but the land is often ruined after a few years of cultivation."

Evander frowned. "That's why Bryon went to India with Lord Harwood. My father sent him to oversee our plantations."

Richard grew thoughtful. "Lord Harwood has boasted often enough about his ventures in India. He owned several such plantations and claimed to be making a fortune." He lowered his voice. "But there's a growing number of groups here in London—reformers, mostly—who are lobbying Parliament to regulate or even prohibit the sale of such estates to foreigners."

"Why?" Evander asked.

Richard's expression turned grave. "Because of the peasants who live there. Many of them are coerced into working for the British planters. They're forced to grow indigo on land they once used to feed their families. The crop is incredibly hard on the soil and it strips the land of nutrients, leaving it barren."

Olivia, who had been listening quietly, set her spoon down with a soft clink. "That's horrible. But what happens if they refuse?"

Richard sighed. "Then they're punished. Beaten. Starved. In some cases... worse. There are accounts of entire villages being decimated for resisting the *Nabobs*."

"*Nabobs*?" she asked.

"It's a term used for British men who go to India and return with vast fortunes, often made through dubious means. It's not a flattering title."

Olivia turned to Evander, her brow drawn with concern. "How can your father support such cruelty?"

Evander's face was unreadable for a moment, then he exhaled slowly. "Because he cares only for what fills the family's coffers. Not the lives that are ruined in the process."

Richard added, "Indigo is in high demand here. It is used in dyeing silks, linens, woolens, and military uniforms. But it's a dangerous business, especially for those with a conscience."

"What are you going to do?" Olivia asked, her gaze fixed on her husband's face.

Before he could answer, a deafening crack shattered the evening calm—a sharp splintering sound that echoed through the dining room like a musket shot.

A large brick came hurtling through the tall sash window, striking the floor with a heavy thud, shattering a pane of glass and scattering shards across the polished wood and patterned carpet. The gust of night air rushed in behind it, fluttering the table linens and extinguishing several candles along the sideboard.

Evander shoved back his chair and rose swiftly to his feet, glass crunching beneath the soles of his boots as he crossed the room. Olivia stood, too, heart pounding in her chest, her hand clutching the back of her chair.

He crouched beside the brick and examined it. "There's a note," he said, reaching down and untying the coarse string that held a scrap of parchment wound around the projectile.

He unfolded the paper and read aloud a single word, harsh and scrawled in thick black ink: "*Nabob*."

Richard was already beside him, his eyes scanning the note with narrowed focus. "This is no jest. It's a warning. We ought to send for the constable."

Evander straightened slowly, tucking the paper into his jacket pocket. "It's not the first threat I've received."

Olivia gasped as she stepped around the table. "What do you mean?"

He met her eyes, reluctant but resigned. "A few days ago, I was accosted outside our townhouse. A man threatened me with a knife. He told me to sell the indigo plantation and to get out of India, or else."

The room fell into stunned silence.

Dosia's hand flew to her mouth, and even Olivia's mother looked visibly shaken. Olivia stared at Evander, her mind racing. "Why didn't you tell me?"

"I didn't want to worry you," he said. "And I had hoped it was an isolated incident. Clearly, it was not."

Richard folded his arms. "You'll need help. Someone who can keep their head when things turn violent."

Evander gave a single nod. "That's why I need to speak with Warwicke."

With a nod, Richard said, "I agree."

A smile came to Evander's lips that looked forced. "I don't wish to let this ruin the evening," he said, gesturing towards the table. "Shall we return to our seats?"

Olivia moved towards him slowly, her voice quiet but steady. "We may continue dinner, but you must promise me something."

"Anything."

"You will tell me everything. No more secrets."

He hesitated for the briefest of moments, then replied, "You have my word."

Though her questions still burned within her—about the plantation, the man with the knife, and what Evander truly planned to do—she forced herself to return to her chair. But she would not forget. Not tonight. Not tomorrow.

She would bide her time.

And when the moment was right, she would insist on answers.

It was still early in the morning as Evander followed Warwicke's butler down the long, quiet corridor of the townhouse. His footsteps echoed faintly on the polished floorboards, the only other sounds the gentle creak of the butler's shoes and the distant ticking of a clock somewhere deep within the house.

The butler halted outside a set of heavy oak doors and gave a discreet knock before opening one. "Lord Westmere to see you, my lord," he announced with a crisp bow.

Baron Warwicke looked up from behind a broad mahogany desk littered with ledgers and scattered correspondence. He raised a brow in acknowledgment, then gestured for Evander to come in as the butler quietly excused himself and shut the door behind them.

"Good morning, Addington... er, Westmere," Warwicke said, the corners of his mouth twitching with the hint of a smile. "Forgive me. Old habits."

"No apology necessary," Evander replied with a polite nod as he stepped farther into the study. "I'm still adjusting to the title myself."

Warwicke motioned to the chair opposite his desk. "Please, have a seat."

"Thank you." Evander settled into the chair.

"I heard about your brother," Warwicke said. "I'm sorry for your loss."

A faint, conflicted smile flickered across Evander's lips. "Bryon was... challenging. But he was still my brother. I am sorry he's gone."

Warwicke's expression darkened. "It's no secret that he and I didn't get along. He once told me outright that I had no right to my title."

Evander sighed. "Yes, well... my brother never did keep his opinions to himself. He could be rather prickly."

"That he could," Warwicke agreed dryly, then leaned back slightly in his chair. "So, what brings you to me at such an early hour?"

Evander straightened. "I came to ask a favor."

"What kind of favor?"

His voice dropped, solemn. "I've been threatened. Twice now."

Warwicke sat forward, his easy manner hardening. "By whom?"

"I don't know," Evander admitted. "A man with a knife confronted me outside my townhouse, and more recently, someone threw a brick through my dining room window."

Warwicke's eyes narrowed. "And do you have any idea why someone would go to such lengths?"

With a reluctant sigh, Evander said, "It has to do with the indigo plantation in India. My father and Bryon purchased it before his death, and now someone wants me to sell it."

Warwicke exhaled slowly, his brow furrowing. "I'm not surprised. There's a growing movement opposing Britain's treatment of India. Reformer groups have sprung up across London and beyond. Some are loud. Others are dangerous."

"What should I do?"

"If I were in your place, I would divest myself of the plantation entirely. Indigo has become... complicated. But I suspect your situation isn't so simple?"

Evander shook his head. "No. My father insists that I manage the estate. He believes it's a legacy worth preserving." He hesitated. "Which is why I came to you. Would you be willing to look into these threats?"

Warwicke sat back in his chair, his gaze thoughtful. "You realize I'm no longer a Bow Street Runner. I've responsibilities now. Estates. Tenants."

"I know," Evander said quickly. "But you still have connections and a particular set of skills. I wouldn't ask if it weren't serious."

A slow smile tugged at Warwicke's lips. "You always were persuasive. Very well. I'll make a few inquiries."

"I appreciate it," Evander said.

"Don't thank me yet," Warwicke warned. "You may learn more than you want to know. And there's always the possibility I find nothing at all."

Evander nodded gravely. "Doing nothing feels far worse."

Warwicke tapped his fingers against the desk. "Do you think your father could be persuaded to sell?"

A shadow crossed Evander's face. "Highly unlikely. He's enamored by the profit margins and refuses to acknowledge the moral complexities."

"Not an uncommon trait among the peerage," Warwicke muttered.

Evander gave a humorless chuckle. "Our coffers aren't as full as they once were. I believe my father sees this as salvation."

Warwicke's tone lightened. "Speaking of new beginnings… I hear congratulations are in order. A wedding?"

Evander's face relaxed into a smile. "Yes. I married Lady Olivia."

"Lady Olivia?" Warwicke's brows rose. "I hadn't realized you harbored an attachment."

"That's because it's complicated," Evander admitted. "My mother… she's ill. It was her greatest wish to see me married before…" His voice trailed off.

"And you don't regret it?" Warwicke pressed.

"No," Evander said. "Not for a moment. Olivia is… she's extraordinary. But it wasn't a love match. At least, not for her."

Warwicke considered him. "Do you love her?"

"I do. And she's my dearest friend. But I had to convince her to marry me."

"Given the scandal surrounding her name, it's an advantageous match for her," Warwicke pointed out.

"Yes," Evander replied, his tone firm, "but that's not why I married her. I didn't do it to save her. I did it because I couldn't imagine anyone else beside me."

Warwicke gave a small nod. "To find friendship and love in the same person is rare. And worth fighting for."

"That's the problem," Evander confessed. "I fear Olivia only sees me as a friend."

"Then you must change her mind."

Evander lifted a brow. "And how, exactly, do I do that?"

Warwicke's lip twitched. "Flowers and sweet treats are usually a good start."

"I've tried flowers and truffles. She appreciated them, of course, but…" He exhaled. "I want more. I want a true marriage."

The amusement faded from Warwicke's eyes, replaced with something more earnest. "There was a time when I would have told you not to bother. But now… now I believe it's worth every effort. My wife changed my life. Loving her changed me."

Evander glanced at the long, jagged scar on Warwicke's cheek. "You seem different. Happier."

"I am," Warwicke said simply. "For a long time, I didn't think I deserved happiness. Especially not after the war. But Dorothea proved me wrong."

Evander's expression softened. "I'm glad for you, truly."

Warwicke met his gaze. "Marriage requires courage. It means allowing someone to see all your vulnerabilities and trusting they won't use them to hurt you."

Evander didn't hesitate. "Olivia would never hurt me."

"Then fight for her," Warwicke asserted. "Show her that friendship can become love. That your marriage can be more than what it began as."

"I intend to."

"Good," Warwicke said.

Just then, the door to the study eased open, and Lady Warwicke stepped in, her red hair neatly arranged into a low chignon at the nape of her neck. She was dressed in a soft morning gown of pale lavender, the color complementing her fair complexion. She stopped short just inside the threshold, her expression momentarily apologetic.

"Oh, I beg your pardon," she said, her hand lightly touching the doorframe. "I didn't realize you were occupied."

Warwicke rose and waved her forward. "You needn't apologize, my dear. Please, come in." He turned slightly, gesturing towards Evander. "You remember Lord Westmere?"

A smile bloomed across her face, brightening her entire countenance. "Indeed, I do." She crossed the room with graceful steps. "How are you faring, my lord?"

Evander stood at once and offered a respectful bow. "Very well, my lady. And you?"

"Well enough, thank you," she replied warmly. "I did not mean to interrupt. I merely came to see if my husband would join me for breakfast."

Warwicke stepped around the desk and took her hand in his. "I would be delighted to." He glanced towards Evander. "Perhaps you would care to join us as well?"

Evander shook his head. "You are kind to extend the invitation, but I must return home. Olivia will likely be awake soon, and I would rather spare her the ordeal of facing my father over breakfast without any reinforcements."

Lady Warwicke's smile turned conspiratorial. "Then we must have you both to dinner soon, at a more civilized hour."

"We would be honored," Evander said, inclining his head.

Warwicke offered his arm to his wife, which she took with a light touch. "And how are you this morning?" he asked softly, his gaze lingering on hers.

"Perfectly well, thank you," she said, her tone affectionate.

As the couple turned to depart the study, Evander followed at a respectful distance. They walked together through the corridor until they reached the front entry hall.

There, Warwicke came to a halt and turned to face Evander once more, his manner shifting subtly back into the serious mode of earlier. "I'll look into what we discussed. You have my word."

Evander met his gaze. "Thank you, Warwicke. Truly."

Lady Warwicke glanced between the two men, her eyes narrowing ever so slightly with curiosity. "Dare I ask what exactly it is you're investigating?"

"A simple enough matter," Warwicke assured her.

Before he could say more, Evander interjected, "I've received two threats—one in person, the other quite literally through a window. Your husband has very generously agreed to help me uncover the source."

Lady Warwicke's expression immediately shifted to one of concern. "Threats? That sounds far from simple. Will it be dangerous?"

Warwicke gave a one-shouldered shrug, the movement deliberately nonchalant. "Possibly. But you need not concern yourself."

She tightened her hold on his arm and looked up at him with tender insistence. "I will always concern myself where you are involved."

"And that," Warwicke murmured, "is why I will forever love you."

Realizing it was his moment to depart, Evander quietly

cleared his throat. "I'll take my leave," he said before he stepped out into the pale morning light.

The air was crisp and fresh, carrying with it the scent of dew-covered hedges and distant chimney smoke. As the door closed gently behind him, Evander drew his coat tighter around his frame and descended the stone steps with slow, measured strides.

He was genuinely pleased for Warwicke. The man had returned from the war scarred in ways both seen and unseen. And yet, in Lady Warwicke, he had found peace, acceptance, and the kind of love that could knit even the most fractured soul back together.

Was such a thing truly possible for everyone? Or only a fortunate few?

Evander wasn't certain.

He had married Olivia for many reasons—duty, friendship, affection—but love had grown in his heart long before she had agreed to take his hand. He loved her with a depth that surprised even him. However… she did not love him in return. Not in the way he wished.

A heaviness settled in his chest as he made his way towards his waiting carriage.

What if she never did?

The thought struck him harder than he anticipated. Was he destined to spend his days pining for a wife who saw him only as a loyal friend?

He didn't regret marrying her—he never could—but he feared he had made a grave miscalculation. Love, unrequited, was a lonely thing.

He glanced up at the morning sky, knowing there was still time. Time to win her heart. Time to build something real.

But it would take patience. Courage. And no small amount of hope.

Drawing in a long breath, he climbed into his carriage, resolved to try.

10

Dressed in a jonquil morning gown, Olivia descended the grand staircase. Her blonde hair had been arranged in a demure chignon, a single pearl comb gleaming in the early light that streamed through the windows. Though outwardly composed, a strange sense of unreality clung to her. She had been married for a full day now—an entire day—and still it felt as if she were playing a part in some elaborate charade.

As she neared the dining room, she smoothed her skirts with a nervous hand. The scent of warm bread and roasted ham wafted through the corridor, mingling with the faint polish of beeswax on the oak paneling. She paused just outside the threshold, peering in.

Lord Everwyck sat alone at the head of the long table, clad in a dark jacket, his silver hair immaculately brushed and the newssheets unfolded before him. There was no sign of Evander.

Olivia's heart sank. Breakfast alone with the Earl of Everwyck was hardly how she wished to begin her second day as a married woman. His dislike for her was not just assumed—it had been demonstrated repeatedly over the years, each interaction laced with disdain.

She took a quiet step back, already retreating in her mind to the sanctuary of her bedchamber, where she could ring for a tray and spend the morning in peace.

But fate intervened in the form of an aged floorboard that groaned beneath her slippered foot.

Lord Everwyck looked over and his expression soured instantly. "Olivia," he said, his voice clipped and void of any welcome.

She dipped into a curtsy. "My lord."

He gestured towards an empty chair. "Will you not join me?"

No, she wanted to say. A hundred times, no. But she was a guest in his house. His daughter-in-law, she reminded herself. It would be unforgivably rude to refuse.

With her chin slightly elevated, Olivia moved to the indicated chair and sat. "Good morning," she said, infusing the words with all the warmth she could muster.

Lord Everwyck grunted and returned his attention to the newssheets, lifting them as though she were no more than a draft of air.

She clasped her hands in her lap, grateful she would not be forced into tedious conversation. A footman approached and set a plate in front of her. She turned politely towards the servant.

"Is chocolate available this morning?"

Before the footman could reply, the earl lowered his newssheets. "We do not indulge in such frivolities," he informed her.

Olivia's smile remained, though a faint strain touched the edges. "Ah. That is disappointing. I am rather accustomed to a cup of chocolate with breakfast."

"You shall have to develop more practical habits," he said. "Juice, perhaps. Or tea."

"I assure you I am far more agreeable with chocolate in the mornings," she quipped, attempting lightness.

He did not so much as blink, already hidden behind the newssheets once more.

Silence settled between them, awkward and heavy. Olivia lifted her fork and began to eat, chewing slowly, wishing desperately for Evander's presence.

A sudden rustle of paper accompanied a low scoff from the earl. "Your wedding has made the Society page," he said with a sneer, tearing out the article. He extended it towards her with reluctant fingers. "You might as well read it yourself."

She accepted the page delicately. The piece was penned by Mr. Fairchild—blunt and factual, but thankfully lacking any biting commentary. Still, the speed with which it had been published startled her.

"I suppose it was only a matter of time before the *ton* discovered our nuptials," she murmured, setting the newssheet aside.

"My son should never have married you," Lord Everwyck said.

The words hit like a slap. Olivia inhaled through her nose, willing herself not to react. "Are we truly doing this now?"

The earl's mouth tightened. "Evander is beguiled by you, nothing more. Once the enchantment wears off, he'll see you for what you are and he'll resent you for it."

"I hope that is not the case," she replied, her voice remarkably even. "I would not wish to become the source of his unhappiness."

"You are a pretty thing," he admitted. "But I do not believe you possess the refinement, nor the fortitude, to serve as countess."

Olivia allowed herself a dry smile. "For once, we find

ourselves in agreement. I daresay I shall make a terrible countess."

A voice cut in from the doorway. "I disagree."

Olivia's head turned with visible relief as Evander entered the room. He crossed the floor with easy confidence and leaned to press a kiss to her cheek before sitting beside her.

"I do believe," he continued, "that Olivia will make a remarkable countess. In fact, she is precisely what Society needs."

She met his gaze briefly and offered him a grateful smile.

"Sorry I'm late," he murmured.

His father snorted. "It's about time. I've been awake for hours."

"As have I," Evander replied, pouring himself a glass of water. "I visited Lord Warwicke. We had a rather illuminating conversation regarding the indigo plantation."

"A waste of your time," the earl snapped. "You should be studying the correspondence and ledgers here. There's much work to be done."

Evander took a sip before answering, "I think we should sell it."

His father looked as if he had been struck. "Pardon me?"

"The more I learn, the more I believe we should sever ties with it."

"And leave a fortune behind?"

Evander's voice was calm but firm. "Is a fortune worth more than our integrity?"

Lord Everwyck scoffed. "That money will help sustain the estate. Without it, what will we do?"

Olivia finally spoke. "Would my dowry not help ease the strain?"

The earl gave her a fleeting, dismissive glance. "It will help. But it is not enough."

Evander's jaw tightened. "We've been threatened twice. I don't wish to see this escalate."

"So you surrender?" his father barked. "You allow reformers to dictate our actions? You grow soft, Son."

"Father—"

"Enough," Lord Everwyck cut in. "We'll discuss this later. Alone. Olivia need not concern herself with such weighty matters."

"I am his wife," she said evenly. "Should I not be informed of matters that affect our future?"

"Women care nothing for serious concerns," the earl said. "They care for gowns and pin money and gossip."

A flare of heat rose in Olivia's chest. She opened her mouth to respond, but Evander quietly placed his hand over hers—a silent gesture of support.

"I believe," Olivia said slowly and clearly, "that I should be involved in the running of the estate."

"Absolutely not!" Lord Everwyck thundered. "You shall see to the household and remember your place."

Her spine straightened. "And what, precisely, do you believe my place to be?"

Before the earl could reply, Evander intervened. "As Mother is indisposed, Olivia is the lady of this house. She deserves our respect."

"Respect is earned," the earl snapped, shoving his chair back. "And I find this conversation intolerably tedious. I shall be in my study until the funeral proceedings."

As the door slammed behind him, silence fell.

Evander turned towards her. "I'm sorry."

She waved it off with a shake of her head. "You've nothing to apologize for. He is grieving, and today—of all days—must weigh heavily upon him."

"That may be so, but grief does not excuse cruelty."

"No," she agreed. "It doesn't. But I would prefer to grant him some grace, considering he has lost a son." She tilted her head, her voice gentling. "How are you faring?"

He released a long, weary sigh, his shoulders rising and falling. "Well enough, I suppose. Bryon and I were never particularly close, and now..." He hesitated, his gaze drifting to the unlit hearth. "Now I am consumed with estate matters and these threats."

Olivia leaned forward, laying a hand gently on his sleeve. "You must give yourself permission to grieve," she said. "You cannot carry it all without consequence. Pain has a way of settling into your bones if left unattended."

He turned his gaze to her. "When did you become so wise?"

She gave a small, impish smile. "I have always been wise. You've merely failed to recognize it."

"Wise?" he echoed with mock incredulity. "Is this the same girl who smeared mud on the back of my trousers and declared to all that would listen that I had soiled myself?"

Laughter burst from her lips, light and unrestrained. "That was a delightful day."

"I was not nearly as delighted," he replied dryly. "Especially as you chose mud from the riverbank. It reeked of something foul and unmentionable."

"You should not have closed your eyes when I told you to," she teased.

He narrowed his eyes in mock suspicion. "Henceforth, I shall keep them wide open whenever you are near."

"Oh, you may trust me now," she said, feigning innocence. "I was far more mischievous at eight than I am at five and twenty."

"I do trust you, Olivia. I always have."

"And I trust you."

Evander's expression sobered. He leaned back, staring up at the ceiling as though searching for strength there. "I'm worried about my mother," he admitted. "She wished desperately to attend the funeral, but her health will not permit it. She doesn't even have the strength to rise from her bed."

"Would you like me to stay with her?" Olivia asked.

He looked at her then, his brows drawn, as if trying to determine whether he had heard her correctly. "You would do that?"

"For you, I would do anything."

For a moment, he simply stared at her. Then a smile curved his lips—small, but sincere—and the fine creases at the corners of his eyes deepened. "I daresay I chose well when I asked you to be my wife."

A warmth spread through her chest. The way he looked at her now reminded her far too keenly of the moment they had kissed. The memory still lingered on her lips, tempting and undeniable.

Her gaze flickered to his mouth.

How easy it would be to kiss him again. All she needed to do was lean forward, close the short distance between them, and—

But before temptation got the better of her, she drew her hand back and straightened in her chair.

"Are you all right, Olivia?" he asked.

"Yes," she replied, smoothing her skirt unnecessarily. "I was merely thinking that I could do with a cup of chocolate."

"I shall speak to the cook at once."

"There's no need," she responded. "Your father informed me that such 'frivolities' are not to be indulged in this household."

Evander huffed, clearly unimpressed. "Let me concern myself with my father's sensibilities. I am well aware of your deep affection for chocolate, and I would not dare deprive you of it. Deliciousness should never be rationed."

Her smile returned, soft and pleased. "Thank you."

"We should eat," Evander encouraged.

Olivia nodded, her smile a touch too swift. "Yes... yes, we should."

She reached for her fork with fingers that felt strangely unsteady, focusing intently on the simple act of cutting a slice of ham, as if the mundane motion might silence the storm quietly brewing within her.

Anything to distract herself.

The last thing she needed was to dwell on these ill-timed, wholly unwelcome feelings rising for her new husband. Feelings that had nothing to do with duty or practicality. No, this was something far more dangerous. Longing. Warmth. A growing desire to lean into his nearness and forget the carefully drawn lines between them.

But that way led to heartbreak. She knew it. She had loved once before, and it had left her bruised in places no one could see. Evander had been her friend, her constant—he was supposed to be safe.

So why had his simple words made her chest ache with unfamiliar hope?

Olivia forced herself to chew slowly, deliberately, willing her thoughts to quiet. It was just breakfast. Just an ordinary meal in a household full of strained silences and buried grief. She could manage this—she must.

She kept her gaze on her plate, not trusting herself to look at him just yet. If she did, she feared he might see too much.

Too much of what she was trying so hard to hide.

Evander stood motionless before his brother's grave, the chill of the morning seeping through his greatcoat, though he barely felt it. A single tear rolled down his cheek, quickly lost to the stiff breeze, but he made no move to wipe it away. Grief settled in his chest like a heavy stone—not only for the brother he had lost, but for all that had never been. They had spent most of their lives sparring like adversaries. Still, despite their clashes, Bryon had been his brother, and he longed for what could have been. But it was too late now. The final words had already been spoken. Or left unspoken.

Beside him, his friends stood in respectful silence—Alcott, Bedford, and Westcott. They didn't speak. They didn't need to. Their presence was a balm of quiet strength, and he found himself grateful for each of them.

He exhaled slowly, the breath misting in the air. It was time.

He turned from the grave, his boots crunching on the gravel, and cast one last look over his shoulder at the cold stone marker. *Farewell, Bryon.*

"Shall we?" he asked, his voice low, roughened by emotion.

Alcott laid a firm hand on his shoulder. "You can stay for as long as you want or need. We'll remain with you."

Evander gave a small, grateful smile. "That's kind of you, but I think I should return home. There's someone I wish to see." *Olivia.* He didn't say her name aloud, but she was the one bright spot in the dim haze surrounding him. Just being near her eased the tightness in his chest.

Alcott gave a single nod and stepped back. "Very well."

They walked in silence, the wind tugging at their coats as they made their way through the iron gates and down the quiet lane towards their waiting coaches.

At his own coach, Evander paused and turned to face the men who had stood beside him throughout the years.

"Thank you," he said. "I know none of you were close with Bryon."

Bedford shrugged one shoulder. "We didn't come for him. We came for you. You're not alone in this."

Evander swallowed hard. "Is it... is it dreadful that I feel something like relief?"

Westcott met his eyes. "It isn't. There is no wrong way to grieve."

"Bryon and I were never close," Evander said. "I spent years avoiding him. His words always cut deep." He looked away. "And yet I still hoped we might find common ground one day. It was foolish of me."

"Family relationships are complicated," Alcott offered.

Evander gave a faint nod. "I should return. My mother was too unwell to attend. I need to check on her."

"Go," Bedford said simply.

He climbed into the coach and let the door shut behind him. The bench felt colder than usual as he leaned back, tilting his head against the interior wall. He closed his eyes, but his thoughts offered no respite. His mother wouldn't be with him much longer and it was only a matter of time before he stood before her grave.

The coach gave a jolt and began to move, wheels clattering over cobblestone as they merged into the late-morning traffic. He loosened his cravat with a sigh, the fabric suddenly constricting. Everyone had watched him at the grave. The new Lord Westmere. The heir. The benefactor of death.

But he hadn't wanted this. He had never asked for any of it. The only good to come from this wretched change in fortune was Olivia. He had won her—by some miracle—and he would spend the rest of his life trying to deserve her.

The coach slowed in front of his townhouse. Without waiting for the footman, Evander opened the door and stepped down. A sharp crack shattered the air.

His heart stopped.

Then—*splintering wood.* A sharp whistle past his ear. He turned in time to see a fresh hole carved into the coach's side.

"My lord!" one of the footmen shouted, rushing forward. "Get inside! Someone's shooting at you!"

Evander didn't hesitate. He bolted up the steps, pushed

open the front door, and slammed it shut behind him, chest heaving. He pressed a hand to his heart and breathed deeply, steadying the panicked rhythm. A few inches closer, and...

"My lord?" Gillingham appeared at once, brows furrowed. "Are you injured? I heard a shot."

"No," Evander said, voice steady only by force of will. "I'm well."

"Shall I send for the constable?"

He hesitated, then shook his head. "No. Not yet. Let's not make a scene."

Gillingham didn't look convinced, but accepted the answer with a slight bow. "As you wish."

"Where is my wife?"

"She is with your mother."

Relief flooded through him. "Thank you," he murmured, handing over his hat. He took the stairs two at a time.

At the end of the corridor, he eased open the bedchamber door.

There she was.

Olivia sat beside his mother's bed, her delicate fingers moving deftly over a small piece of embroidery. The sight of her—calm, composed, surrounded by soft light filtering through the window—unraveled something tight within him.

She looked up and smiled. "Hello."

He crossed to her side. "How is she?"

"Asleep," she whispered. "She's been resting for most of the morning."

Placing a hand on Olivia's shoulder, he said, "Thank you for staying with her. I didn't want her to be alone."

Olivia reached up and curled her fingers around his. "And you? How are you?"

He stared into her eyes and let his guard slip, just a little. "I've had better days," he admitted softly. "But I'm better now... now that I've seen you."

Just then, his mother stirred. Her eyes opened, pale and weary. "Evander?"

He leaned over her. "I'm here."

She tried to sit up and he reached for her at once. "Let me help."

As he supported her, she smiled faintly and brushed her fingers along his sleeve.

Yes. He was still grieving. Still haunted and still overwhelmed. But in this quiet room, with Olivia at his side, he remembered why he kept going.

Because there was still something left to fight for.

His mother leaned back against the pillows, her frail form dwarfed by the carved headboard behind her. Though her cheeks had grown hollow and her voice had softened with age and illness, she still carried herself with quiet dignity.

"Tell me about the funeral," she said gently. "Was it well attended?"

Evander sat on the bed. "It was."

"That is good," she murmured, her gaze distant. "I was worried no one would come."

He looked at her, noting the fine tremble in her fingers as they twisted the edge of her blankets. Even bedridden, she thought first of appearances—of whether Bryon had been mourned properly. She had always believed in upholding dignity, even in grief.

A knock interrupted the quiet.

"Enter," Evander called.

The door opened to reveal a young maid. She dipped into a quick curtsy before speaking. "My lord, a gentleman has requested a moment of your time. Lord Luca Dexter."

Evander furrowed his brow. "I do not know him. Did he state his business?"

"No, my lord. Only that it was urgent."

He considered sending the man away. His instincts pricked

with unease—unannounced callers with vague intentions rarely boded well—but curiosity won out. "Inform him I will be down shortly."

Another curtsy, and the maid slipped away.

Evander rose. "I should see what he wants," he said, casting a glance at his mother. "But I won't be long."

She offered a faint smile, though fatigue dulled its warmth. "I will be waiting. Olivia will stay with me."

That small comfort gave him a measure of peace. He looked at Olivia, meeting her gaze in silent thanks before quitting the room.

As he descended the staircase, he tried to push aside the residual weight of the funeral. Yet the ache remained, threaded now with the sense of growing unrest. First, the attempt on his life. Now this unexpected visitor. Something wasn't right.

He entered the drawing room and immediately spotted the man. Tall and broad-shouldered, Lord Luca stood near the window, back straight, hands clasped behind him as he stared out at the gray sky beyond. There was a calculated stillness to him, as if every movement were rehearsed.

"Lord Luca," Evander said.

The man turned, dark eyes sharp, his expression composed. "Lord Westmere." He offered a shallow bow. "Thank you for seeing me."

Evander remained rooted in his spot. "I must admit I don't know why you're here."

Unfolding his hands, Lord Luca stepped forward with the confident ease of a man who expected to be listened to. "I was hoping to ask you a few questions."

"Questions?" Evander repeated. "Why?"

"You may have heard," Lord Luca said, "I recently purchased *The London Gazette*. I'm writing a piece for an upcoming issue."

Evander's brow lifted. "You're writing it?"

"I am," he said without a trace of embarrassment. "I find it helps to be directly involved in my publications."

"And what, exactly, does this have to do with me?"

Lord Luca's smile didn't waver. "I'm writing on the state of indigo plantations in India, and your family's name, of course, came up."

Evander stiffened. "You wish to speak of the plantation?"

"I wish to speak of your intentions," Lord Luca responded. "Will you be continuing your late brother's barbaric treatment of the locals?"

Evander blinked, stunned by the accusation. "I beg your pardon?"

Lord Luca reached into his coat and withdrew a folded document. "There have been disturbing reports—firsthand accounts—of brutal practices under your brother's management."

Evander took the paper with reluctance and unfolded it. The parchment crackled in his hands.

"My brother may have been... severe," he said, choosing his words carefully, "but he was not a tyrant."

"Severity is often a mask," Lord Luca replied. "Some justify cruelty as business. But if you read the article in your hand, you'll see claims that your brother oversaw the slaughter of nearly a hundred locals who opposed his expansion."

Evander's breath caught.

He scanned the article. Names. Villages. Vague descriptions of retaliation. He felt his stomach twist. *Could this be true?*

He looked up. "And how am I to know this piece wasn't fabricated?"

"You don't," Lord Luca said simply. "Which is why I suggest you speak to your father. He knows far more than you might think."

Evander's fingers curled tighter around the paper. "And what do you want from me?"

"Your plans," Luca said. "Will you continue operating the plantation? Or do you intend to reform it?"

Evander met his gaze squarely. "I have no comment."

Luca stepped closer, voice dropping slightly. "There are reformer groups targeting *Nabobs*. They've grown violent. Some have even killed. Have you received threats?"

Evander remained impassive, though the bullet that had barely missed him earlier echoed in his mind. "No."

The lie sat bitter on his tongue.

"I see." Lord Luca tilted his head. "Well, I'd advise caution. These groups are becoming more brazen."

Evander stepped aside and gestured towards the door. "I believe our conversation is at an end."

Lord Luca hesitated a moment, then nodded. "Very well." He turned towards the door, then glanced back. "Keep the article. You and your father may find it... enlightening."

Without waiting for a response, he exited, boots echoing down the corridor.

Evander stood motionless in the quiet that followed, the article still clutched in his hand. A hundred dead? His brother's legacy, tainted by violence? And his father, what had he known?

He looked down at the paper again, heart pounding. There was more to uncover. And suddenly, it felt like he was standing not at the beginning of his inheritance, but at the edge of a much darker truth.

11

Olivia needed to escape.

Not forever—though the temptation lingered—but for just a few stolen hours. A reprieve from the heaviness of recent days, from the carefully composed expressions and whispered condolences, and from the ache of wishing she could be in two places at once. While Evander buried his brother, she had remained dutifully at Lady Everwyck's side, offering quiet comfort to a woman who had already lost too much.

Now, seated inside the quiet confines of her coach, she pressed her gloved fingers to her temple and exhaled slowly. The soft jostling of the carriage as it trundled along the familiar cobbled streets of London brought no real comfort, but at least the destination did. The circulating library had always been her sanctuary. It was a place where she could lose herself in pages instead of problems.

She leaned her head against the windowpane and closed her eyes briefly, letting the dull rhythm of the wheels soothe her. She wished she could have been with Evander. He had always been there for her—steady and kind, even when she had been reckless and foolish. Their friendship had been one of the few constants in her life, which only made the shift between them feel more unsettling.

That kiss.

He had asked permission, and she had given it willingly, but she hadn't anticipated the storm it would stir within her. They had married out of necessity, not love. She had needed saving, and he had needed to fulfill a dying wish of his mother. It had been a practical arrangement. Logical. Predictable. But that kiss... it had introduced complication, intimacy, the sort of feelings she had not prepared herself to feel. The sort she wasn't entirely sure she wanted to feel.

The coach drew to a gentle stop, jolting her from her thoughts. She waited until the footman opened the door. Taking his gloved hand, she stepped down onto the pavement. For the first time in her life, she moved about London unchaperoned, a married woman with a new kind of independence. It was a small freedom, but a welcome one.

Tugging the brim of her straw hat into place, she lifted her chin and entered the library. The familiar scent of aging parchment greeted her like an old friend. The hush inside was immediate, the kind of reverent silence only a room full of books could command.

She made her way towards the back corner, where the French romances were shelved. But her steps faltered.

There, nestled into the corner with a teetering stack of books before her, sat Lady Jane. Her head was bowed, her eyes rimmed red, and her hands clenched tightly in her lap. Olivia's heart twisted at the sight.

She approached slowly and spoke softly. "Jane?"

Jane looked up, startled. Her lashes were wet, and her lips trembled as she whispered, "Livy... what are you doing here?"

"I needed something to read," she said, unwilling to mention the rest. The heartache. The confusion. The worry.

"Oh. That makes sense." Jane looked away quickly, pretending to busy herself with a book she wasn't truly reading.

Olivia didn't hesitate. She pulled out a chair and sat. "Something is troubling you. What is it?"

Jane released a long, trembling sigh. "My father has arranged a marriage for me."

Olivia's stomach dropped. "To whom?"

There was a pause, and then Jane replied quietly, "The Duke of Brackenford."

Olivia blinked. "But... he's old enough to be your grandfather."

"I know," Jane whispered, her voice breaking. "But he has no heir. Only daughters. And I am the sacrificial lamb."

Olivia leaned closer, voice hushed. "You can't marry him. He's dreadful. I've heard whispers—terrible ones. Some say he beat his last wife to death."

Tears welled in Jane's eyes. "What choice do I have? My father would disown me if I refused. I have no dowry left. No influence. Nothing."

"There must be another way," Olivia said, her mind racing.

"I've thought of everything. I truly have." Jane's voice cracked as she swiped at a tear. "And I keep coming back to the same truth that I have no options."

Olivia sat back in her chair. "I won't let you give up. There has to be a way."

"It's too late," Jane said, her voice flat. "The banns have already been posted. I marry him in three weeks."

"You can always say no."

"And do what?" Jane snapped, her grief bleeding into frustration. "Starve in the gutter? I have no fortune. No relatives who would take me in."

Olivia paused, then offered quietly, "What if you became my companion?"

Jane looked appalled. "I'm the daughter of an earl. I can't take a position. It would be… degrading."

"More degrading than being forced into marriage with a man three times your age who has buried four wives already?"

Jane considered that, lips trembling. "I would be a duchess, and our marriage contract is rather generous to me, should I outlive him. Which shouldn't be hard, considering he's a thousand years old."

Olivia's laughter slipped out despite herself. "He's not quite a thousand. I believe he's only eighty."

"Is there a difference?" Jane asked.

"Perhaps to some," Olivia replied with a half-smile. "But I daresay he appears ancient to you since you only recently turned one and twenty years old."

Jane's face crumpled. "What am I to do?"

Olivia reached for her hand. "You cannot marry him, Jane. The price is too steep. You deserve more than to be bartered away."

"My family believes this to be an advantageous marriage. I would benefit my whole family."

"At what cost?"

Jane tipped her head back, staring up at the painted ceiling. "Even if I ran away, no one would come after me. I'd be truly alone."

"You're not alone. You have me."

Jane offered a weak smile. "Thank you. But I fear I must do my duty."

"Even if it destroys your future?"

"Do I even have one without this match?" Jane whispered.

Before Olivia could answer, a shadow fell over their table.

"Jane," barked a stern voice. Olivia looked up to see Lord Barkley—Jane's older brother—bearing down on them with his usual disapproval. "Why is your maid loitering outside?"

Jane stood quickly. "I needed a moment alone."

The viscount's cold gaze slid towards Olivia. "Lady Westmere." He inclined his head without warmth. "If I may suggest, you should cease encouraging my sister."

"And why is that, my lord?" Olivia asked, meeting his stare.

"Your reputation..." He let the words dangle meaningfully. "I don't believe I need to say it. But you know it, and I know it."

Jane bristled, stepping closer to Olivia. "Lady Westmere is my friend."

"Then you would do well to choose better friends," Barkley said curtly. "Now, we must be going."

"I wanted to check out these books," Jane said, gesturing feebly to the stack.

"Leave them. We have books at home." He extended his arm. "Come. We have matters to arrange for your wedding."

Jane's shoulders sagged in defeat. "Very well."

Olivia watched helplessly as Jane was led away, her steps reluctant, her face pale. She wanted to call out, to defy Lord Barkley on her friend's behalf, but knew it would do no good. Jane had always done her duty—even when it cost her dearly.

And now, it seemed, she was going to do it again.

"Poor Lady Jane."

The voice, soft yet distinct, broke through the silence. Olivia turned and saw Miss Winslow, standing a few paces away, her posture relaxed but her blue eyes holding an unfamiliar shade of earnestness. There was no coyness in her expression, no trace of the usual drawing room flirtation Olivia had come to associate with her. Just quiet compassion.

"I couldn't help but overhear your conversation," Miss Winslow added, stepping forward. She showed not even a flicker of embarrassment for the admission. "It's terrible what they're doing to her. Forcing her to marry that man. The Duke of Brackenford, of all people."

Olivia stiffened instinctively. She had no idea how much Miss Winslow had overheard, and while she doubted Jane's brother had the imagination to send someone to spy on them, she still felt a cautious curl of unease rise in her chest.

She offered a thin, noncommittal smile. "Yes, well… it is what it is, I'm afraid."

A glint of frustration flickered in Miss Winslow's eyes. She tucked a loose blonde curl behind her ear with practiced elegance, though her voice remained genuine. "I wish there were something we could do to help her."

Olivia drew in a quiet breath. *So do I.* But instead, she said carefully, "I'm afraid that as women, our positions are… limited."

"Do you truly believe that?" Miss Winslow asked, her tone somewhere between challenge and curiosity.

No, she didn't believe that. Not really. But saying so aloud—especially to someone she barely knew—felt like opening a door she wasn't quite ready to walk through.

"I don't know what I believe," she said at last. It was not a lie. Merely the edge of the truth.

Miss Winslow placed a hand on her hip, her chin lifting just slightly. "All women have to do is remain silent, and our critics win. That's how they've always kept us small—by convincing us we have no voice. No power."

Olivia blinked, startled. She had never known Miss Winslow to speak so forcefully on any subject that didn't involve dresses, dances, or which gentleman had the finest horses. And yet here she was—animated, impassioned, and surprisingly incisive.

"Everyone knows the rumors about the Duke of Brackenford," Miss Winslow continued, stepping closer and lowering her voice. "He is not a good man. He wasn't a good husband, either."

"But what can we do?"

Miss Winslow bit her lower lip, thoughtful. "If we put our heads together, surely we can think of something."

"And if we can't?"

Miss Winslow didn't flinch. "After everything you've been through, Lady Westmere… do you not believe it's possible to do the impossible?"

Olivia's heart gave a tiny flutter—whether from fear or hope, she couldn't tell. But she nodded. "I do."

A slow smile spread across Miss Winslow's face. "Then let's make the impossible happen."

"Do you have an idea?"

"I might," she said, her smile sharpening with sudden mischief. "I know Mr. Fairchild. I'll ask him to write something. A piece on Lady Jane's situation."

That name gave Olivia pause. "How do you know Mr. Fairchild?"

Miss Winslow waved a gloved hand dismissively. "That's hardly relevant. What *is* relevant is that he owes me a favor and he's not above stirring a little outrage in the press."

Olivia wasn't entirely reassured. "Even if he did publish such a thing, I doubt it would matter. Lord Ketteridge and his son, Lord Barkley, are both stubborn men. They would never be swayed by public opinion."

"No," Miss Winslow agreed. "But the rest of Society might. And if enough tongues start wagging, the scandal might become more of a liability than the marriage an asset."

Olivia considered that. She wasn't sure how far they could push, or how loud their voices would ring, but she had learned something over the past year: women had more power than they were ever taught to believe—they simply had to be willing to use it.

Still, something tugged at her. "Why are you so willing to help Lady Jane?"

Miss Winslow's expression softened, her voice quieter now. "Because once, at a dinner party, I spilled wine on my gown. Bright red. Right down the front. No one offered to help—not the other girls, not the hostess. They only laughed. But Lady Jane pulled me into the retiring room and helped me wash the stain. She offered me her shawl to cover it, so I wouldn't be embarrassed. She was kind when no one else was."

"That does sound like Jane," Olivia acknowledged.

"She didn't have to help me," Miss Winslow added. "But she did. And I haven't forgotten."

Olivia felt something shift in her then—not just cautious respect, but a glimmer of connection. Perhaps Miss Winslow wasn't as frivolous as she had seemed. Perhaps none of them were. Underneath their pretty gowns and painted smiles, they were all navigating a world that too often treated them like pawns.

"All right," Olivia said at last. "Let's do it. Let's try."

A satisfied smile curved across Miss Winslow's face. "I will be in touch, Lady Westmere," she said, her voice brimming with a confidence Olivia had never quite noticed before. With a subtle tilt of her chin and a graceful turn, she strode away, hips swaying with the unmistakable air of a woman who always got what she wanted.

Olivia remained still for a long moment, watching her retreat. What in the world had she just agreed to?

An uneasy alliance with Miss Winslow—of all people. The very thought would have made her laugh a week ago. They weren't exactly enemies, but they certainly weren't friends either. Still, she couldn't shake the strange tangle of curiosity and caution winding through her chest. She had no idea what kind of chaos Miss Winslow might stir up—or how far she was willing to go for Lady Jane's sake. But Olivia did know one thing: doing nothing was no longer an option.

So be it, she thought, straightening her shoulders. If she had to form alliances with unlikely women to help Jane, she would do it. Strange times called for strange companions.

With a quiet sigh, she turned back towards the shelves,

letting the familiar scent of parchment and leather draw her back into the present. She ran her fingers lightly along the spines of the books as she passed, pausing at a shelf of novels in French. Selecting a slim volume bound in worn blue leather, she tucked it beneath her arm, then reached for a second. Two would be enough. She didn't want to be gone too long.

As she walked towards the front counter to check out her selections, a thought pricked at the edges of her mind—*the impossible,* Miss Winslow had said. Olivia had lived through the impossible. Survived it. And perhaps now, just perhaps, she could help someone else do the same.

Evander sat at the desk in his study as the flickering candle cast shadows across the ledgers spread before him. The ink on the page had long since dried, yet he stared at it as if willing the numbers to change. But there was no denying it—his father had been right. The indigo plantation promised a fortune, its projected earnings nothing short of staggering.

And yet, wealth had never felt so cursed.

His shoulders tightened as he leaned back in the chair, the creak of old leather loud in the silence. He had been threatened and shot at. He knew with a chilling certainty that if another warning came, it might be his last.

A knock broke through the tension, followed by the quiet footfalls of the butler entering. "Lord Warwicke has requested a moment of your—"

The sentence died in the air as Warwicke stepped past the butler, his face grim.

"We need to talk," Warwicke said, voice clipped and dark with urgency.

Evander dismissed the butler with a curt nod. "Very well,"

he said, gesturing towards the chairs opposite the desk. "Would you care to sit?"

But Warwicke remained standing. "I've made some inquiries into your brother's death... and I've discovered something I don't believe you'll like."

Evander's spine stiffened. "Go on."

Jaw clenched, Warwicke said, "I think he was murdered."

The words hung between them like a dropped blade. Evander felt the ground shift beneath him. "Murdered? What are you basing that on? Illness broke out on his ship and many of the passengers perished. It is not uncommon for that to happen on a long voyage."

"That's just it," Warwicke said. "Earlier today, I saw that very ship moored on the River Thames, so I went to make some inquiries. None of the crew seemed to remember Bryon or Lord Harwood even making the journey."

Evander blinked, incredulous. "That's impossible."

"I thought the same," Warwicke replied. "Until I spoke to the crew. And there's more—I attended a meeting with certain reformers opposing British rule in India. They spoke of your brother, and let's just say, it wasn't in reverence."

Evander rose from his chair slowly and walked over to the tall windows. "If what you're saying is true... how do we prove it?"

"Give me more time," Warwicke replied. "But until then, you need to be careful. These men—these reformers—they don't operate with mercy. They are methodical. And ruthless."

Evander turned from the window, his expression hardening. "What about Lord Harwood? Do you believe he was murdered, too?"

Warwicke gave a single, sharp nod. "It's highly likely. If the reformers wanted to eliminate anyone involved with colonial trade, disposing of bodies at sea while en route would have been easy—and efficient."

"I want to help," Evander said firmly. "Let me attend one of those meetings."

"No," Warwicke said, his tone brooking no argument. "You're already a marked man. If they spot you, they may not wait for another opportunity."

Evander's hands curled into fists. "I won't stand by and do nothing."

"You must," Warwicke said. "At least for now. Let me do what I'm trained to do. I've already reached out to my contacts at Bow Street. We need solid evidence before we act. Right now, we're blind in the dark."

"I sent extra guards to watch over Olivia when she went to the circulating library earlier. I don't want to worry her, at least unnecessarily, but I fear that whoever might be threatening me might turn their sights on her."

"That was wise."

With a low exhale, Evander returned to the desk, absently gathering the plantation papers. "This indigo venture could make my family immensely wealthy."

Warwicke gave him a pointed look. "That's why men are dying over it."

"Yes. And I know my father won't relinquish his hold without a fight."

"Some fights," Warwicke said, "are worth having."

Evander's gaze narrowed. "You're right. But I fear the cost may be higher than he realizes."

A soft voice from the doorway made them both turn. "I'm sorry to interrupt," Olivia said, her tone polite. "But the dinner bell has rung."

Warwicke turned towards her and gave a respectful bow. "My lady."

She offered a graceful curtsy. "Would you care to join us for dinner, my lord?"

"That's kind of you, but I intend to dine with my wife this evening," Warwicke replied. "If you'll excuse me."

Evander watched his friend go, then turned his attention fully to Olivia. Her pale green gown was a perfect complement to the fair glow of her skin. Her hair, drawn back into a neat chignon, was threaded with pearls that caught the light like tiny stars.

He stepped closer, his voice soft. "You look lovely."

"Thank you," she replied with a smile. "You look rather dashing yourself."

He offered his arm. "My father is out. I hope you don't mind dining with only me."

A mischievous smile danced on her lips. "There are worse ways to spend an evening. But I refuse to play chess with you again. You cheat."

Evander chuckled, grateful for her lightness. "Not the way I see it."

"Then you see it wrong," she teased. "There's a right way and a wrong way to play chess."

"You were simply a sore loser."

She rolled her eyes. "You tried using your wooden soldiers as chess pieces. Those don't belong on a board."

"I disagree. It made the game more exciting."

"You claimed checkmate after one move!"

Evander shrugged. "Those are the rules—my rules."

She laughed, and the sound warmed him. "You are utterly delusional."

As they strolled towards the dining room, he asked, "How was the circulating library?"

"I ran into Lady Jane," Olivia replied, her tone sobering. "She's to marry the Duke of Brackenford."

Evander's steps faltered. "That poor girl."

"We have to help her," Olivia said, eyes burning with quiet determination.

"Of course. But how?"

"She said her father would disown her if she refused. If that happens, could she stay with us?"

"If that's what you want, then yes. She's welcome."

They reached the dining room, and Evander pulled out her chair with a practiced hand. Once she was seated, he took his usual place across from her.

Olivia laid her napkin across her lap. "I spoke with Miss Winslow today as well. She's connected to Mr. Fairchild."

"The man who writes for *The Morning Post*?"

"Yes. And he owes her a favor. She's going to have him publish an article about Jane's engagement."

Evander took a sip from his wine glass. "Do you think that will help?"

"It might. If Society disapproves, it could pressure the duke to withdraw his offer of marriage."

He arched a brow. "That's quite the gamble."

She sighed dramatically. "Must you always be a naysayer?"

He grinned. "My apologies. I think your plan is brilliant and will no doubt save Lady Jane from a terrible fate."

"That's better," Olivia said, visibly pleased. "Now, what did Lord Warwicke wish to discuss?"

Evander paused. He had always been honest with Olivia, but this was different. He wasn't sure how she would take it.

She lifted a brow. "I know what you are trying to do. You're trying to protect me from something, aren't you?"

He gave a small, helpless smile. "How do you always know?"

"Because I know you, Evander," she said. "Tell me."

How he wished he could tell her the truth—that he was in love with her. That every moment spent in her company left him wanting more, craving something just beyond reach. He had loved her for years, quietly, faithfully, completely. But he knew Olivia wasn't ready for that kind of truth. Not yet. Perhaps not ever.

And so, he locked it away behind a practiced expression and steadied his breath.

Taking a deep breath, Evander said, "Warwicke believes my brother was murdered. Over the indigo plantation."

Olivia stiffened, the color draining from her face. "Murdered?"

He nodded grimly. "Yes. And he fears I might be next, considering I've already been threatened... and shot at."

She gasped, her chair scraping slightly against the floor as she jolted upright. "*What?!* You were shot at? When did this happen?"

"Right after the funeral," he admitted reluctantly. "But—"

"You should have told me that!" she cut in, her voice sharp with alarm.

"I didn't want to concern you."

Her eyes flashed as she leaned forward across the table. "So you didn't say anything at all? That was your solution?"

He gave a small, sheepish smile. "Not my finest plan, no."

"No, it wasn't," Olivia said firmly, reaching across the table to grasp his hand. "I don't know what I would do if I lost you."

A soft ache stirred in his chest. "You'd be fine."

She squeezed his hand. "No. I wouldn't. You are my best friend."

Friend.

There it was again—that word. So simple, so devastating. It wrapped around his heart like a ribbon made of thorns. Would she ever see him as anything more? Did she even realize what it cost him every time she said it? He looked down at their joined hands, then up at her face, memorizing the concern in her eyes, the earnest curve of her brow, the way her lips trembled slightly when she was upset.

Moments later, the footmen stepped in with perfect timing, placing steaming bowls of soup before them. Olivia reluctantly withdrew her hand and leaned back in her chair, her gaze still lingering on him with worry.

"What are we going to do?" she asked.

Evander lifted his spoon but didn't touch the soup. "*We* are going to do nothing, but I have to convince my father to sell the plantation. But it won't be easy. He believes this indigo land is the answer to everything and it will keep the estate afloat for decades to come."

"And if he's wrong?" Olivia asked, her brow furrowed.

Evander didn't respond right away. He stared into the bowl as if the swirling broth might yield a solution. "Then we might all lose far more than coin."

Olivia picked up her spoon and took a small sip before placing it back down. "Have you contacted the constable about the threats?"

"No," he admitted. "But Warwicke is looking into it for me."

She tilted her head. "Wasn't he a Bow Street Runner once?"

Evander finally allowed himself a smile. "He was. And I suspect he never quite stopped."

"Well, lucky for you," she said with a forced lightness, though the tightness in her voice betrayed her lingering fear. She looked down at her soup and shook her head. "I must admit, I've lost my appetite. It's hard to eat when knowing that someone tried to shoot you."

He reached out, brushing his fingers briefly over hers again—just enough to feel the spark, to remember it was real. "I didn't mean to frighten you."

"You didn't mean to," she echoed, meeting his gaze. "But you did."

Evander looked at her across the candlelit table, her expression clouded with worry, and knew that this—*this*—was why he hadn't told her earlier. Because it wasn't just about the danger. It was about what came after. What truths might spill out if he gave himself permission to break.

But he wasn't ready for that either.

Not yet.

12

The following morning, Olivia slipped quietly from her bedchamber, her slippers making scarcely a sound upon the carpet as she made her way down the corridor. She hoped to pay a visit to Lady Everwyck before breakfast to ensure she was well.

As she neared the door to Lady Everwyck's chambers, she slowed. The door stood slightly ajar, the soft creak revealing a glimpse of the room within. Curiosity getting the better of her, Olivia leaned in and peered through the gap.

Lady Everwyck lay propped up against a bank of pillows, her face pale and drawn with fatigue. Seated at her bedside was Lord Everwyck, his fingers gently entwined with hers. Their heads were bowed together as they spoke in hushed tones, his voice almost inaudible over the ticking of the longcase clock in the corner. But what struck Olivia most—what nearly stole the breath from her lungs—was the sight of tears tracking down the earl's stern face.

Tears. From Lord Everwyck.

She was stunned. She had never once imagined him capable of such emotion. He had always seemed so rigid, so impervious to sentiment. Yet here he was, utterly undone at his wife's bedside, pressing his lips to her forehead with a reverence that made Olivia's throat tighten.

He rose suddenly, brushing at his face with a trembling hand and turning towards the door.

Panic gripped her. She had no wish to be caught spying on such an intimate moment. With scarcely a thought, she turned on her heel and opened the nearest door, slipping inside.

Only once the door had clicked shut behind her did she realize her error.

Evander stood before the looking glass, his hands adjusting the folds of his cravat. He caught sight of her in the mirror, and a slow smile spread across his face.

"Livy?" he asked, one brow arching in bemusement.

She raised a finger to her lips. "Shhh."

She moved to the door and cautiously cracked it open, peering down the corridor. Was Lord Everwyck still inside, or had he already passed by? The thought of facing him now made her stomach twist.

Evander came to stand behind her, his breath tickling her ear. "What mischief are you about?"

She turned her head slightly, their faces now mere inches apart. The nearness made her pulse quicken, memory rushing in—the last time they'd stood this close, they had kissed.

Her gaze dropped, quite against her will, to his mouth.

Could she?

Would she?

The scent of him—spiced orange, cedar, something warm and masculine—wrapped around her like a memory. She shouldn't be here. Not like this. Not alone with him in his bedchamber.

And yet… they were married.

A flurry of emotions tangled in her chest, but before she

could act—or even decide what she wished—Evander took a small step back.

"I must ask," he said with a teasing glint in his eyes, "are you here to seduce me?"

Her eyes widened. "Heavens, no!"

"That is a shame," he said lightly. "You would find I am very seducible."

Her cheeks burned. "You shouldn't say such things."

"Why not? We are husband and wife. Surely it's permissible to engage in the noble art of conjugal flirtation. Or, as I prefer to call it—the dance of naked bodies."

"No one says that," she muttered.

"It will catch on," he said confidently. "Give it time."

She gave him a withering look. "You are enjoying this far too much."

"I am, my *Kicksy-Wicksy*," he admitted with a grin. He stepped closer. "After all, you are the one who crept into my bedchamber uninvited. What was I to think?"

"That I was hiding," she replied.

"From me?" he asked, mock-offended.

"No," she said with a sigh. "From your father."

Evander blinked. "My father?"

She nodded, tucking a stray curl behind her ear. "I saw him in your mother's room. He was holding her hand… and crying."

Evander's brows shot up. "Crying? Are you sure?"

"Yes, I saw the tears and I panicked. I didn't want to be caught eavesdropping, so I fled into the nearest door. Unfortunately, that door was yours."

He crossed his arms slowly, digesting her words. "I confess, I'm not sure which is more shocking—my father's emotional display, or your daring escape into my chambers."

"He looked… human," Olivia said softly.

"Well, that's a relief," Evander replied. "I had long suspected he was made of stone."

She gave a quiet laugh.

"Did he see you?" he asked.

"No. I was very stealthy. Like a ninja."

"A ninja who stomps everywhere she goes?" he teased.

"I do not stomp."

"You do. But it's endearing."

She narrowed her eyes. "Aren't you supposed to be charming?"

"That depends. Will this conversation end in a kiss?"

"It will not."

He sighed. "Then, no kisses, no charm."

"You are impossible," she said, reaching for the door.

"You married me," he reminded her smugly.

Peeking into the corridor, she gave a small nod. "It's safe. Come along."

Evander followed her out and pulled the door shut behind them. "You know, as your husband, I am legally entitled to be alone with you in my bedchamber. In fact, it's rather encouraged."

"I'd rather not give the servants something to gossip about," she said briskly.

"They'd be delighted. It would add spice to their otherwise mundane lives."

She shook her head as she increased her stride. "I think I've had enough of you for one morning."

"You love me."

"Not today," she tossed over her shoulder.

He caught up with her easily, and they made their way to the dining room together.

Upon entering, Olivia's gaze fell on Lord Everwyck, already seated at the head of the table with the newssheets spread before him. He glanced up, and as always, his expression darkened ever so slightly.

"Olivia. Evander," he greeted tersely, beginning to rise.

Olivia lifted a hand to halt him. "Please, my lord. Don't trouble yourself."

She took a seat as far from Lord Everwyck as the dining table would allow, relieved when Evander followed suit and settled beside her. His presence at her side always offered a strange, welcome comfort.

A footman stepped forward and laid a plate of food before her. She reached for her linen napkin and smoothed it across her lap, inhaling the comforting aromas of toasted bread, soft eggs, and smoked ham. Her stomach gave a gentle protest of hunger, but before she could lift her fork, Lord Everwyck's voice cut sharply through the clink of cutlery.

"Well," he drawled, not bothering to look up from the newssheets, "it would seem your antics have not landed on the Society page this morning. A small mercy."

Evander let out a quiet sigh and began, "Father—"

But Olivia spoke first, keeping her tone light, controlled. "It's quite all right. Your father was merely stating a fact. And I, too, am rather relieved not to find my name smeared across the Society columns."

At that, Lord Everwyck lowered the newssheets just enough to fix her with a pointed gaze. "You may not be mentioned, but it appears Mr. Fairchild has taken issue with the impending union between the Duke of Brackenford and Lady Jane. His article is... less than flattering."

Olivia's hand stilled on her fork. Her heart gave a swift, hopeful beat. *Miss Winslow did it.* She had convinced Mr. Fairchild to wield his pen in Lady Jane's defense. If the duke read it—if the right tongues began to whisper—perhaps the engagement could still be undone.

"That is wonderful news," she said, unable to keep the quiet excitement from her voice.

Lord Everwyck's lips curled into a thin, humorless line. "Wonderful? Hardly. The Duke of Brackenford is not likely to be deterred by the opinion of an inconsequential writer in *The Morning Post*."

"He may not," Olivia agreed, straightening, "but Lady Jane cannot—*must not*—marry him."

The earl blinked slowly, as if the very idea bored him. "And why, pray tell, is that?"

"Because," Olivia said firmly, "he only wants her to provide him an heir. He's old enough to be her grandfather."

"That is often the way of noble matches," he replied with maddening calm. "She should consider herself fortunate. To be a duchess is no small thing."

She turned towards Evander, seeking support. "And what do you think?"

Evander tilted his head, the corner of his mouth tugging in amusement. "I'd be an unwise man to contradict my wife. But," he added, growing serious, "the duke's history with his previous wives is... troubling. The shadows cast by his reputation are long, and not without cause."

His father sniffed in disdain. "You two sound like children with fairytale notions. Lady Jane will have power, prestige, and a fortune beyond her imagination. Do you not see what she stands to gain?"

"But at what cost?" Olivia asked.

Lord Everwyck pushed back from the table with an abrupt scrape of his chair. "I'm finished with this tiresome conversation. I'll be in my study." He turned to Evander. "I'll expect you after breakfast. We've much work to attend."

"Yes... work," Evander echoed with no particular enthusiasm.

Without another word, the earl swept from the room, leaving a strained silence in his wake.

Olivia reached for her cup of chocolate and took a steadying sip, letting the warmth ease her tight throat. "Well," she murmured, "it would appear your father has fully recovered from his emotional state this morning."

Evander gave a dry chuckle. "If you hadn't seen him crying, I would never have believed it possible."

"I do hope Mr. Fairchild's article sets the gossips talking. If public opinion turns, the duke might just withdraw his offer."

"It's a gamble," Evander said. "Mr. Fairchild is sharp, but the duke is stubborn."

"I'm willing to take that gamble for Lady Jane's sake," Olivia said. "She deserves a chance at happiness—not a gilded cage with an old man."

Evander leaned subtly closer, his shoulder brushing against hers. "Not everyone is lucky enough to marry a devastatingly handsome man. You are, undoubtedly, the most fortunate woman in England."

She arched a brow. "You are intolerably cocky this morning."

"Why wouldn't I be?" he asked, eyes sparkling. "You snuck into my bedchamber to seduce me."

Her mouth fell open. "I most certainly did not!" She took a moment to gather herself. "I explained why I was there."

"That you did," he said solemnly. "But it was all rather convenient, wasn't it? You just happened to stumble into my room."

"You are a lackwit."

He placed a hand dramatically over his heart. "You wound me, my *Kicksy-Wicksy*."

Olivia groaned. "Must you keep calling me that?"

"It's an affectionate endearment. Very traditional. And I like it."

"It's appalling."

"It's adorable," he corrected.

She rolled her eyes. "It's astonishing that I tolerate you."

"You do more than tolerate me," he said with a grin that made her chest ache in a most disconcerting way.

She looked back to her breakfast with purpose and picked up her fork. "Can we not simply eat?"

"An excellent idea," Evander said agreeably, turning to his own plate. "I do love food."

Olivia began eating, grateful for the momentary silence. Yet beneath her calm façade, her thoughts tumbled. She loved bantering with him and treasured the easy rhythm of their conversations. But she couldn't deny it any longer—her feelings for Evander were changing, deepening. They were no longer simply friendly affections.

No. These were not the emotions one had for a best friend.

These were the quiet beginnings of something far more dangerous—and that is what scared her the most.

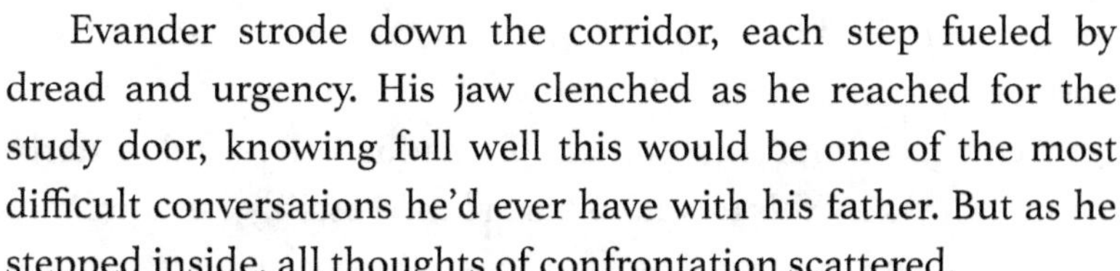

Evander strode down the corridor, each step fueled by dread and urgency. His jaw clenched as he reached for the study door, knowing full well this would be one of the most difficult conversations he'd ever have with his father. But as he stepped inside, all thoughts of confrontation scattered.

His father was slumped over the desk, motionless, and a trail of blood trickled down from his temple. The drapes blew in the breeze of the open window behind him.

No.

Evander's heart seized as he rushed forward. "Father!" he called, already reaching out. The back of his father's silver hair was darkened with blood—matted, sticky. He had been struck, hard.

"Gillingham!" Evander roared. "Send for the doctor, now!"

Dropping to one knee beside the chair, he grasped his

father's sleeve and gave a gentle shake. "Father—can you hear me?" His own voice shook with panic. The coolness of the skin beneath his fingers made his stomach twist.

"Evander..."

He turned at the sound of Olivia's voice. She stood in the doorway, face pale, eyes wide with disbelief. Her gaze dropped to the still form at the desk. "Is he... dead?"

Evander leaned in, willing himself to detect something—anything. Relief flooded his chest as he saw the faint but steady rise and fall of his father's breathing. "No," he murmured. "He's alive."

Olivia moved closer, bending down beside the chair. She reached down and lifted a large rock streaked with blood from the carpet. "There's a paper," she said, pulling it loose and handing it to him.

Evander untied the rough string with trembling fingers. The paper was crumpled, stained, but the words were unmistakable: *This is your last warning.*

He closed his eyes briefly, fury and fear coiling together in his gut. This had been intentional. This was a message—and it had nearly cost his father his life.

"This is about the indigo plantation," he said bitterly. "Whoever threw this meant to harm him. Possibly kill him."

Olivia laid a steadying hand on his sleeve. "Are you all right?"

He turned to her, met her gaze, and showed her the paper. "No," he said flatly. "If we don't sell the plantation, one of us is going to die."

A low groan came from the desk. Evander leaned in quickly. "Father?"

The older man stirred, eyes fluttering open before squinting in pain. "What in the blazes happened?"

"You were struck in the head," Evander said, keeping his

voice calm. "A rock came through the window. You lost consciousness."

His father touched the back of his skull, pulling back fingers slick with blood. He stared at them, dazed. "Who would throw a rock at me?"

Evander set the rock on the desk with a dull thud. "The same people who threatened me. The same people who may have killed Bryon."

"Don't be ridiculous," his father snapped. "Bryon died from illness."

"No," Evander said. "Lord Warwicke saw his ship docked on the Thames yesterday and spoke to the crew. No one seems to recall Bryon even being amongst the passengers."

The color drained from the earl's face. "That's... impossible."

"Who told you Bryon was dead?" Evander pressed.

"Lord Harwood's brother." His father blinked, as though trying to remember. "Joseph. He assumed the title after his brother died."

Olivia's voice was careful. "You don't think Joseph had anything to do with his brother's death, do you?"

Evander shook his head slowly. "I don't know what to believe anymore. But someone tried to kill me. And now they've attacked my father."

His father scoffed. "It's those blasted reformers. They want the indigo for themselves. But I won't bend. That plantation will make us rich."

Evander frowned. "Even if it kills you?"

His father straightened. "Yes."

"And what about me?"

There was a pause. Just long enough. "It won't come to that," his father said, but his tone was less certain.

"It might," Evander replied. "They won't stop."

Before the argument could spiral further, Gillingham reappeared in the doorway. "The doctor has been summoned, my lord."

His father scowled. "For what purpose?"

Evander stared at him, incredulous. "To examine you. You were bleeding and unconscious when I arrived."

"I've had worse," the earl muttered, waving a dismissive hand.

Olivia stepped around the desk and inspected the back of his head. "You likely need stitches."

"And you need to mind your own business," he snapped.

Evander opened his mouth to defend Olivia, but she cut him off.

"I hardly think we need to worry about you dying," she said dryly. "You're far too cantankerous."

The earl actually snorted. "For once, we are in agreement."

Olivia crossed her arms. "You're a fool. No business is worth your life."

"You have the luxury of believing that," the earl replied curtly.

"Perhaps," Olivia said, lifting her chin, "but I am not going to let you endanger Evander's life."

His father narrowed his gaze. "Is that so?"

"It is," she said, stepping forward. There was steel in her posture, fire in her voice—and Evander had never been more proud of her.

"And you speak for Evander now?" his father asked.

"No," she said simply. "He speaks for himself. But it's time someone spoke to you. I've held my tongue out of respect for your wife's condition, but no more. I have a voice, and I will use it."

The earl turned to his son. "Are you going to let a woman fight your battles?"

Evander drew Olivia closer, his arm sliding around her waist. "I would like to think that we fight them together."

Olivia smiled up at him. "I like that thought."

Whatever retort his father had died on his lips. His face turned ashen, and he slumped back into his chair. "I don't have time for this nonsense."

Evander moved quickly to his side. "You need a doctor."

The fight seemed to drain from the older man. His shoulders sagged. "Fine. I suppose I can make the time."

"Can I get you something? Tea?" Olivia offered as the earl now sat slumped, pressing a handkerchief to his bloodied head.

His father scowled. "You do not need to fuss over me, Woman," he growled, though the faint rasp in his voice betrayed his exhaustion.

Evander shot Olivia a rueful glance and gave a subtle shake of his head. "I think he'll live," he said. "Perhaps we should give him a moment to recover his... temperament."

"Thank you," the earl muttered without meeting either of their eyes.

Evander took Olivia's hand and gently guided her towards the door. As soon as they crossed the threshold and the door shut behind them, his tone softened. "You were remarkable in there."

Olivia's lips tightened. "I'm tired of the way your father speaks to me, as though I ought to stay silent. I hope I didn't upset you by speaking up."

"Not in the least bit," he said, pausing to turn towards her. "Quite the opposite. I've never been more proud of you."

She gave him a wry smile. "I suspect your father didn't share the sentiment."

Evander chuckled. "Well, I find it rather comforting knowing you're capable of standing your ground. It saves me a great deal of trouble."

Olivia's amusement faded. "What are you going to do about the plantation?"

His expression turned grave. "I need to persuade my father

to sell it. No business venture is worth this level of danger. And I refuse to watch him bleed—or worse—because of his pride."

"Why is he so resistant?" she asked, clearly baffled.

He exhaled, rubbing the back of his neck. "Because he sees only the profit. The promise of legacy. The power. He refuses to see the risk. Or he does—and believes himself invincible."

"Well," Olivia said pointedly, "in my humble opinion, it's maddening. He's clinging to something that might destroy him. Or you."

Evander smirked. "You know, you and my father might have more in common than you think."

She reared back slightly, playfully. "Did you just compare me to your father? My nemesis?"

"My father is your nemesis?"

"Everyone needs a nemesis or two," she joked. "It keeps things interesting."

They reached the entry hall. Evander slowed his pace, then stopped altogether, letting the quiet weight of the moment settle between them. "I need to speak with Warwicke. He must be told. My father's life was threatened, and whoever is behind this has gone too far."

Olivia looked uneasy. "Are you sure Warwicke is the right person to handle this?"

"I do," Evander said, his voice firm. "He has a particular set of skills, and I trust him."

Still, she bit her lower lip, hesitating. "Do you really think it's safe to leave the townhouse?"

"I'll be fine."

"I just—" Her voice faltered slightly. "I just worry."

He stepped closer, his voice low. "I will always come back to you."

She lifted her chin and searched his face. "You promise?"

He leaned in, brushing a tender kiss against her cheek, his

lips lingering longer than they should. "That is the easiest promise I've ever made."

Olivia's eyes shimmered. "I can't lose you, Evander."

"You won't," he said, with quiet certainty. "You're stuck with me. Now and forever."

Her lips curved into a faint smile. "There are worse fates," she murmured, the words light, almost teasing—but Evander saw beyond them. Beneath the levity, there was something sincere in her gaze. Warmth. Affection. A glimmer of something more.

His chest tightened with the possibility. Was she beginning to care for him, truly? The thought sent a quiet thrill through him, softening the heavy weight of the morning.

Before he could respond, a sharp knock echoed through the front hall. Moments later, Gillingham appeared, emerging from a side passage with his usual silent efficiency. He moved to the door and opened it to reveal Doctor Wentworth, who entered with brisk steps and an earnest expression.

"Where is his lordship?" the doctor asked without preamble.

Gillingham gestured down the corridor. "This way, Doctor. He's in the study."

The two men disappeared down the hallway, leaving Evander and Olivia alone once more.

With a sigh and a glance towards the upper landing, Olivia said, "I think I should go sit with your mother. I don't want her to be alone, especially not now."

Evander reached for her hand briefly, letting his fingers close around hers in gratitude. "Thank you," he said, and hoped his voice carried the depth of appreciation he struggled to express aloud.

Olivia leaned closer, placing a gentle hand over his chest. Her touch was steady and precisely what he needed in the moment. "Go. Do what you must. I'll be here when you return."

He smiled, warmth stirring in spite of the circumstances. "I'm rather glad I married you."

Her eyes sparkled with mischief. "Obviously."

"I'll come back as soon as I'm able," he promised.

But Olivia tilted her head and gave him a look he recognized all too well—the look that usually came before a battle of wits. "Perhaps I should come with you," she said. "I keep a muff pistol in my reticule, and I'm an excellent shot."

Evander immediately shook his head, more sharply than he intended. "And put you at risk? Never. You'll stay here, where it's safe."

She opened her mouth, clearly preparing to argue—but something shifted in her expression. She paused, then exhaled slowly and gave a small, deliberate nod.

"Very well," she said, "but only because there's chocolate in the dining room now. And I have no intention of being heroic on an empty stomach."

She was putting on a brave face for him, but he could see it in the way her smile lingered just a moment too long, the way her posture remained tall even when her eyes betrayed fatigue.

"I'll return as soon as I can," he told her again, his voice gentler now.

She touched his hand once more. "I'll hold you to that," she said.

And he knew she would.

13

Evander stepped into White's, the heavy oak door thudding shut behind him. The familiar scent of smoke and old leather met him like an old adversary. His eyes swept the opulent hall, filled with the usual congregation of idle aristocrats posturing over cigars and snifters of brandy. But Evander had no patience for social niceties. He was here for one man.

Warwicke.

His butler had mentioned that Warwicke had left for the club more than an hour ago. If Evander had been in a better state of mind, he might have shaved the stubble he hadn't noticed accumulating. But decorum was a luxury he couldn't afford—not after what had happened.

He spotted Warwicke near the far corner, seated at a small table with Lord Alcott. Warwicke was half-slouched in his chair, a drink in hand, his expression relaxed. Evander envied that ease for the briefest of moments. Alcott was mid-laugh—something witty, no doubt—but the moment their eyes met, both men fell silent.

Evander crossed the hall in long strides, ignoring the

curious stares that followed him. He came to a stop at their table. "We need to talk."

Warwicke raised a brow, the humor in his face vanishing. "Now?"

"Yes," Evander said, not bothering to soften his tone.

With a slight wave of his hand, Warwicke gestured towards the empty chair. "Take a seat, then."

Alcott began to rise. "I should leave you to—"

"You can stay," Evander cut in, lowering himself into the chair. "It's only a matter of time before this gets printed in the newssheets."

Alcott stilled mid-motion, then slowly sank back into his seat. "That sounds ominous."

"It is," Evander confirmed grimly. "My father was attacked. Someone threw a rock through the study window and knocked him unconscious."

Warwicke set down his glass, his expression hardening. "Is he all right?"

"He'll recover," Evander said, though even now the image of his father slumped in the bloodied armchair still made his stomach clench. "But he refuses to sell the indigo plantation. I don't understand why he's being so blasted obstinate."

"Most likely," Alcott chimed in, "because he doesn't want to walk away from a fortune."

Evander exhaled sharply through his nose. "Yes, but what use is a fortune if he's dead? We've already lost one family member. I'm not interested in losing another."

Warwicke leaned forward slightly, his fingers tapping against the table. "Was there a note?"

"There was," Evander said. "Tied to the rock. It said, '*This is your last chance.*'"

Silence settled between the three men.

Warwicke's frown deepened. "Then the reformers are done

playing games. They've intensified from threats to physical violence."

Evander's voice dropped. "What should we do?"

"Nothing." Warwicke's answer was firm. "Stay at your townhouse. Keep yourself and your father protected. I'll start making inquiries. Discreetly."

Evander sank deeper into the chair. "He has Parliament tomorrow."

"Then try to persuade him to stay home."

Evander gave a dry laugh. "You haven't met my father. Once he's made up his mind, he is not one to back down."

Warwicke stood, tugging down the ends of his finely cut waistcoat. "Then I best change before I go out. I'll stand out far too much where I'm headed."

Evander looked up at his friend. "If I haven't said it already —thank you."

Warwicke gave him a curt nod and disappeared into the crowd.

Left alone with Alcott, Evander reached up to pinch the bridge of his nose. The pressure there did nothing to ease the pounding in his head.

Alcott studied him over the rim of his glass. "How are you faring?"

Evander gave a huff. "You mean besides the fact that someone is trying to kill me and my father? I've had better days."

Alcott signaled to a passing server. "Let me buy you a drink."

"A drink won't fix this."

"No," Alcott agreed, "but it's a start."

Evander gave a half-smile, though there was no humor in it. "Life wasn't supposed to be this complicated. I had it all figured out, and then Bryon died. Everything shifted."

Alcott tilted his head. "Some men would be grateful to inherit a title."

"Not like this." Evander's voice turned quiet. "I'd give it all back if it meant my brother could walk through that door. I miss my life in academia. Quiet. Predictable. Safe."

Alcott swirled the amber liquid in his glass. "And what of your wife? Any regrets there?"

Evander didn't hesitate. "None. Olivia is... the one good thing in all of this."

Alcott chuckled. "A wife shackles a man."

"Not Olivia," Evander said. "Loving her isn't a decision I made. It is instinctive. I couldn't stop if I tried."

Alcott smirked. "You're smitten. It's far too late for you, old boy."

Before Evander could offer a rebuttal, a tall shadow stretched across the table.

"Evander."

He looked up and immediately recognized the voice. Joseph. The newly minted Earl of Harwood.

"Harwood," he acknowledged, rising halfway.

Joseph gave an awkward grimace. "I'm afraid I am still getting used to being called that."

"I know the feeling," Evander said, gesturing towards the empty air beside him. "I keep expecting my brother to walk in behind me."

Joseph inclined his head towards Alcott. "Lord Alcott."

"My condolences," Alcott said. "Would you care to join us?"

Harwood hesitated only a moment before pulling out a chair. "I don't wish to intrude."

"Nonsense," Alcott replied, waving him in. "You are always welcome."

Joseph settled in with a rueful smile, then turned to Evander. "Has anything unusual happened to you recently?"

Evander stiffened. "Define unusual."

Lowering his voice, Joseph said, "I've been receiving threats. Demands to sell our indigo plantations."

Evander's heart thudded in his chest. "You have?"

"Yes. And frankly, I'm beginning to think I ought to take them seriously."

Evander met his gaze. "Then you should know that we've been receiving threats, too."

Joseph's eyes widened, the color draining slightly from his already pale face. "So it isn't just me?"

"No," Evander responded. The truth had a strange weight to it when spoken aloud. "Someone threw a rock through an open window at our townhouse this morning. Hit my father in the head and knocked him unconscious."

Joseph stared at him for a moment. "What are you going to do?"

Evander's jaw tightened. What was he going to do? "I want to sell the indigo plantation. That seems the only sensible path. But my father refuses."

Joseph's brow furrowed. Then, unexpectedly, he asked, "What if I bought it from you?"

"Why would you want to do that?"

Harwood gave a shrug. "It's merely a business decision. Nothing more. Our plantations border each other. If I owned both, they'd make a far more appealing package for the right buyer. Twice the land, twice the return."

Evander leaned back slightly in his chair, considering him. "Are you anticipating difficulty selling yours?"

"Not especially," Harwood said, "but the value increases with scale. It's easier to market a vast, uninterrupted expanse than two smaller, adjacent ones. Buyers want simplicity and control."

"I'll think about it," he said. "Truthfully, I haven't stopped thinking about any of this since the first threat came. And now..."

Harwood's tone shifted, lower, tighter. "I know what you mean. I've been haunted lately. Not just by the threats, but by the whispers. The things people said about my brother, and how he treated the workers. The cruelty."

Evander bobbed his head. "My brother wasn't much better." The admission left a bitter taste in his mouth. "Sometimes I wonder what we inherited, besides their titles."

Harwood gave a quiet laugh, sharp and without joy. "That doesn't make me feel better." He stood then, brushing invisible dust from his trousers. There was a stiffness in his movements, a hollowness behind his eyes. "I should go. My brother's funeral is this afternoon."

Evander stood with him. "I wish you luck."

Harwood closed his eyes, just for a moment. But it was long enough for Evander to catch the glimmer of moisture clinging to his lashes. Grief etched itself across his face, as raw and unguarded as a wound.

"I keep hoping I'll wake up from this nightmare," Harwood murmured.

Evander reached out and rested a hand on the man's shoulder. There were no clever words, no solutions. Only solidarity. "You're not alone in this."

Harwood's eyes opened again. "That's kind of you to say. But you're wrong."

With that, he turned and walked away, shoulders hunched, as if carrying the weight of far more than grief.

Evander watched him go, the echo of Joseph's words clinging to him like fog. He understood the pain of how isolating grief could be, even when surrounded by people who claimed to understand.

"He'll be all right," Alcott said beside him, breaking the silence.

Evander didn't answer at first. He just watched the door

where Harwood had vanished. "I hope so," he said quietly. "I should go, as well."

"Are you sure you don't want that drink?"

Turning towards his friend, he replied, "No, I should return home. Olivia will be waiting, and my mother... well, I don't like to be gone too long."

"How is your mother?"

Evander rubbed a hand down his face, trying to wipe away the exhaustion that clung to him. "She has her good days and her bad. The doctor says she doesn't have long, but he's been saying that for months now."

Alcott's expression shifted, his usual mask of levity giving way to something more sincere. "I know what it's like to lose a mother. It's not for the faint of heart."

Evander swallowed against the lump forming in his throat. "She's always been the center of everything. The glue that held the family together. Even when my father grew distant. Even when Bryon—" He broke off, shaking his head. "I don't know what we'll do when she's gone. I'm not sure we'll hold it together."

"Fortunately, you have Olivia to help you through all of this."

A genuine smile tugged at the corner of Evander's mouth. "That I do. She's been... a miracle, really. I don't know how she manages it—supporting me, my mother, dealing with all this pressure—but she does. Quietly. Steadily."

"You know I'm no advocate for marriage," Alcott said, though the warmth remained in his voice, "but in your case... I daresay it's proven beneficial."

"Don't let anyone hear you say that. Your reputation as a determined bachelor would be forever tarnished," Evander teased.

Alcott grinned. "Exactly. So let's keep it between us. I've

built a carefully composed image of romantic cynicism. I'd hate to see it shattered."

"Still, you'll have to marry eventually. You need an heir. Your estate won't manage itself when you're gone."

Alcott gave an exaggerated sigh. "Yes, yes. One day, I'll find some well-bred lady to tolerate me. It'll be for practical purposes only, I assure you. No foolishness about love."

Evander gave him a dry look. "What a lucky lady she will be."

Alcott appeared unbothered. "Do try to rest, Evander. You look like a man being pulled apart by too many hands."

You have no idea, Evander thought, but said nothing.

With a final glance at the room—a room filled with laughter and men who had no idea what kind of world was unraveling outside its walls—he turned and made his way towards the door, already dreading the quiet heaviness that waited for him at home.

The room was still, dimly lit by the weak afternoon light slanting through the tall windows. Olivia sat by the bedside, her book resting open but unread in her lap. Her eyes drifted away from the page, again and again, to the figure beneath the embroidered coverlet. Lady Everwyck was asleep—truly asleep, not just resting her eyes as she sometimes pretended to. The soft snoring that rose from her was gentle. Olivia found herself listening for it, counting on it, as if its rhythm might ward off the silence she dreaded.

The countess's face was drawn, her skin nearly translucent against the white pillows, but her features were still sharp. She had never been a woman to shrink away from battle, and even now—frail, half in shadow—there was a stubbornness in her jaw that declared she would not go easily. If death had come knocking, Lady Everwyck would not open the door without a fight.

Suddenly, the stillness broke.

"Dear heavens," the countess murmured, her voice scratchy with sleep. "Was I snoring?"

"No," Olivia replied, too quickly, too smoothly.

Lady Everwyck narrowed her eyes in that familiar way, a wry smile playing on her lips. "I daresay you are being kind to spare my vanity."

Caught, Olivia grinned. "Guilty. But I thought it rather soothing, actually."

A huff of laughter escaped the countess. "My snoring has only worsened with age, I fear."

Olivia gestured to the silver pitcher on the side table. "Would you care for something to drink?"

"No, thank you," she said, pushing herself upright.

Olivia stood at once. "Let me help you."

But the countess waved her off. "Do not trouble yourself, my dear."

Olivia returned to her seat, watching carefully as Lady Everwyck arranged a pillow behind her back. She looked impossibly small in the vast bed, the silken coverlet swallowing her whole. Still there was fire in her eyes.

"Do not look at me like that," the countess said, her tone light but pointed.

"Like what?"

"As though I might perish at any moment."

"I'm sorry," Olivia murmured. "I didn't mean to."

Lady Everwyck smiled again, but this one didn't quite reach her eyes. "I know. But I have no intention of giving up. Not yet."

"I'm glad. Evander… he will be devastated when you—" Her voice caught.

"When I die," Lady Everwyck finished softly.

"Yes, but—"

The older woman raised a hand, silencing her. "You don't have to soften the truth for me. I'm dying, Olivia. I've made peace with that."

A wave of helplessness washed over her. "I'm sorry," she whispered.

"For what?" Lady Everwyck asked. "It's not your fault. This body has simply reached its end. There is nothing for you to apologize for."

Olivia reached for her hand, desperate to do something—anything—that felt like comfort. "I just wish I could help you."

"You already have," Lady Everwyck said, squeezing her fingers. "You're taking care of Evander. That is more than I could ever ask for."

"I will always care for him," Olivia promised.

Lady Everwyck's gaze softened. "It is my greatest hope that one day you will love him, as well."

Olivia's heart jolted. "I do love him—"

"Not affection, Child," the countess interrupted. "I'm speaking of that rare kind of love. The kind where you will find friendship and romance—all in the same person."

Olivia looked away, unable to answer. Her feelings for Evander were tangled—deep and steady, yes, but also uncertain. She didn't know what name to give them. Was it love? And if it wasn't... would it ever be?

Lady Everwyck didn't press her. "It's all right. I know why you married him. You did it for me."

"That is partially true," Olivia admitted. "Evander offered his name to protect me. He saved me from ruin. He gave me safety when I had none."

"And he would do it again," Lady Everwyck said. "He would do anything for you."

"And I for him."

That seemed to please Lady Everwyck. Her lips curved into

a genuine smile, one that reached her eyes and crinkled the corners. “You two have always been thick as thieves.”

Olivia laughed. “Only because he used to follow me around.”

“Like the time you dressed as a boy and snuck into his fencing lesson, calling yourself his cousin.”

A laugh bubbled up from Olivia’s chest. “The fencing master didn’t believe me for a moment. ‘Marco’ was not my finest invention.”

“No, it wasn’t,” the countess agreed. “But Evander played along.”

“He always did,” Olivia said, her smile lingering. “I remember when he helped glue feathers onto my arms and convinced me that I could fly. It took hours for the maid to scrub the glue off me.”

Lady Everwyck leaned her head back and laughed, a rich sound that warmed the room. “You were a wild sight. All feathers and bare knees, running across the lawn like you truly believed you’d take flight.”

“I did believe it. But I was only eight.”

The countess’s laughter faded into a thoughtful silence. “I can only imagine what your children will get up to.”

Olivia stiffened. “Evander and I haven’t discussed children.”

“But you will have them?” the countess pressed, tilting her head.

“I… I suppose. One day.”

“Of course you will. Children may be useless little creatures, but they bring more joy than sense.”

Olivia gave a short, uneasy laugh. “I do want children. I think. But I’m afraid.”

“Of what?”

Her voice dropped to a whisper. “Of not liking them. I’ve never cared for other people’s children. They seem so… tedious. And loud.”

Lady Everwyck gave her a knowing look. "Most people feel that way. Until the child is their own. Then you would gladly move heaven and earth for them."

"And if I don't?" Olivia asked, her fear crackling at the edges of her voice.

"There will be days you won't like them. But the good days will make it worthwhile. And on the bad days, you'll be especially grateful for the nursemaids."

Something in Olivia's chest unknotted at that. "I always thought there was something wrong with me."

"No," Lady Everwyck said with quiet certainty. "You're far more normal than you believe. Even Paul was terrified of babies. He used to hold them like fragile glass, convinced he'd drop them."

"I can't imagine that."

"He was just like you. The endless questions from our sons drove him mad. But he loved them all the same."

"I don't think he's changed."

"He has," the countess insisted. "Slowly. And not always in ways you can see." She paused. "Have you ever truly been in love?"

Olivia looked down at her hands, fingers laced tightly in her lap. "I thought I had been. But I was wrong."

"Love is unpredictable," Lady Everwyck said. "Your heart rarely picks with logic. Mine chose Paul."

The word came out before Olivia could stop it. "Why?"

The countess's expression grew amused. "Because beneath his harsh exterior is a deeply tender heart."

Olivia raised a skeptical brow. "Are you quite sure?"

"I am. He was always hard on Evander because he saw his younger self in him. As a second son, he understood how precarious life—and inheritance—could be. He wanted Evander to be prepared."

"He was cruel about Evander's choices," Olivia responded.

"He mocked his love of learning. Scorned his career in academia."

"Because he believed Evander should stay close. Be ready to assist Bryon in case of his untimely death."

"Evander had to make his own way."

"He did, and I've never been prouder."

"I don't think your husband shares that sentiment."

Lady Everwyck sighed. "Paul is not easy to love. But those are the moments he needs it most."

Olivia hesitated, then said, "Evander's relationship with his father is… complicated."

"I know. I won't excuse Paul's behavior, but he does love his son. In his own way."

"Forgive me, but he has a terrible way of showing it."

Lady Everwyck grew quiet, her gaze distant. "Paul's father was a cruel man. He beat his sons for any infraction. Vindictive, brutal. Paul ended that cycle. He refused to lay a hand on his boys. But the anger still lingers sometimes. It slips through."

"I daresay Evander is not like his father," Olivia said. "He's slow to anger, thoughtful. That's one of the reasons he is one of my dearest friends."

Eyeing her curiously, the countess asked, "Does your heart still belong to another?"

The question landed like a stone in Olivia's chest. "No. No, no…" She shook her head, too quickly, her words too vehement. "I fell for the wrong man. He married someone else. At the time, it felt… unbearable, but it was for the best. It had to be."

Lady Everwyck studied her a moment longer, and Olivia had the sudden sensation of being seen more clearly than she liked.

"I do believe that you are meant for someone whose heart won't let go of you so easily."

Olivia didn't answer right away. Her gaze shifted to the window, where the wind had pushed one of the heavy velvet drapes aside. The breeze stirred the stale air of the room, and with it came an aching tightness in her chest. She didn't know how to untangle the mess of feelings she held for Evander. What if she reached for something more, and ruined everything? Their friendship had been a constant in her life—steady, unshakeable. What if she broke it?

Lady Everwyck's voice drew her gently back. "Trust your heart."

Olivia let out a soft breath and turned to face her. "My heart was wrong before," she said. "And I don't trust it anymore."

"Then trust me, my dear." Lady Everwyck's expression was full of that calm certainty Olivia had always admired. "When you fall deeply—truly, irrevocably—in love with someone, that kind of love doesn't vanish. It stays with you."

Before Olivia could reply, a knock at the door interrupted them. It creaked open a second later, and Evander stepped inside.

His smile was easy, familiar. "Good afternoon."

Lady Everwyck's face brightened immediately. "Hello, Evander. We were just talking about you."

"Oh?" he asked, arching an eyebrow.

The countess gave a mischievous nod. "Do you remember when Olivia tried to fly by gluing chicken feathers to her arms?"

Evander chuckled. The sound stirred something warm in Olivia's chest. "How could I forget? We spent weeks collecting feathers. I think it was the only time Cook ever allowed us to waste her glue."

"I maintain it was a rather ingenious plan," Olivia said, lifting her chin with mock dignity.

Evander gave her a teasing look. "Only you would think that. The best part was that your mother had guests on the terrace at the exact moment you came running through the gardens, flapping your arms like a deranged goose."

Olivia laughed, covering her mouth. "She was absolutely mortified."

"And yet," Evander added, grinning, "she helped peel off the feathers herself before hauling you off to the bath."

Olivia groaned. "That was the most painful bath I've ever endured. I promised her I'd never do anything so foolish again."

He smirked. "Until the next time you got into trouble."

She shrugged. "I couldn't help it. I was a curious child. Besides, you were always right beside me, just as eager to misbehave."

"That I was."

Their eyes met for a moment too long. Olivia's smile faded slightly as a peculiar feeling pressed against her heart—fondness, certainly. But also something deeper. Something that scared her.

Lady Everwyck yawned, covering her mouth with a fragile hand. "Pardon me," she said. "But I believe it's time for me to rest again."

Olivia stood at once. "Of course. We'll let you sleep."

"I would like that," the countess murmured, already sinking back into her pillows.

As Olivia followed Evander out into the corridor, the door clicking shut behind them, she asked, "Did you find Warwicke?"

"I did," Evander said, pausing as they reached the end of the corridor. He turned to her. "He's looking into the attack. Into all of it."

A faint wave of relief passed through her. "Good. I hope he can put a stop to these threats. I can't bear the thought of anything happening to you."

Evander looked at her with a steadiness that made her breath catch. "Nothing will happen to me."

But she couldn't let him dismiss it so easily. She reached out and laid her hand on his sleeve. “Do not make light of this situation. I need you to be careful, Evander.”

The air between them seemed to shift as his gaze locked with hers. “I will be,” he said. “Because I’ve never had such a reason to fight before.”

Olivia’s heart gave a small, traitorous flutter. She didn’t speak. She couldn’t. She simply stood there, with her hand still on his arm, and tried to remember how to breathe.

But then Evander stepped back.

It was subtle—just one step, hardly noticeable to anyone else—but to Olivia, it felt purposeful. Her hand, which had rested so naturally on his sleeve a moment ago, fell uselessly to her side.

“We should start dressing for dinner soon,” he said, his tone even, as if nothing had passed between them.

Olivia forced herself to nod, though her throat felt tight. “Yes, we should,” she replied, hoping the words carried more steadiness than she actually felt.

He gave her a smile—gentle, almost private—but it only deepened her confusion. There was something in his eyes she couldn’t name, and before she could search his expression for more, he turned and walked away down the corridor, leaving her alone in the fading light.

Olivia remained rooted in place for a long moment, her heart beating too loudly in the silence he left behind. What had just happened? Had she imagined the moment? The look in his eyes? The weight of his words?

Something had transpired between them, but what it was, she could not say.

14

Evander walked away from Olivia, resisting the overwhelming urge to look back. But if he did, he might not be able to walk away at all. He wanted to tell her—desperately—that he loved her. That he always had. But she wasn't ready, and if he pushed now, he might lose her entirely. Still, every time she met his gaze or touched his hand, his restraint crumbled.

He reached the study and paused briefly at the threshold, composing himself. The scent of brandy and ash hung heavy in the air. His father sat by the hearth, glass in hand, his face turned towards the flickering flames. He didn't move. Didn't even glance in Evander's direction.

"Father," Evander said, stepping farther into the room.

The earl's voice was dry and clipped. "Son."

Evander crossed the room and sank into the worn leather chair opposite him. "How is your head?"

"The doctor said I'll live," his father replied, as if even that were a mild inconvenience.

"I had no doubt," Evander murmured, allowing a sliver of warmth to enter his voice.

Only then did the earl turn to look at him. His eyes were bloodshot but clear. "I've made peace with dying. That should make everything easier."

Evander's brows furrowed. "In what way?"

His father exhaled slowly. "Because I don't know what I'll do when your mother's gone. She's been… the better part of me for decades. Without her—" He shook his head. "I'm not certain there's anything left."

The vulnerability in his father's voice startled Evander. It was a rare, unguarded admission.

"If you loved her so deeply," Evander asked, "why the mistresses?"

The earl gave a careless shrug. "It's what men in our position do. We entertain distractions. I wasn't the first peer to take a mistress, and I doubt I'll be the last."

"And that makes it justifiable?"

"I never said that," his father said, taking another sip. "I was weak. Don't make the same mistake, Son. I know I hurt your mother more than once. And still, she stayed." He gave a dry laugh. "I don't deserve her."

"I intend to be true to Olivia," Evander asserted.

A chuckle escaped the earl. "I doubt she would let you stray anyway. She's an obstinate one."

"She is," Evander agreed, a faint smile tugging at his mouth. "But I love her."

"Well," his father said with a sigh, "I'm glad for you. Truly. You deserve some measure of happiness."

Evander gave him a look of mock suspicion. "How hard did that rock hit you, exactly?"

The earl barked a laugh, some of the tension breaking. "All I've ever wanted was for you to find purpose."

"I had purpose," Evander said. "At Oxford. In academia. But you told me—repeatedly—that I was wasting my time."

The humor fled from his father's face. "Because you should

have been here. With me. With Bryon. That was the path laid out for you."

"No, that was Bryon's path," Evander responded. "I was the second son. I had to make something of myself without relying on inheritance or title. And I did. I was made a Fellow."

His father looked down at his glass. "You don't think I understand that? I didn't want this life either, you know. I only inherited the title after my brother died. If he had lived, I would have been—"

"What?" Evander asked, genuinely curious. "What would you have done?"

A wistful smile curved his father's lips. "I would've become a barrister. My Uncle Alexander was one and I admired him."

"Because you enjoy arguing?" Evander teased.

"Partially," his father admitted, "but mostly because I wanted to make my own way, not just inherit power. Alas, I became an earl instead."

"I'm sorry you never got the chance."

The earl waved a hand, brushing the sentiment aside. "We all sacrifice for the family. That is our duty."

"Duty," Evander echoed bitterly. "I'm so very tired of that word."

His father leaned forward and set his glass on the side table. "I have failed you, Son."

"In what way?"

The earl's expression sobered. "I wasn't going to tell you. But after today, I believe you deserve to know. The estate is... struggling. Gravely." He paused. "I invested in a scheme I believed in. I trusted the wrong men and lost nearly everything. What little remained, I poured into that indigo plantation. It is our last hope."

Evander's mouth felt dry. "And Olivia's dowry?"

"It'll sustain us for now. But it's not a solution. The indigo plantation is the solution. Long-term."

Evander sat back, stunned. "How much did you lose?"

His father winced. "Fifty thousand pounds."

"*Fifty thousand?*" The number hit like a blow. "That's a fortune."

"I'm aware. And I wasn't the only fool. The late Lord Harwood invested, too—and lost it."

Evander rose, walking over to the drink cart with slow, deliberate steps. He poured himself a drink, the clink of glass echoing in the tense room. "There must be another way. Something that doesn't depend on land thousands of miles away. Something that doesn't risk lives."

"If you think of one, do let me know," his father said wearily. "Bryon and I spent many a night at this very fire, asking the same question."

"What about selling off some of the properties?"

"Most are entailed."

"Yes, but with my consent—"

His father shot to his feet. "No. I will not be the man who dismantles our legacy. The plantation is our only course."

Evander stared into the amber liquid in his glass. "And you'd risk your life for it?"

"Yes."

"My life?"

Silence. His father's gaze fell to the hearth. "It won't come to that."

"It already has."

"I will not yield to threats," his father said firmly. "If we cave, we will be weak. And I am not weak."

"It's not about weakness," Evander argued. "It's about survival."

"If we lose that plantation," his father said, voice rising, "we lose everything."

"Then what are our options?"

His father squared his shoulders. "We fight."

A new voice echoed from the doorway.

"I disagree."

Evander turned to see Olivia entering the room, calm and composed. "You do?" he asked.

She stepped fully inside. "I believe that you should sell the plantation—not because of the threats, but because it's the right thing to do."

The earl scoffed. "And what would you know about what's right?"

Unbothered, Olivia came to stand beside Evander. "I know that I don't want to watch my husband die defending a future built on a foundation of cruelty and injustice. Indigo plantations are known for their abuse of laborers. We are better than that."

Evander arched a brow. "How long were you eavesdropping?"

She met his gaze squarely. "Long enough to hear the truth."

"Then you understand why we must keep the plantation," the earl grumbled.

"Why not consider Evander's suggestion?" Olivia asked. "We could sell off some lands and—"

"Absolutely not!" the earl roared, cutting her off with a sweep of his hand. "And you have no right to comment on matters that do not concern you."

Evander saw Olivia's body go still before her chin lifted a fraction, her spine lengthening in that graceful, imperious way she had when offended.

"And why wouldn't this concern me?" she asked tightly. "Is this not my future we are discussing as well?"

Evander barely had time to brace before his father fired back.

"Women do not have the mindset for business. It is not in their nature."

"That," she said, her voice sharp with disbelief, "is the most barbaric thing I have ever heard."

Evander knew it was time for him to interject. "I value Olivia's opinion in all things."

His father did not look impressed. "But she is merely a woman."

Evander reached out and placed a steadying hand on Olivia's sleeve. "She is not merely anything. She is brilliant and more than capable of helping us sort through this mess. I would be a fool not to listen to her."

Olivia turned to glance at him, and he caught the flicker of warmth in her eyes—the silent acknowledgment, the gratitude. Her lips curved in a private smile meant only for him, and for a moment, it felt like the world tilted back into balance.

"Thank you, Evander," she said softly.

He returned the smile, but there was no time to dwell on it. He turned his attention back to his father. "Lord Harwood has offered to buy our indigo plantation," he shared. "Perhaps we should consider his offer."

His father looked at him as though he'd grown a second head. "You cannot be in earnest," he snapped. "We stand to lose a fortune if we sell it now."

Evander met his gaze without flinching. "But we stand to lose more if we keep it, considering I have heard of Bryon's ill-treatment of the peasants."

"I would not give much heed to those rumors. They are vastly exaggerated," his father replied. "Bryon assured me that he was treating the peasants fairly."

"And you believed him?"

His father shrugged. "I had no reason to suspect otherwise."

The dinner bell chimed in the distance, alerting them of the time.

The earl glanced at the mantel clock. "I told your mother I would dine with her this evening," he said stiffly. "We will continue this discussion another time. Perhaps, with time, you'll come to your senses."

He strode from the room without a backward glance, and silence fell in his wake.

Evander exhaled and turned to Olivia. She had folded her arms, though the tension in her shoulders had softened.

"Thank you," she said, "for standing up for me."

"I always will. Even when you're wrong."

She arched a brow. "You think I'm wrong?"

He smirked. "Not this time. But eventually, there will come a moment when you're entirely mistaken. And I look forward to being there when it happens."

She laughed then, just as he had intended. How he loved her laugh. It was a sound that he could get lost in.

He offered his arm. "It would seem we're dining alone this evening."

"I prefer that," she said, slipping her hand into the crook of his arm.

"So do I. But," he added teasingly, "you'll have to improve your conversational skills. I can't be the only one carrying the weight of stimulating dialogue."

She gave him a look. "My conversational skills are just fine, thank you."

"So says you."

"No one has ever complained before."

He began leading her out of the study. "That's because you're beautiful. People rarely argue with beautiful people."

She gave him a sidelong glance. "You truly think I'm beautiful?"

He didn't hesitate. "I always have."

"I don't feel beautiful."

Evander slowed, and his hand shifted slightly, bringing her closer. "Then you haven't seen the way I look at you. To me, you are the most beautiful woman I've ever known."

Her eyes searched his, as if she were looking for the truthfulness of his words. Let her look. He had nothing to hide. Well, almost nothing. There was one truth he hadn't dared speak. That he loved her. And that truth… he kept buried.

Until he was brave enough to tell her the true extent of his feelings.

Olivia's heart was in a state of disarray as Evander led her to the dining room. This evening, there had been something unguarded in the way he'd looked at her. When he said she was beautiful, he had meant it. She saw it in his eyes, felt it in the warmth behind his words. And that frightened her more than she cared to admit.

They had always shared honesty. That was the nature of their friendship, but this… this was different. It was fraught with risk.

Could she tell him the truth?

Yes.

It was time for her to be bold.

As he pulled out her chair, she sat down and blurted out, "I have feelings for you."

Evander froze. "Pardon?"

Heat rushed to her cheeks. She hadn't meant to say it like that. She straightened her posture, trying to recover. "I mean… I don't know precisely what I feel, but I *think* I have feelings for you."

He took his seat at the head of the table, his expression guarded. "You think?"

"I do," she said, quieter now. "But you don't have to say anything. Truly. Perhaps we should just forget I said anything."

"I don't want to forget."

The sincerity in his voice stilled her breath. Still, she pressed her lips together and shook her head. "I shouldn't have said it. But we've always been honest with one another. I didn't want to stop now."

"I'm glad you said something."

Her gaze darted to his. "You are?"

He nodded, slowly. "I have feelings for you as well."

"You do?" The words were barely above a whisper. "Was it... because of the kiss?"

His eyes darkened with something unreadable. "Yes," he said. "It was the kiss that did me in."

Her heart leapt and twisted all at once. "What are we to do now?"

A smile curved his lips—mischievous, familiar. "Well, I daresay we proceed on as we have been, and see if these feelings deepen."

"That's... a good plan," she murmured, trying not to look too giddy.

He picked up his wine glass, adopting a mock-serious tone. "I knew it was inevitable, though. Me being so handsome and all. It was only a matter of time before you fell for me."

She rolled her eyes. "I did not fall for you."

"Your actions say otherwise." He leaned closer, his voice teasing. "I can see you undressing me with your eyes."

Her mouth fell open. "I am doing no such thing!"

"You aren't?" he asked with a playful pout. "Pity." He winked as a footman stepped forward and placed a basket of warm rolls between them.

"You're lucky I don't throw this roll at you," she said, picking one up.

Evander clicked his tongue. "Threatening bodily harm with bread? Livy, I expected better."

She took a bite, trying to hide her grin. But then she said, more softly, "Perhaps we should... kiss more?"

He stared back at her, clearly stunned. "Did you just say what I think you said?"

She met his eyes, bold once again. "I did. If we both started feeling something after that kiss, maybe it's worth exploring further."

His answering smile was all boyish delight. "You'll hear no complaints from me. Shall we start now?" He leaned forward eagerly.

She laughed and placed a hand on his chest, stopping him. "I think we should wait. For the right moment."

Evander let out a theatrical sigh. "I do not like that plan."

"You'll survive."

"I suppose," he grumbled, reclining in his chair. "But the next time we kiss, you should prepare yourself. It will change your world."

She quirked a brow. "Oh?"

"I'm an excellent kisser," he said with mock gravity. "If there were an award, I'd win it."

She shook her head in disbelief. "You're absurd."

"We've only kissed twice and already you're smitten. Coincidence? I think not."

"Perhaps I shouldn't have told you what I was thinking," she muttered.

His teasing faded as his expression sobered. "No. I'm glad you did."

Bowls of soup were placed in front of them, steam rising in gentle tendrils. Olivia picked up her spoon but paused.

"What should we talk about now?" she asked.

Evander didn't answer right away. When he did, his words were firm. "I want to know the real you. Not just what the world sees, but the broken pieces you hide."

Her hand stilled over the bowl. "You already know everything about me."

"I doubt that," he said. "Give me all of you, Livy."

She lowered her spoon and drew in a breath. "There is something… but it's rather embarrassing."

Evander leaned forward. "Now you've definitely piqued my curiosity."

She bit her lower lip. "The truth of the matter was that I was heartbroken when the late Lord Harwood married someone else. That's when I married Mr. Smith. And we both know how that ended."

His features softened. "Do you regret not marrying Harwood?"

"I did. For the briefest of time. But now?" She reached for his hand. "I'm glad I didn't marry Lord Harwood. He wouldn't have made me happy."

Evander held her gaze. "So you're happy now?"

She gave his fingers a gentle squeeze. "I am happy here. With you."

A slow smile spread across his face. "Good. Because you're stuck with me."

"There's no one else I'd rather be stuck with."

He chuckled. "That was beautiful. You should write poetry."

She narrowed her eyes. "Let's just eat. In silence, if you please."

He gave an exaggerated sigh, reaching for his spoon. "Fine. But just know, I'm composing a sonnet about our next kiss."

She rolled her eyes again—but this time, her heart was lighter.

Just as Olivia was reaching for her spoon again, the quiet hush of the dining room was broken by the sound of the door opening.

Gillingham stepped in and bowed. "I apologize for the interruption, but Lord Luca Dexter has requested a moment of your time."

Evander's answer was immediate, and uncharacteristically short. "Send him away."

Before Gillingham could so much as turn, a tall figure entered without invitation. He was striking—dark-haired, well-dressed, and carrying a satchel slung over his shoulder with a casual air that clashed with the intensity in his gaze.

"I assumed you wouldn't wish to see me," he said, his voice smooth and self-assured as he approached the end of the table, "but I must speak to you."

Evander exhaled, slow and annoyed. "Very well. What is it that you want?"

Lord Luca shifted his attention to Olivia and bowed. "Your husband seems to have forgotten his manners. I am Lord Luca Dexter."

"As have you," Olivia replied. "You were not invited into my dining room."

"I assure you that you will want to hear this."

Olivia inclined her head, offering him a polite smile even as her instincts told her to be cautious. "Very well, my lord. Would you care to join us—"

"No," Evander cut in sharply. "Lord Luca will not be staying long."

Her brows lifted. That tone from Evander—cold, clipped—was rare. Even more so in front of company.

Lord Luca didn't seem the least bit bothered. A slow smile crept across his face. "That is true," he said, eyes on Evander. "But your response was rather harsh."

Evander wasn't amused. "Just tell us what you want and be done with it."

The humor dropped instantly from Lord Luca's face, and the air in the room shifted with it. "I heard someone threw a rock at your father and knocked him unconscious."

Evander narrowed his eyes. "How in the blazes did you know that?"

"It's my job to know such things," Lord Luca replied, already pulling something from his satchel. "That's why I'm here. The same thing happened to Lord Lancaster. He was threatened so persistently he had no choice but to sell his indigo plantation."

He withdrew a folded paper and offered it to Evander, but Olivia saw that he was watching both of them now, gauging their reactions.

"You'll never guess who purchased the plantation," Lord Luca said.

Evander unfolded the page, barely glancing at it before muttering, "Lord Harwood."

"Yes," Lord Luca confirmed. "But the purchase was finalized before he died aboard that ship. And the more I dig, the more I suspect his death—and your brother's—were not accidents. Someone is orchestrating all of this. I can't say who yet, but I intend to find out."

"I am not interested in my brother's death being made a spectacle in your newssheets," Evander said, his tone curt.

Lord Luca lifted his hands, palms open. "I'm not trying to exploit anyone. I'm trying to uncover the truth. This is bigger than one scandal or one tragedy."

Evander turned to her then, his expression softening only slightly. "Lord Luca recently purchased *The London Gazette*."

Olivia nodded slowly.

"I did," Lord Luca added, his tone earnest. "But that's not the only reason I'm here. I truly believe there's a pattern—one that might place others at risk. I'm trying to help."

"I don't need your help," Evander snapped. "And I certainly don't want it. Now, if you would kindly leave so my wife and I can enjoy our dinner."

For a moment, Lord Luca looked as if he might argue, but then, just as quickly, he bowed.

"My apologies for the intrusion. Good evening."

As the dining room doors shut behind him, Olivia turned slowly to Evander. "You were rather rude to him."

Evander's gaze stayed fixed on his soup. "He was the one who interrupted our dinner."

She tilted her head, studying him. "But he wasn't wrong about your brother's death. You do suspect he was murdered."

"I do," Evander admitted, his jaw tight, "but I'm not about to trust a man who writes for the newssheets."

Olivia lifted her spoon again, then paused. "But does it matter where the truth comes from, as long as it is the truth?"

"It's not that simple," he replied. "We don't know what Lord Luca's motives are. For all we know, he could be involved."

She stared at him for a long moment. "All right," she said, quiet and measured. "I shall drop it."

"Thank you," he said, though he didn't sound entirely relieved.

She dipped her spoon into the soup, but couldn't quite resist. "Although…"

Evander groaned. "I knew it wouldn't be that easy."

"You could have at least heard him out," she said, giving him a pointed look. "He might know something you haven't thought of."

Evander said nothing for a moment. Then, grudgingly, "Perhaps."

"Now I am done," Olivia said with a gentle smile, letting her tone fall into something teasing and light. "You may eat your soup in peace now."

Evander gave her a sidelong glance before lifting his spoon. He dipped it into the bowl and took a sip—only to immediately grimace.

"It's cold now," he said, his voice flat as he set the spoon back down with a quiet clink against the porcelain.

Olivia didn't miss the subtle shift in his posture. His shoulders had gone stiff again, and his back was too straight. A dozen questions crowded her mind, but none of them made it to her lips. *Should I press him?*

"No," he said, breaking the silence before she could speak.

"No?"

He looked at her then. "I know you," he said. "And no—I do not want to talk about it. I'd prefer it if you told me about your day."

The blunt honesty in his words stilled her. He wasn't dismissing her, not exactly. She could push, certainly. He would let her, if she insisted. But she suspected he needed her silence more than her questions.

She decided to concede. "Very well. I suppose I can manage that." She waved a hand in front of her. "I woke up this morning to the most obnoxious bird chirping directly at my window. Truly, I think it had a personal vendetta against me."

That drew the smallest twitch at the corner of his mouth. Not quite a smile—but close.

Encouraged, she went on. "But the highlight of my morning was the war between two squirrels outside my bedchamber window. I think we might be living in disputed squirrel territory."

Olivia continued talking about her day in great detail, hoping it was the reprieve he needed.

15

Evander sat in a dim corner of White's, cradling a half-full glass of brandy between his hands as though its warmth might somehow steady him. It was early—absurdly early for brandy, though the hour seemed to matter little. He had left the townhouse before breakfast, unable to remain beneath the same roof as Olivia with his thoughts in such a disordered state.

He should be elated. *She thinks she has feelings for me.* Her exact words echoed in his head, unrelenting, uncertain. That single, maddening word—*thinks*—had lodged in his chest like a splinter. He had spent most of the night lying awake, staring at the ceiling, resisting the overpowering urge to go to her room and tell her everything—that he had loved her for years, that he had never stopped, not for a moment.

But to do so might scare her off.

Botheration.

He needed patience. Steadiness. Strategy, even. But none of those qualities came easily when his heart insisted on galloping ahead of his good sense.

"Why do you look like death?"

The voice, dry and amused, came from his left. Evander turned his head to find Alcott standing there.

"Good morning," Evander muttered, lifting his glass in a mock salute.

Alcott slid into the chair opposite him, stretching out his legs with insufferable ease. "Judging by your expression, I'd wager this is about your lovely wife."

"It is."

"Well, out with it, then," Alcott said, folding his arms behind his head and giving Evander his full, expectant attention. "What did she do to cause you to look so utterly despondent?"

Evander hesitated, then sighed, knowing there was no point in pretending otherwise. "She told me last night that she thinks she has feelings for me."

Alcott straightened slightly. "Well, that sounds like progress."

"She *thinks* she does, Alcott. She's not sure yet." He leaned back, the chair creaking beneath him. "That uncertainty is eating me alive."

"You're too dramatic for a man in love," Alcott quipped. "You should take that as a small victory and begin wooing her, assuming you want that."

Evander gave him a flat look. "Of course I want that. I married her, didn't I?"

Alcott's smirk widened. "Plenty of people marry for convenience. You take one end of the house, and she takes the other. A polite nod in the morning, maybe a shared supper once a week. There's a peacefulness in that arrangement."

"That sounds wretched."

"Perhaps," Alcott conceded with a shrug. "But a wife brings a host of complications."

Evander looked down into his glass, watching the amber liquid ripple. "I love my wife," he stated.

Alcott let out a theatrical groan. "And there lies the problem." He leaned forward, lowering his voice mock-conspiratorially. "Have you tried the usual methods? Flowers? Sweets? Grand declarations you don't really mean?"

"I don't make promises I don't intend to keep."

"I suppose sincerity has its place," Alcott said with a grin. "I wish you luck with that."

Evander huffed a laugh despite himself. "So, what brings you to White's at this ungodly hour?"

Alcott's humor faded. "My sister. She's being… difficult."

Evander arched a brow. "What's wrong with Charlotte?"

"She's distraught over the engagement between the Duke of Brackenford and Lady Jane. She wants me to intercede."

"Intercede how?"

Alcott gave a sigh of genuine exasperation. "Charlotte thinks I should marry Lady Jane. That somehow, it would solve everything."

Evander stared at him in disbelief. "Are you even acquainted with her?"

"Yes. Our parents dragged us to all the same events growing up. I'm nearly seven years older, but I've known her for ages."

"And? Do you object to her?"

Alcott lifted a hand. "Lady Jane is perfectly proper. Polished. Pleasant, even. But she's unreadable. I never know what she's truly thinking."

"Olivia's also troubled by the engagement. But marriage to a duke is a coveted match."

"True," Alcott said. "But this particular duke is a vindictive blackguard. I have no desire to provoke him, let alone bind myself to someone I barely know."

Evander tilted his head. "If anyone could survive crossing the Duke of Brackenford and live to tell about it, it's you."

"I'm not afraid of him," Alcott muttered. "But I have no wish to be shackled, either."

"You'll have to marry someday."

Alcott shuddered. "Don't remind me. I'd rather be back on the battlefield."

Evander chuckled. "Your terror of matrimony never fails to amuse me."

But just for a moment, something flickered in Alcott's eyes —an old wound, perhaps. Pain buried beneath layers of sarcasm. And then it was gone.

Before Evander could question it, a third voice joined them.

"Gentlemen," came Lord Wilton's cheerful tone. He approached and dropped into the seat beside Alcott. "I saw your coaches outside and thought I'd stop in for a drink."

He looked between the two of them, eyes sharp with curiosity, and continued. "What's the topic this morning?"

"Marriage," Alcott groaned.

Wilton grinned. "Ah. The one word that makes Alcott break into a cold sweat."

"I do not sweat over it," Alcott snapped. "I simply wish to avoid falling prey to the parson's mousetrap."

Wilton turned to Evander. "Do you share his views?"

Evander shook his head. "No. I'm... actually enjoying marriage, most of the time."

"Then what's troubling you?" Wilton asked.

Tightening his hold on the glass, Evander revealed, "Your sister told me she *thinks* she has feelings for me."

A slow, broad smile spread across Wilton's face. "That's excellent news."

Evander arched a brow. "Is it?"

"You're making headway. In no time, you'll be blissfully in love, surrounded by a horde of noisy children."

"You make it sound so simple."

Wilton met his gaze, his smile softening with sincerity. "It is simple. Just keep loving Olivia, and she'll catch up."

Evander didn't answer at once. Instead, he simply stared at

the swirl of brandy in his glass and tried desperately to believe him. He set his glass down on the table with a soft clink, the final sip of brandy still burning faintly in his throat. The warmth no longer helped. It never did for long.

Rising, he said, "I should return home. I don't want to leave Olivia alone with my father for too long."

Wilton leaned back with a casual air, though his gaze sharpened with interest. "How is she managing him?"

A brief, involuntary smile tugged at Evander's mouth. "Surprisingly well. She holds her own with him. I don't think he quite knows what to make of her. He's used to being obeyed—or avoided—not challenged."

"That is good," Wilton said. "Considering your father can be…" His voice trailed off.

"A brute? A jackanapes?" Evander asked.

Wilton bobbed his head. "Those words describe him rather perfectly."

Evander's smile faded as he dropped his voice. "He refuses to sell the indigo plantation. Says doing so would spell the ruin of the estate."

Alcott spoke up. "And what do you believe?"

Evander hesitated before answering. The question wasn't a simple one. "I believe there are other ways to keep the estate solvent. We could sell off unused land or trim our expenditures. The plantation is a liability, not just financially, but morally." He exhaled slowly. "But he won't even consider it. To him, letting go of any part of the estate is akin to admitting defeat."

Alcott's expression darkened. "My father was the same. Stubborn to the end. He'd have burned the house to the ground before yielding an inch of pride."

Evander studied his friend's face and noticed the subtle tension in his jaw, the flicker of something raw in his eyes. Without thinking, he sat again, and asked, "How have you been faring since he passed?"

Alcott looked away, his gaze drifting somewhere beyond the club walls, beyond the present moment. "I ran from this life, you know. From all of it. But duty followed me to the battlefield. I thought I could lose myself in the war, become someone different. But General Wellington had other ideas. He forced my resignation when word came about my father's dire health." His lips pressed into a tight line. "Now I'm back, tied to the very life I escaped. But I can't leave again. Charlotte depends on me."

A brief silence settled over them, broken only by the muffled sounds of the club beyond their secluded corner. Wilton's voice came low, sincere. "I'm sorry. I know how much being a soldier meant to you."

Alcott turned back to them, and for a moment, all his usual levity was stripped away. "It was the first time I ever felt I had a purpose. Everything out there had weight. I had to earn the trust of my men—it wasn't handed to me because of a title or birthright. They only cared that I kept them alive."

Evander watched as Alcott's hands curled slightly on the arms of his chair. The pain wasn't theatrical or self-pitying—it was real. Worn like old armor.

He knew that pain. The ache of trying to live a life different from the one written for you. The burden of duty.

"I understand," Evander said.

A flicker of relief passed through Alcott's eyes, raw and unguarded. "I know you do," he said. "And I'm glad to know that I'm not alone."

There was a weight in those words that settled between them like an unspoken oath.

Before the silence could stretch too long, Wilton cut in. "This is precisely why you need a wife."

Alcott raised a skeptical brow. "And why is that?"

Wilton, undeterred, leaned back in his chair, his expression annoyingly self-satisfied. "A wife gives you purpose. A reason to wake up each morning. A reason to smile, to hope. Dosia has made me a better man."

Evander couldn't argue with that. He'd seen the change in Wilton—softened edges, sharper focus.

Alcott, however, gave a scoffing laugh. "I'll pass."

Wilton only grinned. "Your loss."

Evander pushed back his chair and rose, smoothing his jacket. "On that note, I'll take my leave. Good day, gentlemen."

He offered a brief nod before turning towards the door. His boots echoed faintly on the polished floor as he walked away, but he wasn't in any particular hurry. The club's familiar hush gave him a moment to think.

He was grateful—grateful for the distraction, for the conversation, for the sense that he wasn't entirely alone in his own struggles. His mood had lifted, if only slightly, the weight of uncertainty about Olivia not quite as heavy as it had been when he'd arrived. But as he reached the pavement, his thoughts turned back to Alcott.

Something was wrong. That flicker of pain in his friend's eyes hadn't left Evander's mind. He knew the feeling all too well. That quiet unraveling, that sense of not belonging in the life you were supposed to live. Duty could shape a man—but it could just as easily hollow him out.

Dressed in a yellow gown with puffed sleeves, Olivia stepped across the threshold of the dining room, her slippers making the faintest sound against the floorboards. The scent of toast and chocolate wafted towards her, but her gaze immediately settled on Lord Everwyck seated at the head of the long table with a newssheet in his hand.

Drat.

She hesitated a fraction too long. She couldn't retreat now or else the earl would know that she was still somewhat uncomfortable around him. He just made every conversation so intolerable.

Squaring her shoulders, she crossed the room and took the seat to his right. A footman silently placed a delicate porcelain cup of chocolate before her, its surface swirling with steam.

She reached for it just as the earl spoke, his voice sharp and without greeting. "I see my son indulges your every whim."

The corners of her mouth curved into a polite smile. "He was thoughtful enough to ensure I had a cup of chocolate each morning."

He gave a derisive snort. "A waste of money, I assure you."

Olivia lifted the cup to her lips, savoring a slow sip before answering. "It is delicious. And I appreciate Evander all the more for it."

The newssheet rustled as Lord Everwyck lowered it to study her more closely. His gaze was penetrating, as if he were attempting to unearth some hidden truth. Then he said, flatly, "You care for him."

It wasn't a question.

"I do," she replied.

"But do you love him?"

The question hit her square in the chest. She faltered, her throat tightening. Of all people to demand such an answer, it had to be Evander's father. Not even Evander had asked her so plainly.

Lord Everwyck seemed to take her silence as an answer. "I see," he murmured.

Her fingers tightened around the delicate porcelain handle. "I—I don't quite know what I feel for Evander. But I care for him deeply."

To her surprise, that seemed to mollify him.

"I told him not to marry you," he shared. "I didn't think you were suitable to be his viscountess."

Olivia didn't flinch. She had known as much. Evander had told her, and she'd long suspected it anyway.

"And yet," the earl added, with something approaching reluctance, "he chose you anyway. I do hope you don't intend to break his heart."

She met his gaze with steady resolve. "Your son has been—and always will be—my dearest friend. I would never hurt him."

His reply was pointed and clear. "I don't think my son is seeking friendship with you."

A flicker of heat rushed to her cheeks, but she kept her voice composed. "And that... is all I can give. For now."

The last two words lingered in the air between them, not quite a promise, not quite a plea. She meant them. At least, she wanted to mean them.

His mouth tightened. "I would hate for you to prove me right, Olivia."

The tension in the room was palpable as they stared at one another. Why this sudden interest in her relationship with Evander? Why now, when he'd never cared before?

But before she could reply, the sound of skittering paws broke through the tension. Finnegan barreled into the room, causing Lord Everwyck to jerk upright.

"What in the blazes is that?"

Olivia reached down and scooped the little creature into her arms. "It is my dog," she replied, stroking Finnegan as he panted happily in her lap.

The earl's eyes narrowed. "That is not a dog. That is a rat."

She bit back a smile. "No, it is a Pomeranian puppy. His name is Finnegan." She lifted him slightly. "Isn't he adorable?"

Lord Everwyck looked appalled. "Get that horrid little beast away from me before I shoot it."

"You shall do no such thing," Olivia said, not bothering to disguise her amusement.

"Does Evander know about that rodent?"

Olivia plucked a small piece of ham from her plate and fed it to Finnegan, who accepted it with glee. "He does, and he said Finnegan was welcome here."

"He would be mistaken," Lord Everwyck said. "And do not feed that thing from the table. What are you—a ruffian?"

Before she unleashed the retort forming in her throat, Gillingham entered with his usual composed air. "My lady, a Lady Jane is here to call upon you."

Olivia rose at once and extended Finnegan to the butler, who accepted him with only the faintest lift of a brow. "Thank you, Gillingham. Inform Lady Jane I shall join her shortly."

As he departed, she took one last sip of her chocolate, setting the cup back on its saucer with care.

Lord Everwyck was not done with their conversation. "I do not want that dog in our home."

"It is my home now as well." She dropped into a graceful curtsy—more mockery than reverence—and continued. "My lord, as always, it has been a pleasure."

And with her spine straight and chin high, Olivia swept from the room before her infuriating father-in-law could say another word.

She reached the drawing room and found Lady Jane pacing anxiously over the floral carpet.

"Jane," she greeted.

Her friend spun towards her. "I want to run away," she said at once. "Somewhere far away where my father and brother will never find me."

"All right," Olivia replied, stepping fully into the room. "What can I do to help?"

Jane's shoulders sagged. "I can't run. I want to, but there's nowhere I could go where they wouldn't drag me back."

"You have reached the age of your majority," Olivia reminded her. "You can make your own decisions."

"Not if I want food and a roof over my head," Jane muttered, sinking onto the settee. "This is hopeless."

Olivia joined her, settling beside her with gentle resolve. "Don't give up yet. We will find a way."

"How?" Jane asked, her voice cracking. "Mr. Fairchild wrote a scathing article about the engagement, and the duke found it *amusing.* Amusing!"

Reaching for the teapot, Olivia asked, "Would you like some tea?"

Jane recoiled. "Good heavens, no! I need something stronger."

With a sympathetic smile, Olivia turned to the maid in the corner. "Please tell Cook we'd like two cups of chocolate at once."

The maid curtsied and disappeared.

Jane placed a hand on her stomach. "My brother won't let me drink chocolate. He says I have to watch my figure to be a proper duchess."

"Your brother is an idiot."

"That he is," Jane agreed with a rueful smile. "He'd be furious if he knew I was here."

Olivia turned towards her. "Where does he think you are?"

"At church," Jane replied with a mischievous giggle. "I told him I needed to consult the vicar about our ceremony."

"You lied?"

"It was the only way I could leave without raising suspicion. I don't expect you to understand."

Olivia grinned. "On the contrary, I wholeheartedly support it."

Jane visibly relaxed, but her worry returned swiftly. "What am I going to do?"

"You can't marry the duke," Olivia said simply. "You'd be miserable."

"I would," Jane whispered.

Olivia reached for her friend's hand, squeezing gently. "We'll find a way."

Just then, the door opened and Evander entered, sunlight catching the golden tones in his dark hair. He smiled at both of them. "Good morning."

Jane sat up quickly, smoothing her skirts. "Forgive me, my lord, I—"

He cut her off with warmth. "There is no need to apologize. You are more than welcome here."

Olivia released Jane's hand and shared, "We were plotting how to rescue Jane from her impending nuptials."

Jane threw up her hands. "It's no use. The duke is too powerful, and I'm trapped."

"We would fight for you," Evander said. "And you're welcome to stay here as long as you like."

Jane blinked at him, astonished. "You would risk the duke's wrath for me?"

"I would," he said, his gaze drifting briefly to Olivia, "because you are Olivia's friend. And I would do anything for her."

Olivia's breath caught. In that moment, her heart did something traitorous—it swelled.

She wasn't sure if it was love yet. But it was close.

"That is kind of you to offer, but I couldn't do that to you or your family," Jane said, rising with a faint, practiced grace that didn't quite mask the strain in her voice. Her hands fluttered briefly at her sides before clasping together, fingers tightening as if bracing herself. "I should go."

"No—don't go, not yet," Olivia said, rising with her. "We could—"

But before she could finish, the door burst open and Lord

Barkley stepped into the drawing room, his jaw rigid and his eyes alight with fury. The heat of his disapproval seemed to fill the air, suffocating and immediate.

A moment later, Gillingham followed with impeccable calm and announced in a resonant voice, “Lord Barkley.”

Olivia’s gaze flicked to Jane, who had gone utterly still. Her complexion, already pale, drained of the little color it had. Her lips parted in a silent breath of dread.

“What are you doing here?” Jane asked, voice low, tremulous.

The viscount’s mouth curled, sharp with contempt. “I could ask you the same thing.”

The tension in the room thickened instantly. Olivia instinctively stepped closer to Jane as Evander spoke.

“Barkley,” he said, his voice curt.

The viscount glanced at him briefly, with barely the decency of acknowledgment. “Westmere,” he muttered, then jerked his chin towards the doorway. “Come along, Jane. You shouldn’t be here.”

Jane looked as though she were walking to the guillotine. Her chin dipped slightly as she approached her brother, each step slower than the last. “I needed a moment to speak to a friend,” she said, tone pleading and soft.

“You should pick better friends,” Barkley said, under his breath but loud enough to wound.

Olivia felt her stomach drop, but Evander reacted faster. He visibly tensed. “I would be careful with the words you say around my wife,” he warned.

A muscle ticked in Barkley’s cheek. “My apologies,” he replied, the words brittle and hollow. He extended his arm towards Jane.

Jane hesitated only a breath before accepting it. Her shoulders were taut, her eyes glassy. Olivia longed to run after her, to yank her back to safety. But the moment had already passed.

With a final, wordless glance towards Olivia, Jane let her brother lead her from the room.

The drawing room door closed behind them with a soft click that sounded far too final.

Olivia moved towards the window. She parted the curtain slightly and watched as Jane descended the front steps and climbed into the waiting coach. The carriage door shut and it rumbled off.

"Poor Jane," she murmured, not even realizing she had spoken aloud until she felt Evander move beside her, close enough that their shoulders brushed.

"I agree with that sentiment," he said. "But unless Jane is willing to stand up for herself… there's little anyone can do."

Olivia knew he was right. That didn't make it hurt any less. "She wants to, I think. She's just frightened."

Evander glanced at her then, his expression gentle. "As anyone would be."

For a moment, they both stared out the window in silence, the quiet between them heavy with unspoken worry. Then, with a soft touch, he placed a hand on her sleeve.

"Are you hungry?"

She turned to face him, welcoming the change in subject, however slight. "I could eat."

"I'm sorry I missed breakfast," he said, his thumb brushing lightly over the fabric at her arm before he let go. "I stopped at the club because I thought it might help clear my head."

Olivia tilted her head, studying him. "Did it work?"

A small, tired smile curved his lips. "No. But it was worth a try." He extended his arm, and she slipped her hand into the crook of his elbow. "May I escort you to the dining room, Wife?"

"Thank you, kind sir," she replied with a smile of her own. As they strolled from the drawing room, Olivia glanced at him sidelong. "I had the most interesting conversation with your father this morning."

"Oh?" he said warily. "Dare I ask what about?"

"He was rather concerned about the state of our marriage. And whether or not I would make you happy."

Evander's brow creased with surprise. "That doesn't sound at all like my father."

"No," she agreed. "I was confused, too."

They entered the dining room, and Olivia saw at once that the table was nearly cleared. Lord Everwyck had already gone. She breathed a sigh of relief. It was peaceful now—just the two of them. The air felt warmer, less sharp. Safer.

And that was when the truth crashed down upon her—swift and unrelenting.

It had always been Evander.

Not in some dramatic, sweeping way she could have predicted, but in quiet moments—a shared glance across a crowded room, the comfort of his voice when her world was unsteady, the way he saw her not as an obligation, but as Olivia. Fully. Clearly. With maddening patience and unshakeable care.

It was, it *is,* it *will be*—only Evander.

The realization settled into her bones with a strange kind of peace. Not the exhilarating jolt of new affection, but the deep, steady certainty of belonging. It was terrifying, yes—but more than that, it was true.

Evander had become the center of her world. She could lie to others, to herself, even to him. But not to this moment.

This, she could no longer deny.

16

Evander watched Olivia across the breakfast table, his appetite forgotten. Something about her was... different. A shift in the air, subtle but undeniable. Her posture was rigid, her fingers toying with the edge of her napkin, and when she lifted her gaze, the warmth he usually found in her eyes was noticeably absent.

He leaned forward, concern tightening in his chest. "Olivia... is something troubling you?"

Her smile came, but it was all wrong—strained, tight, the kind one wore when pretending all was well. "There is, actually," she murmured.

"What is it?" he asked softly, his voice careful, coaxing.

Her lips parted, and she started, "I... uh..." but whatever she meant to say vanished as Gillingham stepped into the room.

The butler gave a respectful bow. "I apologize for the intrusion, but Lord Harwood has arrived and requested a moment of your time."

Evander's jaw tensed. Of all the wretched timing. He did not care to speak with Harwood—not now, not when Olivia had clearly been on the brink of revealing something important.

With a brisk wave of his hand, he dismissed the suggestion. "Inform Lord Harwood this is not a good time."

"Yes, my lord." Gillingham bowed once more and turned to leave.

But Olivia's voice stopped him. "Wait." She turned to Evander. "You should go speak to him."

Evander frowned. "I would rather have breakfast with you."

She reached across the table and placed her hand atop his. The warmth of her touch contradicted the guarded look in her eyes. "I know, but I will be here when you get back. You should see what he wants."

He studied her, unsure what he was seeking—an opening, perhaps. An invitation to stay. "Very well," he relented, though every instinct told him not to let the moment pass. "But I want to hear what you were about to say before we were interrupted."

Color rose to her cheeks, pink and sudden.

Interesting. That reaction was new. Olivia was not a woman easily flustered, especially not by him.

He rose and stepped towards her, then bent low and pressed a kiss to her cheek. "I will return, my *Kicksy-Wicksy*."

She made a face. "I would prefer if you called me something else."

He smirked, keeping close. "I could call you 'my dear.' It would be perfectly proper, considering we are married, after all."

Her lips curved into a small but genuine smile. "I would like that."

"Good," he murmured. "Then it is settled."

He lingered for a moment too long, committing to memory the gold flecks in her blue eyes, the slight tremble in her breath. Something was shifting between them—and for once, it felt like it might be in his favor.

But Olivia, ever composed, gently broke the moment. "You should go. Lord Harwood is waiting."

He groaned. "Let him wait."

She tilted her head in mock reprimand. "That is rather rude. He came all this way to see you."

Evander sighed and straightened, tugging down the hem of his waistcoat. "Very well. But that is only because you requested it, not him."

The smile she gave him then was the one he had been waiting for—warm and real. "I will be waiting for your return."

He returned her smile with a nod and turned on his heel, his thoughts still lingering on her unfinished words as he made his way to the drawing room. Whatever Harwood had to say had best be worth the interruption.

He found the man standing near the hearth, already pacing.

Harwood's eyes lit with urgency the moment he entered. "I'm sorry to disturb you so early, but I'm afraid it couldn't wait."

Evander folded his arms. "What is it that you need?"

"I intend to sell my indigo plantation," Harwood began. "And I've found a buyer—on the condition that your land is included in the deal."

Evander's brows lifted. "Who is this buyer?"

"I don't know his full intentions. He claims to represent a company, Walter Textiles, which is looking to expand its holdings in India. Gave the name *Mr. Robert Taylor.*"

That name landed uneasily in Evander's mind.

"I'll pay you one hundred and ten percent of what you paid for your land," Harwood added, his tone clipped.

Evander strode to the drink cart, unease curling in his gut. "Why wouldn't I just deal with Mr. Taylor directly?"

"You could," Harwood allowed, "but has he approached you?"

Evander took his time uncorking the decanter. “Would you care for a drink?”

“Not at this time,” Harwood said impatiently. “This is a good deal. You should take it.”

Evander poured himself a measure of brandy, slowly. “We both know the land is worth far more.”

“Which is why I’m offering ten percent more.”

Glass in hand, Evander turned back to him. “What is he offering you?”

Harwood shifted in his stance, clearly uncomfortable. “That doesn’t matter.”

“But it does. To me.”

Harwood moved a step closer. “I’m tired of the threats. I want out of India. I want to start over.”

Evander sipped his drink and watched the man carefully. “I would like to meet Mr. Taylor myself.”

“Whatever for?”

“To know who’s buying up these lands. And why.”

Harwood’s expression darkened. “Why do you care? Aren’t you tired of fearing for your life?”

“Of course I am. But that doesn’t mean I can sell our family holdings without my father’s approval.”

A flicker of frustration crossed Harwood’s face. “I’m trying to help us both.”

“By profiting more than you let on?” Evander said. “Because I suspect you’re getting a far better price if I hand over my share.”

“That land never should have been yours. My idiot brother sold it to Bryon without my knowledge.”

Evander narrowed his gaze. “Why is that land so important?”

Harwood hesitated, then shrugged. “It’s not. Not on its own. It’s the combined holdings that make the difference.”

Evander didn’t believe him. “Then you shouldn’t mind if I

speak to Mr. Taylor myself. Unless you have something to hide."

Harwood's jaw tightened. "We've known each other for years, and you accuse me of deception? That's insulting."

"No," Evander said. "That's business."

Harwood's composure cracked. "Someone threw a rock into my mother's bedchamber. She's shaken."

Evander's eyebrows rose. "Is she all right?"

"She'll recover. But it rattled her—and me. That's why I want out. You'd be wise to follow suit."

"I shall think on it."

Harwood scoffed, throwing up his hands. "What is there to think about?"

Evander took another drink, more to buy time than anything else. Harwood's outburst felt too practiced. Too performative. "It's my father's decision, not mine."

Harwood muttered a curse. "Then convince him to sell before it's too late."

He strode past Evander, clearly done with the conversation. Evander turned to follow and found Olivia standing in the entry hall.

Her eyes flicked between the two men. "I heard shouting."

Harwood offered a stiff bow. "My apologies, my lady. I was merely venting some of my frustrations."

"Is everything all right, Joseph?" Olivia asked.

A tight, unconvincing smile stretched across Harwood's lips. "It is," he said with ease. But it was too smooth, too measured. "Your husband and I were just discussing some business."

Evander's jaw tensed. That wasn't business. It had been pressure veiled as persuasion, and Harwood knew it.

"By shouting at one another?" Olivia questioned.

Stepping closer to her, Evander informed her, "Harwood was just about to leave."

"I was," Harwood agreed, his exit abrupt and purposeful as he disappeared out the main door.

The moment the door clicked shut, Evander felt Olivia's gaze land squarely on him. When he turned, she had already placed one hand on her hip, and her expression was all demand.

"Would you care to explain what that was about?"

He did not want to explain. Not when they'd been teetering on the edge of something unspoken earlier. He would have much rather returned to that—her unfinished sentence, her blush, the way she'd looked at him like she might let something slip.

But Olivia, he knew, would not let this go.

With a sigh, he ran a hand down his waistcoat. "Harwood wants me to sell the indigo plantation to him."

"Would that be a terrible thing?"

"As you know, I'm not opposed to selling the plantation. I've considered it. But something about the deal feels... off. Too tidy. As if it's already been decided without me."

She tilted her head. "Do you think Joseph would cheat you?"

That was the heart of it. It was the question that had been gnawing at him since Harwood first brought up the deal. "I don't know," he admitted.

Olivia stepped closer. "I've known Joseph for a long time," she said. "He's always been kind to me."

He grinned. "People tend to be kind to beautiful people."

"That wasn't why."

Evander lifted a hand and set it gently on her shoulder. "I'd rather not talk about Harwood anymore. I'd prefer if we could return to our previous conversation. The one we started over breakfast?"

At his words, the color bloomed in her cheeks again, and

her gaze dropped to his chest as though unable to meet his eyes.

"I would prefer not to," she murmured.

Evander's hand shifted. He brought his fingers under her chin, tilting her face upward until her eyes met his.

"What has you so flustered, my dear?"

The endearment caught her by surprise. He saw it in the slight widening of her eyes, the way she hesitated before answering.

"I'm not flustered," she attempted, but the softness of her voice betrayed her.

"You are," he responded, his thumb brushing along her jaw. "And it is rather adorable."

Her blush deepened to something almost crimson.

"I feel..." she began, and then faltered.

His pulse ticked up. "You feel?" he prompted, careful not to push too hard.

Her lips parted, but before she could form the words, a sharp knock echoed from the main door. Both of them turned at once.

Gillingham appeared, striding across the entry hall. He pulled open the door, and there stood Warwicke, broad-shouldered and grim.

His eyes locked on Evander. "We need to talk," he said, his tone brooking no argument.

Evander felt Olivia shift beside him. She stepped back and said, "I'll leave you both to it."

He watched her retreat down the hall, and the urge to follow her nearly overwhelmed him. He didn't want to speak to Warwicke. He wanted Olivia to finish that sentence. He wanted to know what she had felt.

Warwicke stepped forward, drawing Evander's attention back to the present. "We can talk in your study."

Evander's irritation returned with a low grumble. "This had better be important."

"It is," his friend assured him.

And yet all Evander could think about was Olivia—her blush, her silence, and the answer he hadn't been allowed to hear.

Evander led Warwicke into the study, closing the door behind them with a soft click. The early morning light streamed through the tall windows, casting long shadows across the carpet. He turned to face his friend, still a bit weary from the restless night before. "What is so important that it couldn't wait until a more civilized hour?"

Warwicke's expression was grave—far more so than usual. "I looked into Lord Luca Dexter, as you suggested. And I discovered something... troubling."

Now Warwicke had his full attention. He straightened, every muscle in his body coiled with tension. "What did you discover?"

"I attended a meeting of the reformers last night," Warwicke said. "He was there. Slipped in after it started and stood at the back. But there was no mistaking him."

A curse hovered on Evander's lips, but he swallowed it. "Did he see you?"

Warwicke shook his head. "I don't believe so, though I can't be certain."

Evander exhaled slowly, dragging a hand down his face. "So it's him, then. Lord Luca is the one behind the threats."

"It could be."

"Could be?" Evander's voice sharpened. "Who else would it be?"

Warwicke gave him a pointed look. "We shouldn't leap to conclusions. But now that we've placed him near the reformers, I'll dig further. See what else he's hiding."

Evander crossed the room to the drink cart, tempted to pour something strong to steady his nerves. He reached for the decanter and asked, "Would you care for something to drink?"

"No, thank you. I need a clear head."

With a nod, Evander set the decanter back down, the crystal clinking softly against the tray. He turned, leaning one hand on the edge of the cart. "What do we do now?"

Warwicke didn't hesitate. "You stay here at your townhouse. Hire more guards. Keep Olivia and your father close. At least until we know more."

Evander gave a short, humorless laugh. "That will be easier said than done. My father is at the House of Lords today. He refuses to be cowed. Says silence only encourages tyranny."

"Foolish pride," Warwicke muttered. "It'll get him—or you—killed."

Evander walked slowly to the leather armchair and sank into it, the weight of responsibility pressing heavily on his shoulders. "Even if Lord Luca is involved, how do we make the threats stop?"

A faint smirk played across Warwicke's lips. "Leave that to me."

Evander's brows lifted. "What exactly does that mean?"

"It means I can be very persuasive when I need to be," Warwicke said lightly, but his eyes were hard.

Evander met his gaze and gave a slow nod. There was steel beneath his friend's charm—danger, even. "I trust you."

"Good." Warwicke crossed the room and sat opposite him. "I saw Lord Harwood leaving your townhouse earlier. What did he want?"

Evander's jaw tightened at the mention. "He wants to buy the indigo plantation."

Warwicke's brow rose. "Interesting."

"He claims it's just business. Says combining our plantations would increase the value when he sells."

"That's what he told you?"

Evander nodded, though unease was starting to prickle at the back of his neck. "Yes. Why?"

"Did he mention who the buyer was?"

"A Mr. Taylor," Evander said. "He represents Walter Textiles."

Warwicke gave a dry chuckle. "How convenient."

Evander frowned. "I've known Harwood for years. He's brash and arrogant at times, but he's always acted out of duty."

"Duty and ambition are not mutually exclusive," Warwicke said, settling deeper into his chair. "I think I'll look into Harwood next."

Evander gave him a cautious look. "You think he's involved in the threats? He claimed to have received them himself."

"So he says," Warwicke murmured, unconvinced.

"But why would he lie about that?"

Warwicke's grin was almost mocking. "Greed. Power. Leverage. Any number of motives, depending on what he stands to gain. Or lose."

Evander glanced towards the closed door, his thoughts turning to Olivia. "I should be able to convince her to stay here, at least until we sort this out."

Warwicke tilted his head. "You two looked close when I arrived. That's good, isn't it?"

"It is," Evander admitted. "We're making progress. But sometimes I look at her and I wonder what she's thinking. If I'll ever be enough."

Warwicke chuckled. "That's the wish of every good husband."

Evander paused, then asked, "What if I can't get her to love me?"

At that, Warwicke sobered. "Love doesn't work that way. If it is meant to be, it will happen. It is given. Freely. Unexpected."

"That doesn't sound very promising."

Leaning forward in his seat, Warwicke said, "I tried pushing Thea away, convinced I was unworthy. But she didn't care. She proved her love through every word, every gesture. That's what changed me."

Evander stared up at the ceiling. "I see the questions in Olivia's eyes but she is stubborn."

"Aren't all women?" Warwicke asked, rising. "That's what makes it worth the fight."

Warwicke stepped towards the door and continued. "I'll let you know if I find anything else. Be on your guard."

Evander gave a sharp nod. "I always am." But even as he said the words, he knew they rang hollow.

The door shut quietly behind his friend, and the study fell into stillness once more. Evander leaned back in his chair, the leather cool against the nape of his neck, and closed his eyes. He should have been planning, strategizing, doing something —*anything*—to get ahead of the threats looming over his family. But instead, his mind veered—again and again—to Olivia.

She was always there, just beneath the surface of every thought. He tried to shake her, to push her from his mind, but she came back stronger. Every smile, every skeptical look, every quiet breath she took near him—it consumed him. And that, he thought grimly, was the problem.

A knock at the door broke the silence.

"Pardon the interruption, my lord," came Gillingham's voice as he stepped inside, bowing slightly. "Your mother is requesting a moment of your time."

Evander straightened with a sigh and rose. "Thank you."

As he walked through the corridors towards his mother's bedchamber, he tried to rehearse what he would say to Olivia.

He needed to convince her to remain here, where it was safe, but Olivia was no meek lady. She'd balk at being confined, and she'd demand answers he couldn't yet give. He had no certainty to offer her—only shadows, and the hope that Warwicke would unearth something solid.

When he reached the familiar door to his mother's chambers, he knocked once before stepping inside. The drapes had been pulled back, and sunlight poured in, illuminating the soft pink of her bedclothes and the thin lines around her eyes. But her posture was alert, and her color was better than he'd seen in weeks.

"Mother," he greeted, stepping to her side. "How are you feeling?"

"Well enough to live another day," she replied, voice dry as always.

He gave a brief smile and sat beside her on the edge of the bed. "You asked to see me?"

She nodded. "I did. Olivia visited me this morning. She was troubled. Is everything all right?"

No, he thought. But he said, "It will be."

His mother gave him a look that reminded him he hadn't been able to lie to her since he was six years old. "I know something is going on. Your father didn't slip and hit his head, did he?"

He winced slightly. "That's what he told you?"

She crossed her arms with impressive vigor. "I'm not some simpering miss, Child. I can handle the truth."

"Mother..."

"The *truth*, please."

Evander exhaled, knowing it was inevitable. "We've received threats. Someone wants us to sell the indigo plantation."

"You've been threatened, too?"

"I have. But you mustn't worry about it." He squeezed her hand gently. "You need to focus on your recovery."

"Oh, pish-posh," she said, waving off the concern. "I do nothing but lie here all day waiting for death. Let me be of some use."

"You are not going to die," Evander said firmly, his voice low with emotion. "You're going to live forever just to keep Father in line."

She smiled faintly. "If you will me to live, I'll obey. I'll try," she said. "Now, what do you intend to do about these threats?"

"They're being investigated by someone I trust." He paused. "I won't let anything happen to any of us."

"That's a relief," she murmured, eyes softening.

His gaze wandered towards the bright window. "You've opened the drapes."

"Olivia insisted," his mother said, glancing towards the light. "She said I needed more sunlight. And I do believe she's right—it lifts the gloom in here."

Evander stood, his heart beginning to thump faster in his chest. "I need to speak to Olivia."

"You'd best hurry," she informed him. "She mentioned visiting her brother this morning."

His blood ran cold. "She left? Now?"

"She didn't say when, but—Evander?"

But he was already out the door.

His boots thudded against the floor as he raced down the corridor to Olivia's bedchamber, his chest tightening with every step. He knocked hard, too hard, and the door opened a moment later.

A maid stood before him, blinking in surprise. "My lord?"

He craned his neck, his heart hammering. "Is my wife here?"

"No, my lord. She left for her brother's townhouse a few minutes ago. You may still catch her—"

He didn't wait for the rest.

He spun on his heel and sprinted down the stairs two at a time. He burst through the front door just in time to see the crested coach blending into the flow of traffic at the far end of the street.

"Botheration," he muttered, his voice tight with panic.

Behind him, Gillingham's calm voice drifted into the morning air. "Is something wrong, my lord?"

Evander turned, jaw clenched. "Yes. Ready my horse at once."

As the butler disappeared to carry out the order, Evander forced himself to take a deep breath. *She's only going to her brother's. It isn't far. It's broad daylight. She'll be fine.*

But even as he repeated it in his head, the unease in his gut refused to dissipate.

She had to be safe.

She had to be.

Because the alternative was unthinkable. And Evander didn't think he could survive losing her—*not now*.

17

Olivia kept her gaze fixed on the window as the coach brought her closer to her brother's townhouse. Rows of tidy brick houses and flickering lamplight gave way to shaded trees and cobbled lanes, but she scarcely noticed. Her thoughts were too loud, too persistent.

She hadn't needed a break from Evander himself—far from it. She needed space because being near him stirred feelings she could no longer contain. There had been a time when friendship was enough, when the quiet safety of their camaraderie had been all she desired. But that kiss... that blasted kiss had upended everything.

Now, she couldn't look at him without remembering the way his lips had moved over hers—tentative at first, then certain. It had been the kind of kiss that left one unsteady, the kind that lived in the memory long after it had passed. And ever since, something in her had shifted. She didn't want a marriage of convenience. She wanted *him*. In every sense.

But what if he did not feel the same?

Her heart gave a nervous flutter. Evander would never mock her or respond with cruelty—she trusted him too much to believe that—but rejection from someone she had come to love would be its own kind of devastation. How could she return to being simply friends after that?

The coach rocked slightly as it slowed, the sound of the horses' hooves softening on the stones. She turned just in time to see the door open, startled to find Lord Harwood climbing in.

Her brow arched with suspicion. "What, pray tell, are you doing here?"

"I needed to speak with you," he said, settling across from her. He spoke as if that alone excused the impropriety of it all.

Before Olivia could gather her wits enough to retort, the coach door swung open and one of her footmen appeared, his face a mask of alarm and hostility as he sized up the uninvited passenger. "Get out!" he ordered.

Lord Harwood didn't so much as flinch under the glare. Instead, his gaze remained fixed upon her. "Please, Olivia. Just hear me out."

Olivia pursed her lips together. How dare he, knowing full well the danger he posed to her reputation? "You do realize the precariousness of the situation you put me in?"

"I do," came his simple reply.

She exhaled slowly. "Very well. I will hear you out."

The footman looked to her for confirmation, then—albeit reluctantly—closed the door. The coach jerked back into motion, causing Olivia to sway slightly in her seat.

She narrowed her eyes. "And you do realize what would happen if anyone saw us alone like this?"

"We are family friends."

"I am a married woman, Joseph," she said sharply. "Everything has changed. We are not children anymore."

He gave a rueful smile. "If my brother hadn't been such a fool, you would have been married to him."

Olivia's stomach twisted, but she kept her tone composed. "It was for the best."

Joseph tilted his head. "I'm not entirely sure that's true. He was miserable after he married. He did it for the dowry, not for love."

"Well, that was his decision. Not mine."

He leaned forward, his voice softer. "You were the best thing that ever happened to him."

She drew back slightly. "It matters not. What's done is done." Her voice was firm. "And I am married to Evander now."

Joseph didn't miss a beat. "Do you love him?"

Her breath caught. "I beg your pardon?"

"The question is rather simple. Do you love him?"

She could feel the blush creeping into her cheeks and despised herself for it. "I heard you. But I will not answer that."

His smirk deepened. "You do. I know it."

Trying to regain her composure, she crossed her arms and asked, "Is there a purpose to this conversation?"

"No," he said, shrugging casually. "But I am happy for you. I never thought it fair how the *ton* painted you."

She glanced out the window, trying to keep her voice light. "I made a mistake."

"One mistake in an otherwise unblemished life," he said, not unkindly.

Olivia turned back to him, her gaze steady now. "Why are you here, Joseph? You didn't risk both our reputations just to chit-chat about the past."

His features sobered. "I need your help. I need you to convince Evander to sell the indigo plantation."

"Why would I do that?"

A flicker of genuine distress passed over his face. "Because I fear your life may be in danger."

She drew back further. "Why? I have nothing to do with the plantation."

"True, but the reformers are growing desperate. We are running out of time," he said grimly. "I've been threatened, and so has my mother."

The mention of Lady Harwood made her gasp. "Not your mother."

"She's already endured more than her fair share. I can't burden her with this, too."

"I understand, but—"

"No, Olivia," he interrupted, his tone steelier than before. "You don't understand. Neither does Evander. What's at stake here is greater than you know."

She held his gaze. "Then explain it to me."

He hesitated, then ran a hand through his hair. "There is a growing movement in India. They're determined to dismantle the power of the *Nabobs*. An uprising is coming. We need to pull out before we lose everything."

For a long moment, Olivia simply studied him. There was real fear in his eyes—an urgency that made her chest tighten.

"I will speak with Evander," she said. "But I promise nothing."

"He will listen to you. I know he will." He knocked against the ceiling of the coach. "This is my stop."

The vehicle came to a halt, and Joseph exited as swiftly as he had arrived, leaving her alone with her racing thoughts once more.

Only minutes later, the coach drew up before her brother's townhouse. As she descended, she looked up at its familiar windows and realized with a pang that it no longer felt like home. Her home was now with Evander.

The door opened before she could knock, and Dosia stood on the threshold with a bright smile. "What a delightful surprise! Do come in."

Olivia climbed the steps, allowing herself to be pulled into a warm embrace.

"I'm so glad to see you," Dosia declared. "I've missed you."

The sincerity in her voice brought an ache to Olivia's chest. She hadn't realized how much she missed the comfort of true friendship until now.

"Are you hungry? Thirsty?" Dosia asked, stepping back. "I can have chocolate or biscuits sent up."

Olivia laughed for the first time that morning. "Chocolate sounds heavenly."

Dosia turned to the butler. "Two cups, if you please." Then she linked her arm with Olivia's and led her to the drawing room. "Now then, what brings you here at this hour?"

"Can't I simply visit my dearest friend?"

"You can—and must—but you are rarely up so early without cause."

Once seated in the drawing room, Olivia let go of Dosia's arm and faced her fully. It was time to speak the truth.

"I made a mistake," she revealed.

Dosia's brows lifted. "Oh?"

"I think… I think I've fallen in love with Evander."

"You *think*?"

Olivia moved to the settee and sank down, the admission tumbling out with a sigh. "No, I don't think. I know. I love him."

Dosia gave a knowing smile. "That is not surprising."

"But it could ruin everything," Olivia whispered. "What if he doesn't feel the same?"

"And what if he does?"

She tipped her head back, staring at the plasterwork on the ceiling. "We've always been friends. Can I risk that?"

Dosia joined her on the settee. "It's frightening to bare one's heart, I know. But you cannot continue pretending all is the same."

"Why not?" Olivia asked. "It's safe."

"True love isn't about safety. It's about truth. And truth has a way of growing, whether you like it or not."

"That sounds rather painful."

Dosia grinned. "Sometimes it is. But more often, it's wonderful. There is nothing better than being in love."

Before Olivia could respond, the sound of voices and hurried steps echoed through the entry hall. A moment later, Evander burst through the doorway.

"Olivia!" he said, relief etched in every line of his face.

She rose at once. "Is everything all right?"

"No!" He ran a hand through his hair. "You shouldn't have left the townhouse."

Her brows furrowed. "Why not?"

He took her hand gently. "It's not safe. Warwicke believes someone may target you next."

"Joseph said the same."

Evander stilled. "You saw Harwood?"

She nodded. "He stepped into the coach on my way here. He wants me to try to convince you to sell the indigo plantation."

His jaw tensed. "You should not have been alone with him. What if someone saw you?"

"It wasn't my choice."

"Regardless, we should get you home where it is safe," Evander said, his hand tightening around hers.

Olivia looked down at their joined hands, then up into his face. There was a solemn intensity in his eyes—protective, almost fierce. The furrow in his brow, the set of his jaw... he meant it. He wasn't just repeating Warwicke's warning. He was worried for *her*.

She might have argued that her brother's townhouse was secure enough, that Dosia and the staff would never let harm come to her. But whatever protest had formed on her lips melted beneath the weight of his concern. And truth be told, it warmed something in her—something soft and fragile that had been growing ever since that kiss.

"Very well," she said at last. "Let's go home."

His features relaxed at once, the tension easing from his shoulders. "I was expecting more of a fight from you."

"I can't become too predictable," she teased. "Besides, you now owe me a cup of chocolate for dragging me away."

"That is easily arranged." He turned to Dosia with a nod of gratitude. "Forgive the intrusion."

Dosia offered him a gracious smile. "You are always welcome in our home."

Evander shifted Olivia's hand, tucking it into the crook of his arm with a familiarity that sent a little flutter through her. She allowed herself to lean into him slightly.

"Shall we return?" he asked.

"I suppose," she said, feigning reluctance, though her heart was quietly soaring. She felt it—every step, every breath, the certainty of it. This—*he*—was where she was meant to be.

As they stepped through the entry hall and out onto the front stoop, the sun filtered through the clouds, casting the gravel driveway in a gentle light. Olivia's eyes fell on the waiting coach. But something was off.

The horses were harnessed and still, but there was no movement. No driver on the box. No footman at the door.

Her fingers instinctively tightened on Evander's arm.

He stopped, just as still. She felt the change in him—the way his body went taut beside hers.

"Wait here," he murmured.

She nodded, though unease prickled at the back of her neck. The world felt oddly silent. Too still.

Then—a sound behind her. Footsteps? No—too fast. Too close.

She turned, or tried to—but something struck the back of her head with brutal force. A flash of pain burst behind her eyes.

The last thing she heard before the darkness swallowed her was the sharp crack of a pistol.

And Evander shouting her name.

"*Westmere*!"

The name pulled at the edges of Evander's consciousness like a ripple across still water. It echoed, urgent, but distant. Everything was dark. Heavy. He wanted to retreat, to let the weight of unconsciousness pull him under again.

"Westmere!"

The second cry was accompanied by a jolt—someone shaking him. His skull throbbed in protest, a hot pulse at the back of his head. Why did it hurt? He tried to recall—

Olivia.

A coach. A pistol. Warwicke shouting. Olivia slumped in someone's arms.

Had he imagined it?

Evander's eyes flew open. "Olivia!"

Shapes swam into view—Warwicke and Wilton, crouched over him, their faces drawn tight with concern.

He sat up abruptly, wincing at the flash of pain. His gaze swept the room in a frantic search. "Where is Olivia?" The question tore from his throat, raw and frantic.

Wilton hesitated. "She was abducted."

The words landed like a physical blow.

Abducted.

"No," Evander said, the denial reflexive, automatic. "How?"

Warwicke's voice was steady, but his eyes were weary. "I had been following you, concerned for your safety. When I heard you scream, I ran over to you as fast as I could. But I was too late. They were already fleeing. I managed to stop them from taking you as well."

Evander shoved his hand through his hair, breathing hard. "You should have gone after her!" he barked, the rage in him snapping like a whip. "You should have—*blast it,* Warwicke, you should have saved her!"

"I know you're angry, but you need to calm down—" Warwicke started.

"Don't you dare tell me to calm down," Evander growled. "She's my wife! I was right there, and I did nothing. I couldn't stop it. I failed her."

"You were ambushed," Wilton revealed. "They were waiting for you to leave our townhouse. This wasn't random."

Evander's jaw clenched. "Who is *they*?"

The two men exchanged a look—tense, uncertain.

"We're not entirely sure," Wilton admitted.

Evander surged to his feet, only to stumble as dizziness slammed into him. The room tilted sideways, and he had to drop back onto the settee, bracing his elbows on his knees.

"You need to have a doctor look at you," Wilton urged.

"I don't need a doctor," Evander bit out. "I need my wife."

Warwicke sat beside him, calm but insistent. "You need rest, Evander."

Evander almost laughed. *Rest?* His heart felt like it had been ripped from his chest. "Would you rest if Dorothea had been taken?"

Warwicke shook his head. "No. I wouldn't."

"Then don't ask it of me," he replied. "I won't sit here waiting for something to happen. I have to find her."

"Then we'll find her," Warwicke said evenly. "But we have to be smart. Until we receive word, there isn't much to go on."

Evander's mind reeled. The reformers. Threats. The meeting.

"Lord Luca," he said suddenly. "Could he be behind this?"

Warwicke raised an eyebrow. "It's possible... but I've heard nothing of this through my contacts."

"Then we ask him," Evander said, rising again—more slowly this time. "We speak to him now."

"I don't think—" Warwicke began.

"I don't care what you think is wise," Evander snapped. "I'm going, with or without you."

Wilton moved to block his path, his expression grim. "We all want Olivia back. She's my sister. But running off without a plan helps no one."

"I've listened to everyone long enough," Evander said, pushing past him. "All I've got is the drive to do *something*."

Warwicke stood. "Fine. I'll go with you. But you must promise you won't do anything reckless."

"I won't make promises I don't intend to keep," Evander said. "Not when Olivia's life might depend on it."

"I can respect that," Warwicke muttered. "For now."

As they stepped outside, the brisk air hit Evander like a wave. And then the memories came flooding back to him.

The coach.

A man stepping from the shadows.

Olivia crying out—then crumpling to the ground.

His own shout of horror.

Then the pain.

He closed his eyes, cursing himself silently. *I was careless. I let my guard down. She paid the price.*

"Westmere?" Warwicke's voice broke through his spiraling thoughts.

"I'm fine," Evander replied tersely.

Wilton lingered at the doorway. "I'll remain here, in case the abductors make contact."

Evander nodded faintly, barely hearing him. He stepped into the fully manned coach, staring blankly out the window as it pulled into traffic. He could feel Warwicke watching him, waiting for him to break. But he would be disappointed. He had a purpose now.

"She means everything to you," Warwicke said after a long moment. "I can see it in your eyes. You'd die for her."

"I would," Evander answered quickly.

"Then stay alive," Warwicke said. "You dying doesn't save her. It only makes it harder for the rest of us."

Evander turned to meet his friend's gaze. "Then what do I do? Just wait? Hope for the best?"

"No," Warwicke said, his eyes steely. "You fight. But you fight smart."

Evander nodded slowly. "Do you have an extra pistol?"

Warwicke shifted his coat, revealing the one tucked at his waist. "No. And I'm not giving you this one."

"Why not?"

"Because I'll be the one to threaten Lord Luca, if it comes to that."

Evander didn't argue. Truth be told, he'd never liked pistols. He used them on hunts but hated the recoil, the way they shattered silence—and lives.

"We don't know Lord Luca is responsible," Warwicke said. "Don't let desperation cloud your judgment."

"He was at the reformers' meeting. That's enough for me."

Warwicke's brows pulled together. "Westmere…"

He cut Warwicke off with a raised hand. "Don't lecture me. Tell me honestly—what would you do if someone tried to kill Dorothea?"

Warwicke looked away, a shadow passing over his features. "They did try, and it nearly destroyed me. But I had to keep my mind clear until I knew the truth."

"I don't think I have that kind of patience."

"You must," Warwicke asserted. "Until we find Olivia."

Evander stared ahead, jaw set, heart hammering with grief,

rage, and dread. *Wherever you are, Livy... hold on. I'm coming for you.*

The coach lurched to a stop in front of a whitewashed townhouse, pristine and imposing against the gray sky. Evander didn't bother to wait for the footman and flung open the door himself, boots hitting the cobblestone before the wheels had fully ceased turning. His blood was pounding in his ears. He couldn't waste a moment.

He took the front steps two at a time, fury giving speed to his limbs, and pounded on the door with the side of his fist.

The door creaked open. A tall, gaunt butler with white hair and an expression of long-suffering patience appeared in the frame. "May I help you?"

"I need to speak to Lord Luca," Evander said sharply. The effort to keep his voice controlled made his jaw ache.

"I'm afraid Lord Luca is not home," the man said with a rehearsed apology. "If you would be so kind as to leave your calling card—"

Evander stepped forward, barely restraining himself. "Where is he?"

The butler's expression didn't change, but a hint of discomfort flickered in his eyes. "I am not at liberty to say, sir. But as I said, if you leave your card—"

"That is unacceptable," Warwicke's voice cut in behind him, calm but firm.

The butler's mask slipped for a second and annoyance flashed in his eyes. "I wish I could help you, but as I said—Lord Luca is not home."

He began to shut the door.

Warwicke stepped forward and stopped it with his hand, pressing it open just enough to slide inside. "And I find that unacceptable," he said, stepping into the entry hall.

The butler jerked back, scandalized. "If you don't leave immediately, I will send for the constable."

Warwicke smiled, but it didn't reach his eyes. "Please do. I'm acquainted with most of them." His voice dropped, losing all trace of politeness. "Now tell us where Lord Luca is."

"No," the butler said again, though his voice had lost its earlier confidence.

Warwicke's smile faded. "It wasn't a request," he asserted.

The butler visibly swallowed. Evander saw the way his hands twitched at his sides, uncertain whether to hold his ground or bolt.

"I could be dismissed," he said, his voice barely above a whisper. "If I say anything."

Warwicke took one slow step closer. "And I could be far less pleasant if you don't."

Evander almost felt pity for the man. Almost.

The butler cracked. "He's at his office," he said quickly. "But he isn't alone. His employees are with him."

"Thank you. That wasn't so hard, was it?" Warwicke leaned in just enough to be intimidating. "I imagine you're thinking about sending a messenger ahead to warn him."

The butler hesitated.

"I wouldn't," Warwicke said with a dismissive wave of his hand. The gesture was casual, but the butler flinched as though it were a threat. "We want this visit to be a surprise. You wouldn't ruin a surprise, would you?"

The man shook his head.

"Good," Warwicke said, turning.

Evander didn't speak as they made their way back to the coach, their boots echoing hollowly against the stone. He climbed in wordlessly, and the moment the door shut, the coach jolted forward again into the churn of London traffic.

Only once they were moving did he turn to Warwicke and say, "You terrified that poor man."

Warwicke didn't even look his way. "He'll live."

Evander allowed himself the smallest twitch of a smile. "Do you think he'll warn Lord Luca?"

"Absolutely," Warwicke said. "But it hardly matters. If Lord Luca is involved, he's expecting us already."

Evander grew quiet. A single question had been digging at his insides the entire ride. "What if he's not involved?"

Warwicke turned to face him fully, his voice serious. "Then we find who is."

Evander exhaled through his nose, but the knot in his chest didn't loosen. "And what if we're too late?"

For a moment, Warwicke didn't answer. Then he said, "Focus on what you can control. Don't let fear in. That's how you lose."

Evander stared at the passing streets, their orderly windows and manicured hedges mocking his turmoil. *Don't let fear in.* But fear was already there. It was curling in his stomach like ice.

"That's easier said than done."

"It is," Warwicke agreed. "But if they meant to kill her, they would have. Abduction means they want something."

Evander's throat tightened. His fists clenched against his knees. "I should have protected her," he said under his breath.

"You were ambushed," Warwicke reminded him. "Blame the ones who took her, not yourself."

Evander said nothing. His mind was already racing, calculating what they would do next. But one thing was for certain: He would not stop. He would not rest. Not until he had Olivia back in his arms.

18

Pain lanced through the back of Olivia's skull, yanking her from unconsciousness. She gasped and instinctively reached up to cradle her head. Her fingers brushed against a tender lump, and she winced. Slowly, she blinked her eyes open. The world came into focus in wavering shadows and harsh light. She was lying on a straw-stuffed mattress—coarse, foul-smelling, and threadbare. The only other furnishing in the small, dingy room was a warped chair slumped in the corner.

Her head throbbed as she pushed herself upright. Panic fluttered at the edge of her mind, but she forced herself to breathe. Steady now. Think.

A grime-smeared window offered a sliver of the outside world. Judging by the filtered daylight, it was sometime in the late afternoon. How long had she been unconscious? A few hours? A day?

The last thing she remembered was being in her brother's townhouse... then darkness. Someone had struck her. But who? And why?

Below her, rough laughter erupted—slurred and raucous.

Men. Several of them. From the timber and the scent of ale wafting upward, she guessed she was above a tavern or an inn. Perhaps a coaching house? That, at least, gave her a hope of being in a public place. A place from which she might escape.

She swung her legs off the mattress and stood, though the motion made her sway. Her head pounded in protest, but she gritted her teeth and staggered to the door. The handle refused to turn. Locked. Of course. No surprise there.

Her gaze darted back to the window and to the tree branch that swayed just beyond it. She felt a stirring of hope. It was close enough to reach. If she could get the window open...

Crossing the cramped space in a few hurried steps, she braced her hands against the grimy panes. They were stuck. She shoved harder. The frame groaned under the pressure, reluctant but not unmovable. With a final heave, it slid open, shrieking in protest. A rush of cool air hit her face, and with it, a strange exhilaration.

There was no time to second-guess her decision. Footsteps echoed in the corridor outside her door. They were coming closer. Louder.

She clambered up to the sill and reached for the branch. The bark scratched her palms as she hauled herself up and out. Her gown snagged and tore, but she didn't stop. Inch by inch, she crept along the limb towards the trunk. Her breath caught as she lost her footing momentarily, but she didn't fall. Not today.

At last, her boots met solid earth.

A shout rang out from above.

She didn't wait to see who had called her name.

Olivia ran.

The street was unfamiliar, dingy, and crowded. A weather-worn sign swung from a rusted bracket above the door of the building she had just escaped: *The Dragon's Head*. She burned the name into her memory.

People stared as she ran past them, but she didn't stop. A hackney stood at the far end of the lane, the driver half-dozing atop the box.

She stumbled to a halt beside him. "I need a ride."

The portly man squinted at her. "I don't give rides to unescorted women."

"Please," she said, glancing over her shoulder. "I was abducted. I need to get home."

He grunted. "Likely story. Do you have any money?"

"No. But—"

The driver cut her off. "No money, no ride!"

"Wait!" she pleaded. "I am Lady Westmere. If you take me to Mayfair, you will be rewarded."

He scoffed. "A lady? In your state? Do you expect me to believe such a tale?"

She looked down. Her once-elegant gown was ruined. Mud clung to her ripped hem. Her hands were scraped. She likely looked mad.

But she stood straighter. "I swear it. I give you my word."

His gaze lingered on her for a moment too long, and she thought he might turn her away. But at last, he jerked his head. "Get in. Before I change my mind."

"Thank you," she whispered, nearly sobbing with relief.

The interior of the hackney was vile—stained seats, a sour stench—but she barely noticed. As the carriage began to move, she huddled low. Two men rushed out of the tavern's side entrance, scanning the street. Searching.

She ducked further.

Each jostle of the hackney felt like an eternity, but finally, blessedly, she recognized the familiar curve of their street. Their townhouse. Home.

Before the coach even rolled to a full stop, she flung the door open and stepped out. A footman rushed down the steps, but she ignored him.

She had made it.

Then—

"Olivia!"

She turned her head to see Evander step out of their crested coach. He sprinted towards her and she barely had time to breathe before his arms wrapped around her, pulling her tight against him.

She relaxed into him. "I'm all right," she whispered, though she wasn't sure she believed it. All she knew was that she was home. In his arms. Where she belonged.

A sharp voice came from behind them. "Lady, I don't have all day!" the hackney driver declared.

Olivia leaned back and explained, "I promised him a reward if he brought me home."

Without hesitation, Evander pulled a velvet pouch from his coat and tossed it up. The man caught it mid-air.

"All this for me?" he asked, eyes wide.

"Thank you for bringing my wife home... to me," Evander said, his voice full of emotion.

The man nodded and flicked his reins, disappearing down the street.

Evander turned back to her. His eyes searched hers. "How are you here?"

"I escaped."

"Yes, I gathered that," he said. "How?"

"I climbed through a window and down a tree."

Lord Warwicke appeared beside them, his brow knit in concern. "Perhaps we should continue this conversation inside."

Evander took her hand in his. "I'm not letting you out of my sight."

"You'll hear no protest from me," she murmured.

Inside, Evander immediately gave instructions for tea, a

bath, and a doctor. She tried to object, but he silenced her with a look.

She didn't argue again.

In the drawing room, Lord Warwicke's tone was all business. "Start at the beginning. Tell us everything."

She recounted what she could about the inn and the escape. When she revealed the name of the tavern she was being held in, Lord Warwicke sucked in a breath.

"The Dragon's Head?" he repeated sharply.

With a nod, she said, "The sign was above the main door."

"That's where the reformers meet," Lord Warwicke said grimly. "It's where I last saw Lord Luca."

Evander's jaw clenched. "Then Lord Luca's behind this."

"Maybe. He didn't speak at the meeting. He just observed."

"Then he might at least know who orchestrated it," Olivia offered. "But why would he target me?"

"Because the reformers are getting desperate. They want Westmere out of India." Lord Warwicke began pacing, thoughtful. "But why make the effort to kidnap you… only to let you escape?"

"They didn't let me," Olivia said, indignant. "I climbed out of a window, and it wasn't an easy feat."

Evander pulled her close again. "They underestimated you."

Lord Warwicke shook his head. "Something's off," he muttered. "Why would Lord Luca align himself with reformers? He is the son of a duke."

Evander dismissed the speculation with finality. "All I care is that she's home. And she stays here, until this is over."

"I wholeheartedly agree," Olivia said.

He smiled down at her. "Care for that bath?"

She sighed. "Desperately. I must look a fright."

Lifting a hand to her cheek, Evander said, "To me, you've never looked more beautiful."

The warmth in his eyes threatened to undo her. Did he mean it? Was this love?

Before she could speak, Lord Warwicke cut in. "I'm going to speak with Luca. Westmere, would you care to join me?"

Evander looked conflicted. "I don't want to leave her, but..." He stopped. "I would like to be there to beat him to a bloody pulp, should he confess."

"You should go," Olivia encouraged. "I'll be here when you return."

"Promise me?"

The vulnerability in his voice sliced through her. She longed to say *I love you*. But fear kept her silent. So instead, she nodded. "I promise."

"Before I go, I will assign footmen to guard your every move. I won't let anyone hurt you... ever again."

The conviction in his tone sent a tremor through her. "Thank you."

He brushed his thumb against her cheek, then turned and followed Lord Warwicke to the door.

The door clicked shut behind Evander and Lord Warwicke, leaving Olivia alone at last. She crossed the room in a daze and sank onto the settee, the upholstery sighing beneath her. Her hands trembled in her lap. She clasped them tightly to still them.

She was safe. She had escaped. But the truth of it—the full weight—was only just beginning to settle on her shoulders.

A shiver worked its way down her spine as she thought of the locked room, the window that had resisted her touch, and the boots thudding outside the door. If she hadn't climbed out in time...

She curled her fingers into the fabric of her ruined gown. *Don't think about that. You're home.*

A knock at the door stirred her, and the butler stepped inside with a bow. "Your bath has been prepared, my lady."

"Thank you," she said, rising on unsteady feet.

She climbed the stairs more quickly than she'd expected her legs to carry her and stepped into her bedchamber.

Her lady's maid was already there, setting out fresh linen. At the sight of Olivia, she gasped. "My lady! Are you hurt?"

"No, I am all right," Olivia replied. She gave the maid a reassuring nod, though she doubted it looked particularly convincing.

Annie approached cautiously. "Shall we get you out of that gown?"

"Yes, please," Olivia murmured, turning around and lifting her heavy hair out of the way.

She stared blankly at the wall as the buttons were slowly undone, the whisper of fabric loud in the quiet room. Her gaze shifted to the hearth where the water basin waited, steam curling lazily upward. The scent of lavender drifted through the air, soft and familiar.

And still, her heart wouldn't stop racing.

She should have felt relief. Joy, even. She was home, whole, alive. But an uneasiness clung to her, as stubborn as the dirt beneath her nails.

The gown slipped from her shoulders and pooled at her feet. She stepped out of it and moved towards the warmth waiting near the fire.

She placed her hand on the rim of the basin and inhaled deeply, the steam enveloping her like a protective cloak. But the words echoed in her head.

You escaped.

But from what—and for how long?

She closed her eyes.

Let me have this moment, she thought. *Let me believe—for a little while—that I'm safe.*

But deep down, Olivia knew the real danger had only just begun.

Evander's hands were balled into fists, so tight that his knuckles ached with the strain. He sat rigid at the coach window, his gaze fixed on the blurred, soot-stained buildings of London streaming past. His thoughts—sharp and burning—refused to be stilled. If Lord Luca had anything to do with Olivia's abduction, if he had dared to touch her, frighten her, *use* her—then no rank nor title would save him. Not even a duke for a father would shield him from the consequences.

The very idea sent a fresh wave of fury through him.

Warwicke's voice was a thin intrusion into the storm. "You need to calm down."

Evander turned his head sharply. "How can you ask that of me? Olivia was abducted and you want me to be calm?"

"We don't know Lord Luca was behind it," Warwicke said calmly. "Not for certain."

"Then *who*?" Evander demanded. "Who else had motive? Who else threatened my family, had an interest in the plantation, and now dares suggest I sell?"

Warwicke raised a hand, placating. "Let me do the talking when we get there. We'll get to the truth—but not if you storm in like a man possessed."

Evander didn't answer. He knew Warwicke was right. He just didn't care. The threats against him were one thing. But Olivia? That had crossed a line. A man only had so much restraint and his had already been stretched past breaking.

The coach slowed, then stopped before a squat red-brick building with faded shutters. A sign over the door read *The London Gazette*. Evander was out before the footman reached the step, striding forward with grim purpose.

Inside, a young clerk rose awkwardly from behind a desk, his quill still in hand. "May I help—"

"I need to speak to Lord Luca. Now," Evander demanded.

The clerk blinked, caught off guard. "I'm afraid that's not possible since he's in a meeting at the moment—"

"I don't care," Evander snapped, advancing. "Tell him Lord Westmere is here, and I will not wait."

The clerk hesitated, but Evander didn't. He swept past him, pushing open the main door and stepping into the heart of the newsroom. The clatter of low conversation filled the space. Desks lined the floor in long, chaotic rows, and at the far end, a closed door marked a private office.

Footsteps pounded behind him. "Sir—you can't go back there!"

"I'm not asking permission," Evander responded.

Warwicke caught up beside him, matching his stride. "Westmere, I'm warning you not to go in half-cocked."

He couldn't promise that. Not when he still saw Olivia's pale face in his mind, her eyes haunted from whatever she had endured. No. He wouldn't be calm. Not for this.

He reached the back office, grasped the handle, and threw open the door.

Lord Luca looked up from behind his desk, clearly startled. "Lord Westmere," he said, rising slightly. "To what do I owe the pleasure?"

Evander stepped forward, his words hard. "We need to talk."

Behind him, the clerk stammered, "Should I send for the constable?"

"No," Lord Luca said quickly, smoothing his expression. "That won't be necessary. I'm sure Lord Westmere and Lord Warwicke are merely… passionate. Gentlemen, shall we proceed civilly?"

Warwicke interjected. "That depends on how honest you're prepared to be."

Lord Luca's brow furrowed slightly as he leaned back. "And what would I have to lie about?"

Warwicke shut the door behind them. "What we're about to say is off the record. Do we have an understanding?"

"That depends entirely on the subject." Lord Luca's tone remained composed, but Evander saw the flicker of wariness beneath.

"The abduction of Lady Westmere," Warwicke said bluntly.

Lord Luca's head turned towards Evander. "Your wife was abducted?"

Evander folded his arms across his chest, his voice like steel. "She was. She escaped." And he would never forgive himself for not preventing it.

"That's... troubling," Lord Luca remarked. "Do you believe it was connected to the threats made against your family?"

Evander's gaze narrowed. "That's the assumption."

"Well then, given everything, perhaps it's time to sell the indigo plantation. That would be the reasonable course, wouldn't it?"

Evander stepped closer to the desk. "Is that what you want? For me to sell?"

Lord Luca eyed him curiously. "Why would my opinion matter?"

Leaning forward, Evander planted his palms on the polished surface. "Because I think this was your aim all along. So I'll ask again—what do you gain if I sell?"

"Nothing," Lord Luca responded.

Warwicke's voice cut in, sharp. "How long have you been working with the reformers who want Britain out of India?"

"I beg your pardon?" Lord Luca asked, his eyes widening.

"You heard me," Warwicke said. "I don't know how to make the question any simpler."

"I am not aligned with reformers," Lord Luca insisted.

Warwicke crossed his arms. "Yet you attend their meetings."

Lord Luca's composure slipped a fraction. "How would you know that?"

"I have my ways."

Standing, Lord Luca replied, "The only way you'd know that is if you were there yourself."

Warwicke smirked. "Correct. I'm assisting Westmere in investigating the threats against his family."

Lord Luca turned to Evander again. "So it wasn't only your father—*you* were threatened as well?"

Evander held his stare. "Yes. But you already knew that, didn't you?"

"I swear I didn't," Lord Luca replied, lifting his hands. "I had no part in it. Nor in Lady Westmere's abduction."

"I don't believe you," Evander said flatly.

"You're welcome not to," Lord Luca remarked. "But I've been here all morning. Ask my staff. I couldn't have orchestrated anything."

"You could have hired someone."

"I could have," Lord Luca agreed, "but I didn't. I've been investigating the truth behind the plantation dealings. I've found some troubling things."

Warwicke stepped forward, skeptical. "Such as?"

Lord Luca lifted a stack of papers from his desk. "You're not the only one who's been pressured to sell. Two others were also threatened and all their plantations were bought by the same company. Walter Textiles."

"I've heard of them," Evander remarked.

"They now control the majority of British-held indigo plantations in India," Lord Luca said. "And no one noticed. It was done quietly."

Warwicke grew solemn. "Who owns Walter Textiles?"

"No one really knows," Lord Luca admitted. "Although it's a business that exists on paper, it doesn't actually do any real work. I suspect it is a dummy corporation to disguise ownership or shift funds around. I've been attending the reformers' meetings hoping to get a lead, but they're just as in the dark."

Evander took a step back, his pulse pounding. If Lord Luca was telling the truth, they were no closer to unmasking the one responsible.

He turned to Warwicke. "What do you think?"

But inwardly, the question twisted: Was Luca telling the truth? Or was he simply a better liar than Evander had given him credit for?

Warwicke stared at Lord Luca for a long moment, his mouth drawn into a tight line. At last, he spoke. "I believe him," he said. "But I don't trust him. Not entirely."

Lord Luca gave a faint shrug, utterly unruffled. "I can live with that," he responded before shifting his attention to Evander. "What do you intend to do with your indigo plantation?"

The question struck like a blow to the chest.

Evander exhaled hard and dragged a hand through his hair, still trying to collect the pieces of everything that had been said. "It isn't my decision to make," he muttered. "My father owns the plantation."

But Lord Luca's expression sharpened. His brows lifted as if Evander had said something naïve. "You don't know, do you?"

Evander's gut tensed. "Don't know what?"

"Your brother left the indigo plantation to you in his will."

For a moment, Evander just stared at him. The words didn't make sense. They couldn't make sense. "That's impossible," he said firmly, shaking his head. "Bryon wouldn't do that. He would've left it to the estate."

Lord Luca lowered himself back into his chair, folding his hands atop a stack of papers. "His will was filed with the probate court. I reviewed it last week, with full permission. It was a clear directive. The indigo plantation was left to you. Solely."

Evander's breath caught as a chill spread through his chest.

Why would Bryon do that? Why would he put him in charge, bypassing their father entirely? And why hadn't his father said anything about that?

He spoke more to himself than to the others. "Why would he leave it to me and not the estate?"

Luca gave a small shake of his head. "I can't say. Perhaps he didn't trust your father to manage it. Or perhaps... he knew what was coming." He held Evander's gaze. "Whatever the reason, the decision is yours now. To keep it. Or sell it."

Evander turned away, unable to answer. His steps carried him to the narrow window, the glass smeared with dust. Outside, the city pulsed with life as carts rattled over cobblestones and pedestrians weaved through crowded streets. Yet everything in him had gone still.

The weight of the decision settled heavily on his shoulders.

Could he sell it? Walk away from the land his brother had entrusted to him?

But if he kept it, if he refused to sell, would that put Olivia in danger again?

Warwicke's voice drew him back. "What we do know is that Olivia was taken to The Dragon's Head," he said. "But she escaped before more harm could befall her."

Evander turned back, his mouth drawn in a tight line. Even now, the idea that she had endured something so harrowing while he was miles away still made his blood boil.

Lord Luca's brows furrowed. "I heard nothing about the reformers planning to abduct Lady Westmere."

"That doesn't mean it wasn't done by one of them," Warwicke replied. "Or someone acting in their interest."

Luca nodded slowly. "There's a meeting in an hour. I could ask around and see if anyone knows something. If I hear anything useful, I'll report back."

Warwicke offered a brief nod of approval. "That would be appreciated."

Lord Luca's lips curled faintly. "I'm relieved we've come to some sort of understanding."

Evander didn't bother responding. He turned on his heel and followed Warwicke out of the cramped office and into the bustle of the newsroom. The hushed conversations and rustle of paper faded behind him as they stepped back into the corridor, then out into the waiting coach.

Only once the door shut behind them did Evander let out a long, frustrated breath. He dragged a hand over his face and slumped back into the seat.

"We're no closer," he muttered. "No closer to knowing who took Olivia. Or who's behind the threats."

Warwicke adjusted the cuffs of his sleeves and leaned back. "We did gain a potential ally."

Evander stared out the window as the coach began to move again, but he didn't respond right away. The streets of London blurred past, but his thoughts were rooted elsewhere—on his brother's will, on the plantation, on Olivia's haunted eyes.

"A reluctant one," he said at last. "And we still don't know if we can trust him."

Warwicke grew silent. "True. But it's more than we had yesterday."

Evander's fingers curled into his gloves. That may have been true. But it still wasn't enough.

Not until he had answers.

Not until Olivia was safe.

19

Olivia sat in the drawing room, a book open in her lap, though she hadn't turned a page in some time. Her gaze was fixed on the fireplace, its soft glow unable to melt the cold coil of unease in her stomach. The memory of waking in that wretched tavern gnawed at her—not just the fear, but the fury. She had been taken. Used as leverage. And she had been lucky to escape. That luck might not hold a second time.

She wasn't weak. She wouldn't let them make her feel small.

The door opened, and Gillingham stepped into the room with his usual composed air. "Lord and Lady Wilton have arrived—"

He didn't finish. Richard and Dosia entered the room, their expressions drawn and anxious.

Her brother's gaze swept over her. "Are you all right?" he asked, the question more of a demand than an inquiry.

Olivia carefully closed the book and rested it on her lap. "I am well," she said, lifting her chin slightly.

Dosia didn't hesitate. She crossed the room and sat beside

Olivia on the settee. "What happened? Please, tell us everything."

For a moment, Olivia closed her eyes. Just long enough to summon a thread of composure. "I woke up in a tavern. In a part of Town that I would never willingly go near. But I found a window, climbed out, and managed to escape down a tree."

Dosia's breath caught. "That sounds… horrifying." She gave Olivia's hand a gentle squeeze. "You were so brave to think clearly and get yourself out."

Olivia looked away, ashamed of the tremor that ran through her. Brave? She hadn't felt brave. She had felt desperate.

Richard stepped forward, arms crossed. "I think we should take you back to our home until this threat is over."

Olivia's eyes snapped to him. "I am home."

"You know what I mean," he said with a sigh. "I do not like the thought of you being here while someone is clearly trying to harm you."

"I am safe here," Olivia asserted.

Richard frowned. "Assuming you stay away from windows and don't leave the townhouse."

Olivia leaned forward and placed the book on the table with quiet finality. "I appreciate your concern, Richard. But I am not alone. Evander will keep me safe."

He looked unconvinced. "Need I remind you that you were abducted while Westmere was mere feet away?"

A flicker of doubt crept in, but she pushed it down. "I am not leaving my home. Or Evander. And need I remind you that I was abducted outside of *your* townhouse, not mine?"

Richard let out a noise of exasperation and turned to his wife. "Dosia, will you try to talk some sense into my obstinate sister?"

Dosia gave Olivia a small, knowing smile. "You must know he only speaks this way because he's worried about you."

"I know," Olivia responded. "But I trust Evander with my life."

With a bob of her head, Dosia replied, "Then you must stay here."

"That's not what we discussed," Richard muttered.

Dosia shot him a look, her smile growing. "We must respect Olivia's decision. Besides, it's not as though we could force her."

"Whyever not?" Richard grumbled under his breath.

Dosia's eyes twinkled with mischief. "Because women tend to stand by the men they love."

Richard lowered himself into a chair across from Olivia, his expression softening. "Is it true?"

The air seemed to thicken around her. She could lie and claim it was nothing more than friendship. But something inside her refused to pretend any longer.

"It is," she admitted. "But I haven't told Evander yet. I'm afraid he won't… that he doesn't feel the same."

Dosia tightened her grip on Olivia's hand. "It's natural to be afraid. But don't let that fear silence you."

"My admission would change everything."

Richard gave a faint nod. "Yes. But for the better. This—this love—is what our parents would have wanted for you. To love, and be loved in return."

Olivia bit her lower lip. "But what if he doesn't return my feelings? What then?"

Her question hung in the air. Richard and Dosia exchanged a look—meaningful and unspoken. It only made her heart pound harder.

Richard cleared his throat. "When I told Dosia how I felt, I was terrified. But I loved her too much to remain silent."

"And I'm glad you told me," Dosia added, giving her husband a fond glance.

"Life is full of uncertainty," Richard said, "but Evander doesn't have to be one of them."

Before Olivia could respond, the door opened and Evander entered the room with a purposeful stride. His eyes found hers instantly, and in that moment—despite everything—she felt the knot inside her begin to loosen.

"Olivia," he said gently. "How are you faring?"

She rose to her feet, her heart steadying. "I am well."

"I am relieved to hear that."

Richard's voice cut in, sharp with protectiveness. "What are you doing to keep my sister safe?"

Olivia turned her head towards Evander, suddenly aware of how still he'd become. But when he answered, his voice was calm, unyielding. "I've hired more footmen. They're stationed throughout the townhouse. No one will get to her again."

She felt a rush of warmth at his words, though she knew they were more for Richard's benefit than hers. Evander had been on edge since she returned. Vigilant. Watchful. As if he blamed himself.

"Good," Richard replied, though he didn't sound fully appeased. "I would prefer if she returned home with me—"

"She is home," Evander stated, his voice clipped. "Now, and forever."

Olivia's breath caught. Not because of his defiance but because of the quiet certainty in his voice. He meant it. Every word.

Richard studied Evander for a long moment. Then, finally, he nodded. "Then I expect you to protect her with your life."

"That goes without saying."

Before Richard could say more, Gillingham stepped into the drawing room with practiced formality. "Your father has requested your presence in the study, my lord."

"Inform him we'll be there shortly," Evander responded.

Richard turned to Dosia and held out a hand to help her rise. "We can see ourselves out."

Olivia offered her sister-in-law a grateful glance. Dosia gave her a small smile and a wink before they left, and the room fell into a quiet hush.

Evander turned to her, his gaze moving over her as if seeing her for the first time since their guests had arrived. "How are you doing—truly?"

Olivia hesitated, then gave a small, rueful smile. "My head aches a bit, but I'll survive."

Her attempt at lightness didn't reach him. The seriousness in his eyes deepened. "I'm sorry I failed you."

Her heart clenched. "You didn't—"

"It was my fault," he said, his voice low and thick with emotion. "You were taken. And I wasn't strong enough to stop it. I wasn't enough."

She stepped forward without thinking, her hand finding his. "Don't say that. You were—are—everything I needed. You didn't fail me, Evander. The people who did this... they did. Not you."

But he didn't seem to hear her. His shoulders were tight, his jaw clenched. "What kind of husband lets harm come to his wife?"

She reached up and cupped his cheek, gently forcing him to meet her gaze. "The best kind. The kind who cares so much he'll carry the blame even when it doesn't belong to him."

His eyes grew moist. "You deserve better."

"It is you that I want. Because no one else makes sense."

She drew in a breath. *Say it. Tell him.*

"I love—"

Gillingham reappeared, clearing his throat. "Pardon the interruption, but your father is rather insistent that you join him in the study."

Evander closed his eyes for a brief moment, then gave a humorless smile. "My father is anything but patient." He took a step back but kept hold of her hand. "I'd like you to come with me."

"Are you sure?"

"Where I go, you go," he said simply. "No more secrets."

That one sentence stole the air from her lungs. She nodded, letting him lead her. Her hand remained wrapped in his, warm and certain. As they walked down the corridor, she could see the tension around his mouth. His grief and guilt hadn't left him—not yet. But perhaps they could face it together.

They entered the study, and Olivia felt Evander's hand tense slightly in hers.

Lord Everwyck sat in one of the wingback chairs, a glass in his hand and a scowl etched across his weathered face. He barely glanced at them. "Why is Olivia here?"

"I asked her to join me," Evander replied.

The earl gave a huff of disapproval and took a sip. Then his eyes, sharper now, turned to Olivia. "I heard you were abducted."

"I was," Olivia said, her voice even.

A flicker of something passed across Lord Everwyck's face—regret? Guilt? She couldn't be sure. "I am relieved beyond words that you escaped unharmed."

The sincerity in his tone startled her. "Thank you, my lord."

He leaned forward, setting his glass down with a soft clink. "I believe the time has come to seriously consider selling the indigo plantation."

Evander's brow creased. "You were opposed to that before."

"I was," the earl admitted. "But whoever is behind these attacks won't stop until we are all in the ground. I can't allow that to happen."

Olivia studied him quietly. There was a weariness about him, one she hadn't noticed before. The stubborn pride that usually defined him had been dimmed. He looked... tired. Human.

Evander's voice cut into her thoughts. "It's not your decision to make, is it?"

Lord Everwyck's head lifted slowly. "What do you mean?"

"I know that Bryon left the plantation to me in his will."

The earl stiffened, his knuckles tightening around the arm of the chair. "That plantation belongs to the estate. It never should have been in Bryon's name in the first place. He used funds that he acquired from gambling."

"But it was. And now it belongs to me," Evander said. He glanced towards Olivia. "What are your thoughts? Should I sell it?"

Her eyes widened, not just at the question, but at what it meant. He *trusted* her. He *valued* her.

Lord Everwyck gave a scoffing laugh. "What kind of man asks his wife for advice on estate matters?"

Evander didn't blink. "A smart one."

Olivia's heart swelled. She looked at the man beside her and realized—utterly, completely—that he was her home, her haven, her future.

Evander turned to her. "What do you think, my dear?"

My dear.

The words sent warmth flooding through her chest and she gave his hand a gentle squeeze. "I'll support whatever decision you make."

He arched a brow. "That doesn't help," he teased softly, though his eyes were still shadowed with concern.

Before she could say more, a knock came at the door and Gillingham entered once again. "Lord Harwood is requesting a moment of your time."

"Inform him that we are not taking callers..." Evander started.

"Send him in," Lord Everwyck ordered, speaking over his son. "I want to see what he wants."

As Gillingham turned to leave, Olivia tightened her hold on Evander's hand and whispered, just for him, "After this... we finish our conversation."

Because she wouldn't let the moment pass again.

She would tell him she loved him.

And this time, nothing would stop her.

Evander stood beside Olivia, her presence grounding him even as his mind churned with the weight of his decision. The indigo plantation had once been nothing more than a grim inheritance—now it had become a battleground. He didn't want to sell. Selling would mean relinquishing a fortune. But how could he cling to principle when it might cost Olivia her life?

He glanced at her out of the corners of his eyes—so composed, so beautiful, and so very vulnerable in the wake of her abduction. No, he couldn't risk her safety. Nothing mattered more than that.

Before he could speak, the door opened and in stepped Lord Harwood, the familiar frown fixed on his mouth. His eyes immediately found Olivia.

"I heard you were abducted," Harwood said, the words too casual for Evander's liking.

Olivia gasped. "How did you hear it so fast?"

Harwood offered a smooth, apologetic smile. "News travels quickly through the *ton*. I am relieved to see you well."

"Thank you," Olivia murmured, her voice guarded.

Harwood's attention shifted to Evander. "Do you intend to sell the indigo plantation now that the reformers have turned their attention to Olivia?"

Evander hesitated—but only for a moment. "I think that would be for the best," he said, the words leaving a bitter taste in his mouth.

Harwood visibly relaxed. "I'm glad to hear that. I'll have my solicitor draw up the contract tomorrow." A pause. "You're doing the right thing."

Just then, Warwicke's voice rang out from the doorway. "Is he?"

Evander turned sharply, heart tightening at the sharp edge in his friend's voice. Warwicke entered the room, his expression unreadable, yet charged with intent.

Harwood gave him a dry smile. "I think it's only wise, given the circumstances."

"And what circumstances are those, exactly?" Warwicke asked.

Evander frowned. "Is there a problem?"

Warwicke looked straight at him. "My contacts uncovered something curious. It seems Harwood is the sole owner of Walter Textiles."

Turning towards Harwood, Evander asked, "Is that true?"

Harwood gave a nonchalant shrug. "It's not illegal to own a business."

"No," Warwicke agreed, "but it becomes rather problematic when you're coercing landowners into selling to you."

Harwood's eyes narrowed. "I've never forced anyone's hand."

Evander stepped forward. "Why didn't you disclose you owned Walter Textiles when you first expressed interest in the plantation?"

"I've worked hard to build that company," Harwood replied, voice tightening. "I didn't think it necessary to share every detail."

Evander studied him, and he saw the shift now, the small cracks forming in Harwood's polished exterior.

"It makes me wonder what else you haven't shared," Warwicke pressed.

Harwood let out an irritated breath. "Why are you even here?"

Warwicke wandered over to the mantel, his movements deliberately casual. "Because once I discovered your little secret, I dug deeper. And do you know what I found?"

"I don't care—"

"Your company owned the ship that supposedly carried your brother and the late Lord Westmere to India. The one they allegedly died on."

Evander stiffened.

"That's a coincidence," Harwood snapped.

"Is it?" Warwicke's smile was thin. "Because when I tracked down the captain, he didn't remember your brother or Bryon ever boarding the vessel. Though their names were on the manifest."

Harwood's expression remained impassive. "A clerical oversight."

Evander's mind raced. Nothing about this was a coincidence. Too many puzzle pieces were falling into place.

Warwicke stepped closer. "Let's consider this, shall we? Olivia was taken to The Dragon's Head. It is well known as a reformers' stronghold. Too convenient, don't you think?"

Evander's chest tightened. "You're saying someone wanted it to appear the reformers were behind it."

"Exactly. But what if they weren't?" Warwicke's eyes turned determined. "What if it was someone who stood to gain the most from you selling your plantation?"

There was only one name left in the room.

"You," Warwicke said, eyes locked on Harwood.

Harwood gave a derisive laugh. "This is absurd. Wild speculation. You have no proof of what you are saying."

"Interesting that you mention proof," Warwicke replied. "Because once I got hold of Walter Textiles's financial records, I found the payments—direct, traceable—made to the men who threatened Westmere and his father."

Harwood blanched. "That's impossible."

"Your man of business is very bad at keeping things secure," Warwicke added. "He really should lock his desk drawers."

"You're lying," Harwood growled.

"I am many things," Warwicke said, "but being a liar is not one of them."

Evander's father, who had remained deathly silent, now rose to his feet. "Are you telling me that *this man* was behind my son's death?"

"I had nothing to do with Bryon's death!" Harwood exclaimed, visibly rattled now. "Don't believe him."

"I wish it weren't true," Warwicke replied. "But the money trail is undeniable."

Evander stepped forward, cold fury building in his chest. "You killed my brother?" he asked, his voice a low growl. "Why?"

Harwood raised both hands in a calming gesture. "Evander, you know me. Do you really think I'm capable of murder?"

Warwicke's expression darkened. "It turns out Westmere's indigo plantation property comes with the water rights. Which means Harwood has to pay him a fortune every year to maintain his factory."

Harwood let out a disgusted sound. "I don't know what my brother was thinking, selling it to Westmere, but that's irrelevant now."

"You were furious," Warwicke said, lifting a vase from the mantel and studying it absently. "You built everything up. Property by property. And then your brother threw a wrench in your empire."

"I was," Harwood admitted. "He didn't understand what I was building. He kept losing money with bad investments."

"And worse yet," Warwicke said, his voice dropping, "he wanted Bryon to marry your sister."

Harwood sneered. "Bryon was a cad. Jemima deserved better."

"And what did you do about it?" Warwicke asked.

"Nothing," Harwood asserted. "But I won't pretend I mourned him."

"You made a mistake," Warwicke said.

"I don't make mistakes."

A new voice rang out from the door.

"You underestimated how much the reformers despise you," Lord Luca said as he entered, his expression grim.

Harwood let out an exasperated sigh. "Wonderful. You've decided to join the circus."

Lord Luca nodded towards Warwicke. "The men who abducted Olivia are in Newgate. They've started talking. And they've named Harwood as the person who orchestrated it all."

Olivia gasped behind Evander. He didn't need to look at her to feel her betrayal.

Harwood rolled his eyes to the ceiling. "They're lying. They want the plantation for themselves."

"I've been tracking the indigo operation for months," Lord Luca said. "You were the one piece I couldn't confirm—until now. Faking a reformer attack was brilliant. But not brilliant enough."

Evander turned fully to Harwood, his voice steady but low with rage. "Is it true?"

"Good gads, no!" Harwood cried. "You'd take their word over mine?"

Evander stared at him for a long, agonizing moment. "Yes," he said. "I would."

Harwood's voice was filled with scorn. "You are a fool, then," he responded. "And I don't have to stand here and listen to these blatant lies."

He turned as though to leave, but Lord Luca moved quickly, blocking his path. "You should know that everything I've uncovered will be printed in the newssheets in the morning," he said. "It's over."

Harwood's jaw tensed. "Then I shall enjoy suing you for slander."

"Nothing I've written was untrue," Lord Luca said. "And you know it."

A smirk slowly crept onto Harwood's face. "It matters not," he sneered. "You'll all be dead soon anyway."

Before Evander could react, Harwood gave a sharp whistle.

Evander immediately stepped closer to Olivia, his instincts on high alert.

"If you're waiting for your thugs to come bursting in, you should know," Warwicke drawled from beside the hearth, "the constable rounded them up before I stepped into the room. Every last one."

The smirk slipped from Harwood's face. "Impossible," he muttered, the first flicker of uncertainty entering his eyes. "They were stationed just outside the door. Waiting for my signal."

In the next instant, Harwood's hand moved fast—too fast. He drew a pistol from inside his jacket and pointed it directly at Olivia.

"I am leaving and taking Olivia with me," Harwood shouted.

Evander surged forward, placing himself squarely in front of her. "Over my dead body," he growled. If Harwood thought he'd so much as touch Olivia again, he'd have to kill him first.

With a tsk, Warwicke said, "It is always a shame to see someone unravel right before our eyes."

"Be quiet!" Harwood shifted the pistol towards Warwicke. "Perhaps I'll just shoot you and be done with it."

Warwicke remained calm, as ever. "You have one shot," he remarked. "I wouldn't waste it."

Harwood's hand shook slightly, but the rage in his voice grew. "Why did you have to get involved?" he shouted at Warwicke. "Everything was going according to plan! I was going to be the largest landowner in India. No one would have dared disrespect me again!"

Evander's stomach twisted. "This was about... respect?"

Harwood's lips thinned. "My brother always acted superior. My mother adored him. He could do no wrong. But I—*I*—was the smart one. I was the one building something. I was the one who made everything work. And still, he looked down on me."

"So you killed him?" Evander asked.

"I did what was necessary," Harwood snapped. "He deserved it. So did Bryon. And now, I'm leaving. And if anyone tries to stop me, I'll kill Olivia."

Evander didn't flinch. His voice was quiet but resolute. "I can't allow that."

"You don't have a choice," Harwood said, amusement flickering back into his expression.

But Warwicke spoke up behind him. "Actually, he does."

Evander turned his head and saw that Warwicke had drawn a pistol of his own, aimed directly at Harwood's chest.

"We both have one shot," Warwicke said. "And I assure you, mine will count. Lower your weapon, and you can live another day."

Before Harwood could respond, another sound rang out.

A loud crack, sharp and deafening.

Harwood cried out and collapsed to the floor, the pistol clattering from his hand as blood spread from his shoulder.

Evander jerked towards the source of the shot and saw his father standing behind the desk, smoke curling from the barrel of a flintlock pistol.

"You killed my son," the earl said in a voice that sent a chill through the room. "You deserve to die."

Harwood writhed, clutching his shoulder, but he still managed to scoff. "You think you've won?" he spat. "I'll claim privilege of the peerage. I'll walk free."

Warwicke stepped forward and kicked Harwood's dropped

pistol aside. "We'll see about that," he said. "There's a long list of charges waiting. And I made sure your name is on every one of them."

At that moment, a tall, broad-shouldered man stepped into the room. Evander recognized him immediately—Constable Banfield. His no-nonsense presence filled the space.

"I heard everything," the constable said grimly. "I'll see to it he's taken straight to Newgate."

"Thank you, Constable," Warwicke said as the man took Harwood by the arm and began dragging him out of the study.

As soon as the door shut behind them, silence fell. Then Evander felt a gentle touch on his sleeve. He turned, already knowing who it was.

Olivia. Her eyes, full of compassion and worry, searched his.

"I'm sorry," she whispered.

He placed his hand over hers. "I'm not," he said softly. "I'm glad we finally know the truth."

And he meant it.

Because no matter the cost, the shadows had been banished —and she was still by his side.

20

Olivia stood in the aftermath, her pulse thrumming so loudly in her ears she could scarcely hear anything else. It didn't feel real—none of it. Joseph, a man she had known for most of her life, had turned out to be something else entirely. A liar. A traitor. A coward. She had never suspected the darkness behind him, and now she saw him for what he truly was.

Joseph had demanded respect from others. But Evander had never demanded anything from others. Or her. He simply lived with such quiet integrity, such gentle steadiness, that respect—and eventually love—had bloomed of its own accord. He had been her refuge through all of this, patient and constant, even when she had pushed him away. And now, she could no longer pretend.

The truth beat against her ribcage, frantic and desperate for release.

She turned her attention to Lord Warwicke, barely registering the conversation as he crossed the room to take the pistol from Lord Everwyck.

"I understand why you shot Harwood, but that was foolish,"

Lord Warwicke said, his voice edged with tension. "You could have missed."

"I never miss," Lord Everwyck replied, his tone steely as he handed the pistol over. "I want him to pay for what he did to Bryon."

Warwicke gave a nod, grave. "He will. I'll make sure of that."

Lord Luca cleared his throat, shifting with visible discomfort. "I do believe I will be on my way now."

Evander turned towards him. "Thank you for what you did."

"It was nothing," Lord Luca deflected quickly. "I only hope Harwood gets his comeuppance for what he's done."

As the conversation faded, Olivia's heart pounded harder. Now. She had to speak now, before her courage fled.

Her hand reached out before she could stop herself, gently brushing Evander's sleeve. "Can I speak to you?"

He turned to face her fully, his gaze softening the moment their eyes met. "Always. Is something troubling you?"

"No..." she whispered, heart in her throat. "I just need to talk to you."

A slight furrow formed between his brows. "You can speak freely here."

Not this. This couldn't be said in front of an audience.

She took a breath, shaky and full of unspoken longing, and whispered, "I love you."

His brow lifted slightly. "As a friend?"

She shook her head, adamant. "No. I love... love you."

A pause. A moment of silence that stretched painfully between them. Then Evander turned and addressed the others, his voice calm but commanding. "Gentlemen, may we have a moment?"

The men, to their credit, needed no further prompting. They cleared the room silently, leaving Olivia standing with the man who had always seen her.

He looked back at her. "You were saying?"

"I... uh... love you," she repeated, aware of how small her voice sounded. "Truly."

"You said that already," he murmured, the corners of his mouth lifting just slightly.

She stared at the front of his coat, the weight of her confession making her throat tighten. "I know my timing is horrid. But after that kiss... everything changed. It made me realize a part of me has always loved you, and I would follow you to the end of the earth."

He stepped closer and one gentle finger slid beneath her chin, guiding her to look up at him. "Are you quite sure, Livy?"

"I am."

His gaze searched hers. "What do you expect me to say? That I love you and my heart beats for no one else?"

She swallowed. "You don't have to say anything—"

"But that is precisely how I feel," he said simply.

"You do?"

A slow smile curved across his lips. "I can't recall a time I didn't love you. From the moment you marched into my life with grass in your hair and dirt on your boots, I knew I'd never be the same. You had a place in my heart before I even understood what love was."

"Why didn't you tell me?"

He shrugged, almost sheepish. "Because I was afraid. Afraid if you knew how deep it ran, you might pull away. I couldn't bear to lose you."

Her throat tightened at the truth in his eyes. He had been waiting all this time. And maybe, just maybe, she had been walking towards him without realizing it.

"I wasn't ready before," she admitted. "But I am now."

He reached for her hands and held them between his own, warm and steady. "Then I propose we make this a true marriage."

"I am in agreement."

"Good," he said, leaning forward just slightly. "And you'd best get used to me kissing you."

Her gaze dropped to his lips. "You'll hear no complaints from me."

And when he kissed her, it was unlike anything that had come before. It was slow, reverent. A promise made in the hush between heartbeats. A kiss that didn't rush or demand, but cherished.

When he drew back, his eyes were filled with wonder. "I can't believe this moment is real. I've loved you for so long... sometimes I thought it might break me."

"I'm sorry it took me so long."

His thumb brushed against her cheek. "No. Your timing is perfect. I never thought I'd be lucky enough to earn your love."

"You never had to earn it," she whispered. "You love me without trying to change me. You never have. You've always seen me for who I am—and loved me anyway. That means everything."

He touched her face, tender and adoring. "Should we host a ball?"

She laughed softly. "I'm not sure that's wise."

"I want the world to know how madly, irrevocably in love I am with you," he said. "It's no less than you deserve."

"Are you certain?"

He smirked. "Just as certain as when I followed you around as a boy and got scolded for tracking mud into your mother's drawing room."

She grinned. "We did get into a lot of mischief."

"And I promise we'll continue to do so," he said, leaning in.

Their lips met again, and this time she kissed him back with everything she had. This wasn't the beginning of something new—it was the homecoming she never expected. And she knew, without a shadow of a doubt, that she would love this man for the rest of her life.

A soft knock at the door shattered the warmth of the moment, as if the world had suddenly remembered them again.

Evander pulled back, though only slightly, their breaths still mingling between them. Olivia's gaze shifted to the doorway where Lord Everwyck stood, his hands clasped behind his back.

"May I have a word, Son?" he asked, stepping farther into the room.

Now? Olivia barely suppressed a groan. Could they not have five uninterrupted minutes?

Evander's voice was reluctant. "Can it not wait?"

But Lord Everwyck didn't pause. He moved towards them with a measured gait, and there was something in his expression Olivia hadn't seen before—something that looked suspiciously like humility.

"I feel as if I owe you—and Olivia—an apology."

Evander seemed skeptical. "You do?"

Stopping just in front of them, Lord Everwyck gave a solemn nod. "I thought this marriage was a mistake. I believed Olivia would hurt you. I let my assumptions cloud my judgment, and I was wrong. Entirely wrong. The truth is that you two are perfect for one another."

Olivia stood very still, unsure how to respond. She had braced herself for his disapproval for so long that his unexpected contrition knocked the wind from her.

Beside her, Evander looked as though he were trying to determine if this was some elaborate jest. "Thank you, Father."

Lord Everwyck's eyes, so often sharp with criticism or cool with detachment, filled with tears. "I know I haven't been the best father. But I want what is best for you. I always have." He paused. "I also wanted to apologize for not telling you about

Bryon's will. That was wrong of me. I should have trusted that you would do what was best for the estate."

Olivia felt the air shift. Not dramatically, but just enough to crack something inside her. Perhaps not forgiveness—at least not yet—but something that resembled grace. She stepped out of Evander's arms and walked up to Lord Everwyck, hesitating only briefly before wrapping her arms around him.

His body was stiff, startled, but after a moment, he returned the embrace. Lightly. Awkwardly. But he didn't pull away.

When she stepped back, he cleared his throat gruffly. "That's all I wanted to say."

And without waiting for acknowledgment, he turned sharply on his heel and exited the room.

The door closed with a soft click.

Evander's eyes stayed fixed on the door. "I never thought I'd hear my father admit he was wrong."

Olivia looked up at him, her voice quiet but hopeful. "Perhaps it's the start of something new between you."

He exhaled, almost a scoff, though not unkind. "I'm not naïve enough to think he'll change overnight. But still... it's something. And I would have loved you, with or without his approval."

Her lips curved. "That's why I love you."

"I don't think I'll ever tire of hearing you say that."

Olivia tilted her head, suddenly mischievous. "I was merely wondering if you might be interested in getting into a bit of trouble right now."

One of Evander's brows lifted. "What sort of trouble?"

She slipped her fingers into his, threading them tightly together. "Why don't you come with me and find out?"

His steps matched hers instantly as she tugged him towards the door.

"Where are we going?" he asked.

She glanced over her shoulder at him with a smile that was

all challenge and promise. "I believe it's as good a time as any to make this a true marriage."

His grip on her hand tightened. "Lead the way, my *Kicksy-Wicksy*."

Olivia groaned and laughed at the same time. "I thought we had agreed to retire that ridiculous term."

"But it suits you so nicely," he said with that insufferable grin that always made her want to both kiss him and mock him in equal measure.

She rolled her eyes, but her heart was soaring. She felt light. Whole. Free.

This was what love felt like—safe and thrilling all at once.

It was him.

Always would be.

"And that is how Olivia begged me to love her," Evander declared with a grand flourish of his hand, reclining just slightly in the chair near his mother's bedside.

Olivia's laugh filled the room. "That is not how I recall it happening."

He cocked an eyebrow and gave her a devilish grin. "Well, you would be wrong. There was a great deal of pleading on your part, if memory serves. And me, being the magnanimous gentleman I am, consented. I couldn't very well let you pine away for me, now could I?"

His mother chuckled softly from her place in bed, her thin hands folded atop the coverlet. Though still pale, she looked stronger than she had in days. "That was kind of you, Son," she said dryly. "But I suspect the truth lies somewhere in the middle."

Placing a hand to his chest with mock offense, Evander

gasped. "I do not know why either of you are acting so surprised. Olivia has always wanted this." He waved a hand over his person. "And can you blame her?"

Olivia rolled her eyes in a dramatic fashion. "Do you even hear yourself speak?"

A grin tugged at his lips. "I do," he replied. "And yet, you are stuck with me."

She met his gaze, soft now, genuine. "You'll hear no complaints from me."

That quiet admission lodged somewhere deep inside his chest. Even in jest, her affection grounded him.

His mother gave a contented sigh. "I am so pleased that you two have finally come to terms with your feelings. I always knew you cared for one another—far more than either of you would admit."

Before Evander could respond, a knock sounded at the door.

"Enter," he called, straightening slightly.

A young maid stepped in and dipped a quick curtsy. "Lord Alcott has requested a moment of your time, my lord."

Evander nodded. "Inform him I will be down in a moment."

As the maid withdrew, Evander leaned forward and reached for his mother's hand. "I won't be long."

She patted his hand with a smile. "Do not rush on my account. I'm rather eager to hear Olivia's version of the tale."

He looked back towards his wife. "I'm sure she'll leave out the part where she nearly swooned from my kiss. It was quite something. She tried to play coy, but truly, she was overwhelmed."

"Overwhelmed by your ego, perhaps," Olivia quipped. "Your kissing skills are merely adequate."

He turned, aghast. "Adequate? Take that back, Wife."

Her eyes danced with mischief. "I might be wrong, but I suppose we'll have to kiss more to find out."

His chest tightened at the thought. How he wanted to whisk her away upstairs, away from his duties, away from the world. But now was not the time.

He cleared his throat and turned back to the door. "I should see what Alcott wants."

As he exited, he caught a final glimpse of Olivia settling beside his mother, the two of them falling easily into conversation. That image—his mother smiling, Olivia beside her, both of them at peace—lodged itself in his heart. He never would've thought he could have this. And now that he did, he would never let it go.

Downstairs, the drawing room was empty save for Alcott, standing with his usual rigid posture, his hands clasped behind his back. He looked every bit the soldier—composed, guarded, as though ready for battle.

"Alcott," Evander greeted as he crossed the room. "Would you care for something to drink?"

"I would," came the reply, though his tone was subdued.

Evander reached for the decanter. "Is something troubling you?"

There was a pause. "I'm considering taking a wife."

Evander's hand stilled mid-pour. "A wife?" He looked up, startled. "You?"

Alcott gave a curt nod, though his jaw tightened. "Not because I want to, not really. But I believe it would benefit my sister. And… I need an heir."

Evander resumed pouring, slowly, before handing his friend a glass. "That is not the best reason to marry."

"I don't claim it is," Alcott admitted, studying the amber liquid in his glass.

"Do you have a young lady in mind?" Evander asked, suspicion already curling in his gut.

"No." Alcott's voice was flat, devoid of any real emotion.

Evander frowned. "That could be problematic."

Alcott glanced towards the doorway, as if wary of being overheard. “I saw Warwicke at the club. He said things are going well between you and Olivia.”

“They are. Better than I ever hoped.”

Alcott gave a short nod. “I’m happy for you. I doubt I’ll be as lucky.”

“I’ve loved Olivia since we were young,” Evander admitted. “She walked into my life like she already knew there was a place for her deep within my heart.”

Alcott’s expression turned solemn. “What do you intend to do with the indigo plantation now that the immediate danger has passed?”

Evander shrugged. “There will always be threats, so long as reformers still exist. But for now… I hope we’ve reached a temporary peace. I intend to treat the workers fairly.”

“Wise,” Alcott murmured as he moved to set his glass down. “I should go.”

Evander studied him carefully. There was tension beneath the surface—something unsaid, something eating away at him. “What’s wrong?”

Alcott hesitated before admitting, “I wish I was still fighting on the Continent. Life was simpler there. There was clarity. Purpose.”

“Some might say it’s easier to be a viscount,” he joked.

“Those people would be wrong.”

The humor drained from Evander’s face. “I was where you are once. Conflicted. Lost. But I came to terms with my duty.”

“Duty.” Alcott spat the word like it tasted sour. “It’s just another name for shackles.”

Evander took a slow breath. “Did something happen?”

“Yes,” Alcott said after a pause. “But I don’t wish to trouble you. Not now.”

“You’re not troubling me—”

"I'll tell you more when I know more," Alcott interrupted. "But I should go."

Evander stepped forward and placed a steadying hand on his friend's shoulder. "Whatever it is, you don't have to go through it alone. You have friends. Me, included."

"I know," Alcott said, though he didn't sound convinced. "How does one even go about finding a wife?"

"You're serious, then?" Evander asked.

"I am. The sooner the better."

Evander opened his mouth to respond, but faltered. What could he say? What advice could truly help a man who didn't believe he deserved love?

Before he could speak, Alcott raised a hand to stop him. "I'll figure it out."

As Alcott turned to go, Evander watched him—his friend's shoulders sagging, his steps slower than usual.

"Wait," Evander called after him. "My only advice is don't rush into marriage. Find someone you could come to love."

Alcott stopped in the doorway, but didn't turn back. "Love?" he echoed, almost mockingly. "I'm not foolish enough to believe I deserve love. I'll settle for a practical marriage of mutual toleration."

Evander's reply was quiet, but firm. "Everyone deserves to find love."

"You were fortunate. Not everyone is so lucky."

And then he was gone.

Evander stood in the quiet room, a heaviness settling in his chest. He didn't know what haunted his friend, but he could feel it—Alcott was slipping into something dark. And Evander only prayed he could reach him before it consumed him entirely.

Olivia appeared in the doorway. "Your mother is resting now," she informed him.

Evander set his glass of brandy on the side table and

crossed the room without hesitation. "I love you," he said, the words leaving his lips with more force than he expected.

Her whole face lit up. "And I love you."

He drew her into his arms. "Thank you for loving me," he murmured against her temple. "I do not know what I ever did to deserve you."

She looked up at him then, her brow knitting slightly with concern. "Did something happen with Lord Alcott?"

Evander exhaled a sigh. "He says he's ready to marry," he replied. "But only for convenience. Duty, security, heirs. He believes love is beyond his reach."

"But that's how we began, and look at where we are now."

He smiled. "There's a difference, Livy," he said, his voice low. He brought a hand to her cheek, tracing the curve with his thumb. "You didn't know it then, but I was never *not* thinking of you. Not once. From the moment you first walked into my life with those fierce eyes and stubborn opinions, you've consumed me, body and soul. You were in my thoughts every hour, in every breath I drew."

Emotion welled in his chest, thick and overwhelming. It had taken him years—too many—to say those words aloud. And now that he had, the truth of them nearly undid him.

Olivia didn't speak right away. She didn't need to. She reached up, her fingers curling behind his neck, and brought her lips to his with a kiss that silenced the world.

When she finally pulled back, her eyes shimmered with the same feeling that had taken root in his own soul. "Then let's not waste a moment," she whispered.

He felt the last remnants of restraint crumble. With a rough laugh that caught in his throat, Evander kissed her again—fiercely, reverently. She was everything he had ever wanted, everything he'd once believed he could never have. And now, she was his.

Forever.

EPILOGUE

SEVEN YEARS LATER…

"It's here!" Olivia called, her voice breathless with excitement as she carefully descended the staircase, one hand braced along the banister, the other cradling her heavily pregnant belly. Each step felt slower these days, but the package waiting on the entryway table gave her new energy.

She reached the bottom and paused in front of the brown-wrapped parcel, her heart giving a delighted little leap. *Finally.* Gillingham was already slicing through the twine with his usual precision, stepping back once the box was open.

Olivia reached inside and pulled out the green leather-bound book, its cover supple and cool beneath her fingers. The scent of fresh parchment rose to meet her—clean and crisp, full of promise. Her lips parted in a smile. *After all those years... all those nights of quiet scribbling... it was real.*

Clutching the book, she turned on her heel and headed for the rear of the townhouse, passing familiar portraits and polished side tables, until she reached the open study door. Sunlight streamed in through tall windows behind Evander's mahogany desk. He was bent over a stack of correspondence, but two familiar heads—dark and tousled—were on the carpet beside him, deep in battle with wooden soldiers and dramatically whispered cannon fire.

"Your book is here," she announced, pride coloring every syllable.

Evander looked up sharply, eyes wide, and pushed his chair back with a scraping sound. He was on his feet a moment later, striding towards her.

"I can't believe it," he breathed as he took the book from her. "I never thought I'd actually be published."

Olivia's heart swelled. "I don't know why you sound surprised. You're the smartest man I know."

He glanced at her with a lopsided smile. "You have to say that, Wife." But there was wonder in his voice as he read aloud from the cover: *"The Rise and Fall of the Roman Empire by Evander Addington, the Earl of Everwyck."*

She stepped closer and brushed a kiss to his cheek. "You did it."

He turned to face her more fully, his eyes unexpectedly tender. "Thank you for encouraging me. None of this would've happened without you."

"I merely cheered you on," she countered softly. "You're the one who stayed up until all hours, muttering about Caesar's military campaigns and questioning footnote placement."

A small voice interrupted. "Will you read us that book, Father?" asked six-year-old Edward, sitting up and hugging a wooden soldier to his chest.

Evander's smile turned playful. "Do you have any interest in the Roman Empire?"

Charles, only four and always eager to contradict his elder brother, wrinkled his nose. "It sounds boring."

Edward frowned and promptly punched his brother's arm. "Don't say that! You're boring!"

"I am not boring!" Charles shouted—and promptly lunged at him.

Olivia took a step forward to intervene, but Evander caught her arm gently. "Let them have their fun."

"They're going to hurt each other," she warned, already half-wincing.

But instead of cries, there came only a tangle of limbs and bright giggles as the boys wrestled. It was chaos, of course, but familiar chaos. Home.

She rested a hand on her stomach, where the baby had begun to stir again. "For my sanity's sake, I'm hoping this one is a girl."

Evander smirked. "If she's anything like you, she'll terrorize the boys and rule this house before her first birthday."

Olivia chuckled and lifted the book again, flipping open to the title page. Her fingers traced the simple, heartfelt dedication: *To my mother.*

"I'm glad you dedicated your first book to your mother," she murmured.

"My first book?" he asked, surprised.

She nodded, her voice sure. "I have no doubt it'll be the first of many."

Evander glanced down at the leather spine again, something proud and disbelieving in his gaze. "Let's hope the public agrees and it flies off the shelves."

Olivia arched a brow. "It may not be a French romance novel, but it is very good."

Evander snorted. "Surely there's a better use of your time than reading such sentimental nonsense."

"There isn't," she declared. "Not when the doctor insists I rest so much. There's only so much needlework a woman can do."

At that moment, their sons reappeared, faces flushed. "Can we name this baby?" Edward asked eagerly.

Olivia's instincts flared. "That depends. What would you name it?"

The boys exchanged a look before Edward leaned in to whisper something to Charles. Whatever it was, it nearly sent the younger boy into a fit of laughter.

"If it's a boy," Edward announced with mock gravity, "we should name him Fitznibble Doggington."

Olivia's lips twitched. "And if it's a girl?"

"Dorcus Figgle," Edward said proudly.

Olivia pressed a hand to her mouth to suppress the laugh that threatened to burst free. "Those names are certainly... unique. But I think your father and I will manage the naming this time around."

A dark-haired nursemaid appeared in the doorway. "It's time for the boys' riding lesson."

Charles immediately perked up. "Can I ride your horse, Father?"

Evander tousled the boy's hair. "Let's stick to your pony a little longer, shall we?"

Charles scowled, dragging his feet as though on his way to the gallows. Edward lingered just long enough to murmur, "That was a good decision. Charles isn't very good at riding."

"I am good!" Charles hollered, bursting back into the room and tackling his brother again.

Olivia rolled her eyes, stepping out of the way as the room devolved into playful mayhem. Evander joined in with mock growls and roars, and she, wisely, made her way to the settee. Lowering herself with a huff and propping her feet on the table, she waited them out.

Eventually, Evander stood and clapped his hands. "All right, riding lesson time. Out with you!"

The boys scampered away, and Evander sank beside her with a dramatic sigh. "I don't think they ever get tired."

"And you do?" she teased.

"I'm old," he declared. "I hurt my back just sleeping these days."

The baby kicked, and Olivia sucked in a breath. Evander turned to her at once and asked, "What is it?"

"Nothing bad," she assured him. "Just... this one is strong." She paused. "If it's a girl, I'd like to name her after your mother."

Evander's expression softened. "I'd like that very much."

She grinned mischievously. "And if it's a boy... Fitznibble still sounds good."

"The Honorable Fitznibble Addington?" Evander shuddered. "I beg you, don't do that to him."

Her laughter melted into a quiet moment. "When do you leave on your book tour?"

"In two months," he replied. "I will be gone for three weeks. Are you sure you won't miss me terribly?"

"Of course I'll miss you," she said. "But we'll be fine. I have a whole household staff to tend to my every need, and my mother is just down the street. Furthermore, the baby will be almost a month old before you are set to leave."

He placed his hand on her belly again. "I can't believe I get to lecture again. Even briefly."

"I know how much you've missed academia."

"I have," he admitted. "But I love the life we have built together."

She reached for his hand. "I have no doubt that your father would've been proud of how much you have accomplished in such a short time. The estate is profitable, the coffers are filled, and you were finally able to sell that indigo plantation."

Evander grew solemn. "I am glad that he is no longer in pain."

Olivia yawned suddenly, blinking against the pull of fatigue. "I'm sorry. I do want to hear more, but I need a nap before dinner or I'll fall asleep in my soup."

Evander stood and offered his hand. “Allow me to escort you to our bedchamber, my dear.”

She rose with effort and a groan. “It’s getting harder to lift myself off these settees. I feel like a waddling hippopotamus.”

He bent to kiss her cheek. “You are radiant.”

She snorted. “You are delusional.”

But his voice was earnest, reverent. “To me, you are—and always will be—the most beautiful woman I have ever known.”

She slipped her hand into the crook of his arm. “Well, then. I suppose I’ll keep you.”

“Good,” he said with a warm smile. “Because I’m not going anywhere.”

As they left the study together, Olivia rested her head lightly against his shoulder. Her heart brimmed with love—for her husband, for her children, for this life she had once thought beyond her reach. And now, it was hers.

All of it.

The End

NEXT BOOK IN THE SERIES

Society turned its back. So she rewrote her fate.

Lady Jane Lyttelton had always done precisely what was expected of her—until the moment she stood at the altar beside an aged duke. Rather than seal her fate, she ran. Disowned by her family and shunned by Society, her future seemed hopeless... until an unexpected inheritance offered her a chance at independence and a second chance at life.

Alistair Winslow, Viscount Alcott, returned from war with more than a title and scars. Haunted by what he had been forced to do to survive, he now shoulders the weight of protecting his sister and upholding the family name. When Jane saves his life in a dark London alley, he finds himself drawn into her troubles and into feelings he cannot afford to have.

But danger lurks in every shadow. As Alistair's investigation regarding the questionable deaths of men in his Army company takes a deadly turn, Jane refuses to remain safely out of harm's way. To protect her, he must confront his past and the man intent on destroying them both. Yet the greatest battle he faces may be against his own heart, for to love her could cost them everything.

ABOUT THE AUTHOR

Laura Beers is an award-winning author. She attended Brigham Young University, earning a Bachelor of Science degree in Construction Management. She can't sing, doesn't dance and loves naps.

Laura lives in Utah with her husband, three kids and her dysfunctional dog. When not writing regency romance, she loves skiing, hiking and drinking Dr Pepper.

You can connect with Laura on Facebook, Instagram or on her site at www.authorlaurabeers.com.

www.ingramcontent.com/pod-product-compliance
Lightning Source LLC
LaVergne TN
LVHW010641110826
845149LV00014B/2913

9781962703376